PENGUI

A NEW C
THE
LITTLE *Penguin*
BOOKSHOP

Jo worked for many years as a writer and producer on soaps ranging from *The Archers* to *EastEnders*, before creating her own fictional world in her popular Shop Girls and Victory Girls sagas, set in a department store in World War Two.

A New Chapter at the Little Penguin Bookshop is the second in her new series that began with *The Little Penguin Bookshop*.

She lives near Bath.

Also by Joanna Toye

A Store at War

Wartime for the Shop Girls

Heartache for the Shop Girls

Christmas for the Shop Girls

The Victory Girls

Wedding Bells for the Victory Girls

The Little Penguin Bookshop

A NEW CHAPTER AT THE LITTLE PENGUIN BOOKSHOP

JOANNA TOYE

PENGUIN BOOKS

PENGUIN BOOKS

UK | USA | Canada | Ireland | Australia
India | New Zealand | South Africa

Penguin Books is part of the Penguin Random House group
of companies whose addresses can be found at
global.penguinrandomhouse.com

Penguin Random House UK,
One Embassy Gardens,
8 Viaduct Gardens, London SW11 7BW

penguin.co.uk
global.penguinrandomhouse.com

Penguin
Random House
UK

First published 2025
001

Set in 10.4/15pt Palatino LT Pro
Typeset by Jouve (UK), Milton Keynes
Printed and bound in Great Britain by Clays Ltd, Elcograf S.p.A.

The authorised representative in the EEA is
Penguin Random House Ireland, Morrison Chambers,
32 Nassau Street, Dublin D02 YH68

A CIP catalogue record for this book is available from the British Library

ISBN: 978–1–804–94603–9

To my readers, who make it all worthwhile.

Chapter One

Late January 1941

'So what did you do? What could you do?'

Carrie stopped with her soup spoon halfway to her mouth.

They were having lunch at The Ginger Cat. The soup was supposed to be oxtail, but these days, wherever you went it was basically Bovril with added Bisto.

Mike looked at her, head on one side, his blue-grey eyes teasing and challenging.

'What would *you* do, faced with a couple of drunken Spaniards waving knives?'

Carrie marvelled at how this man she loved so much could make light of the danger he'd been in while he was desperately trying to get back to England after Dunkirk. But she met Mike's challenge with her own.

'It's not very likely, is it, running the bookshop at Brockington Junction! But tell me anyway – what? Wallop them with a copy of *Death on the Nile*?'

'If only I'd had one.'

Mike grimaced. Carrie knew he'd had to sacrifice all the books she'd pressed on him before he left, giving them away to soldiers going on leave or on their way to the field hospital.

He'd used the final one as kindling to boil water for a wounded man in his platoon.

'No, the only way out,' Mike went on, 'was to get them more drunk. The guide who showed me over the mountains from France had given me a flask of some home-made hooch – a kind of brandy, I think – so I waved that in their faces. They could see I'd got nothing else worth stealing.'

Carrie laid down her spoon.

'But weren't you worried they'd turn you over to the authorities?'

Spain was neutral in the war – in theory. But Mike said it was crawling with Gestapo, and General Franco's police rounded up anyone they considered anti-Nazi and threw them in prison.

'They'd hardly do that.' Mike shrugged away her protest. 'They were operating outside the law themselves.'

As always, thought Carrie, he wasn't going to admit to the sick fear that he must have felt, even as a trained soldier, meeting two thugs on a narrow mountain path in the dead of night. Certainly not here, with the elderly couple at the next table looking over with fond smiles, easily translated as: 'What a handsome couple – and so in love!' Both of which were true.

But Carrie knew that what Mike had seen and done since he'd set off for France the year before had left its mark on him. There'd been many lonely months of silence after his loving letters had stopped, but since his miraculous return on Christmas Day, she'd gradually pieced together what he'd been through.

There was too much of it to tell all in one go, and she

wasn't sure she could have stood to hear it that way. Instead, the story had leaked out – was still leaking out – bit by bit.

Semi-conscious on a French beach, with a badly wounded shoulder, Mike had been picked up by the local Resistance, who'd sheltered him at huge personal risk. They'd smuggled him from barn to outhouse and attic to cellar while his shoulder healed – partially, at least. Then they'd sent him off with false papers to travel the length of France from one cell of resistance to another, by bicycle, train or hidden in the back of a cart. Finally he'd reached the small town of Saint-Girons, the start of a passage across the Pyrenees to Spain – the so-called 'Path to Freedom'.

'You're not having your soup,' Mike said now.

Carrie snapped back to the present.

'No, I'm not . . . Do you want it?'

Mike nodded.

'Waste not, want not, and all that.'

They swapped plates and Carrie watched him as he ate.

Mike was still getting his strength back. His shoulder had been operated on in France – by the local vet, if you please, with brandy and a horse pill for an anaesthetic – but the army medics who'd examined him since had conceded it was a pretty good effort under the circumstances. There was more good news. Mike was having physiotherapy at a local hospital and had been signed off active duty for three months. And he'd been promoted to full lieutenant.

Mike finished eating and looked at her.

'If you're really all done, we've got some shopping to do.'

'Shopping?'

'Well, I have something to collect. OK?'

Carrie frowned and glanced at the clock above the counter. Her watch was losing time and she couldn't rely on it.

'I know, I know,' Mike grinned. 'I know how devoted you are to your customers. You'll be back well before the afternoon rush.'

'I don't like to take Uncle Charlie for granted, that's all.'

Carrie – short for Caroline – had been named for her father's bachelor brother and he'd always had a soft spot for her and her twin brother, Johnnie. Charlie ran a garage business with a friend, but as he'd put up the money to get her started, he came over when he could to 'keep an eye on his investment', as he teasingly put it, and to give Carrie a break. For the rest of the time, she ran her little station bookshop – or 'the little Penguin bookshop', as people called it, since she sold so many of the popular paperbacks – on her own.

Mike called for the bill and laid a few coins on the little dish. He stood up and helped Carrie into her coat – always the gentleman, another of the many things she loved about him. Then she reached up to help him into his army greatcoat. Movement in his right shoulder was still limited.

Carrie was a regular at the homely café, so she gave the proprietress a little wave, which won them another fond smile. Feeling warm inside despite the bitter cold, she let Mike hurry her along to Brockington's main shopping street. Once there, he headed for Lovells, the small town's smartest department store.

'Right,' he said. 'Are you ready for your Christmas present?'

'Oh, Mike—' Carrie began, but he cut her off.

4

'I'm sorry it's late, but there wasn't much of a chance to shop before I got back. And not much to buy. I didn't think you'd appreciate a five-day-old mackerel.'

Spanish partisans had finally smuggled him back to England in the hold of a fishing boat.

'I don't need anything,' Carrie insisted. 'My present is having you back!'

'And mine is being back with you,' declared Mike. 'But that didn't stop you giving me a whole stack of books to replace the ones I'd lost, did it?'

Their shared love of reading had brought them together and Carrie smiled at the memory. Then Mike pulled her, still protesting, through the double doors and into the relative warmth and (for wartime) luxury of the ground-floor perfume hall.

Carrie was intrigued. What could Mike possibly have bought – without consulting her – that he needed to collect? A dress? A winter coat? Her old camel one was pretty shabby. It was a bit of a risk, but it could be . . . He must have asked them to save whatever it was until he could collect it with her. A handbag, maybe? A silk scarf?

It seemed not. He led her past Accessories, and they didn't head upstairs to Ladies' Fashions either. Instead, he led her downstairs and straight for the little cobbler's booth in the corner. There, he fished in his jacket pocket and produced a ticket.

'Ah, yes,' said the elderly man behind the counter. Like many retirees, he must have come back to work to replace a younger man who'd been called up. 'Prepaid. I remember, sir. I put it up here for safekeeping.'

He stretched to a high shelf and turned back to them, holding a long, slim black box.

Mike opened it, turned over something inside and smiled.

'That's perfect, thank you,' he said.

Carrie could hardly contain herself. A long, slim box . . . But Mike had given her a beautiful locket the previous Christmas, and she'd had a silver bracelet from Uncle Charlie for her eighteenth. Mike thanked the elderly chap again and led her away. He found a quiet spot behind a pillar.

'It's not the most romantic location, but then life isn't a film,' he grinned. 'Even if we did get our happy ending.' He bent down and kissed her. 'Happy Christmas, Carrie.'

And at last he handed her the box.

Carrie opened it and saw a watch. Its face was an oblong with tiny gold numerals on a black corded strap.

How typical of Mike! In the few weeks since his return, he'd noticed how unreliable her own watch was. She couldn't go by the train times; the rolling stock was so old they were often late or cancelled. There was the station clock, of course, but she needed a reliable timepiece of her own.

Overcome by his thoughtfulness, she could only whisper a quiet 'Thank you.'

'Turn it over,' Mike instructed.

Carrie extracted the watch and did so. On the back was a simple inscription that read: '*All my love, Mike*'.

'It's so lovely. And so lovely of you.'

'I'm glad you like it,' Mike smiled, then, more seriously, added: 'He asked if I wanted a date on it, but I said no. I didn't want to pin it down. Then I'll always be close to you, whatever the date, wherever I am, and you can think of me every time you look at it.'

'I don't need a watch to make me think of you!' said Carrie, then bit her lip. 'Sorry, that sounds ungrateful – you know I don't mean it like that. Of course I'll wear it every day, but I shan't need it to remind me. I'm always thinking of you.'

'Well, that's a fib for a start!'

Mike was wonderfully open in expressing his feelings, but he always knew when to stop things getting too sentimental. It wasn't helpful in wartime: anyone might be here today, gone tomorrow. However much in love you were, with that dizzy, floating-on-air feeling it could give you, you had to keep your feet on the ground.

'You know I come second to your beloved bookshop,' Mike went on. 'And then there's your family . . .'

'That's rubbish and you know it! Stop fishing!' Carrie shot back, picking up his tone. 'And talking of my bookshop . . .'

'You'd better get back. I'll walk part way with you, then I'm off to the hospital for more rotator-cuff exercises. Can't wait! But first, let's put your new watch on.'

Mike draped the watch around her wrist and fastened the small buckle. Carrie held out her hand admiringly.

'It's perfect,' she said. 'Thank you again.'

She stood on tiptoe and kissed him. Mike hugged her close.

'I was wrong, you know,' he said. 'This has turned into quite a romantic location after all.'

*

Carrie hurried back to the station, partly to relieve Uncle Charlie, but just as much to show off her present to Penny and Bette. The three of them had become fast friends.

Bette was a woman in her fifties who ran the station refreshment room and didn't stand for any nonsense. She'd been the first to welcome Carrie when she'd opened up her bookshop in the early months of the war.

Penny was a newer arrival. About Carrie's age, dark-haired and dark-eyed, she'd arrived as a porter to replace Bette's son, Eric, after he was called up. She'd seemed rather standoffish at first, but that had been explained when Carrie had found out more about her and the three of them got on famously now.

Carrie got her usual thrill as she emerged from the booking office onto the platform and turned towards her bookshop. Strictly speaking, it was a bookstall: a large, green-painted cabin standing on the platform under the shelter of the station roof. Carrie sold newspapers, magazines and stationery oddments as well, doing a brisk trade, but it was for the books, the Penguin paperbacks in particular, that she'd become known.

It still thrilled her to see her name painted over the counter in clear white letters:

C. Anderson: Books, Newspapers, Magazines

Uncle Charlie was serving a customer a *Picturegoer* magazine and gave her a thumbs-up.

'Aye, aye, here she is, businesswoman of the year! Nice lunch, love?'

In reply, Carrie held out her wrist to show him the watch.

'Christmas present from Mike.'

Uncle Charlie gave a low whistle.

'That's a nice piece! That didn't fall out of a cracker, did it?'

'I'm very lucky,' Carrie acknowledged. 'Where's Penny? I'd like to show it to her, if you can hang on for ten minutes.'

'Last seen going into the tearoom on her break,' said Uncle Charlie. 'With your brother!'

Chapter Two

Carrie hurried down the platform, past the poster urging people to ask themselves: 'IS YOUR JOURNEY REALLY NECESSARY?'

It made Mr Bayliss, the stationmaster, so indignant, he huffed and puffed like one of the engines. As if he was going to be out of a job, what with the number of troop trains halting at Brockington Junction, the airmen disembarking for Biggin Hill and Kenley, and the soldiers doing the same for Caterham Barracks. Carrie glanced into his office as she passed and saw him brushing his bowler hat, his back to the fire. Fussy, self-important little man!

Then she came to the tearoom, with its battered metal signs advertising Brooke Bond tea and Fuller's walnut cake, the door with the jangling bell above and the doormat set into the mosaic-tiled floor. There, at the table nearest the stove, two dark heads were bent over a newspaper, chuckling together.

'Aha!' Carrie exclaimed. 'Two birds with one stone!'

Penny sat back and Johnnie jumped up to greet her. 'I heard you'd skived off!'

'I was not skiving!' Carrie gave her brother an affectionate punch on the arm. 'What's your excuse?'

'You don't mind if I have twenty-four hours off from

helping to defend the skies?' Johnnie retorted. 'So you can sleep safe in your bed?'

Johnnie was a pilot, and not just any old pilot. He was one of 'The Few' – the Spitfire pilots who'd defeated the Luftwaffe in the Battle of Britain. He was so good, in fact, that he'd been given a training role, but he was itching to get back in the air and Carrie knew it wouldn't be long before he wore his superiors down and they had to let him. For now, she was enjoying the relief. She and her parents had had enough scares when he was flying, and if he was ground-based, he was at least a tiny bit safer.

'D'you want one?' He indicated the half-drunk cups of tea on the table.

'No time,' said Carrie. 'Talking of which . . .'

She extended her wrist from her coat sleeve and Johnnie whistled.

'So that was the police cars we heard. Daring daylight raid on a jeweller's?'

'You are a clot,' Penny spoke up. 'She's had lunch with Mike, hasn't she? I bet that's a present from him.'

'Spot on,' Carrie admitted. 'Like it?'

'It's gorgeous,' Penny said kindly.

And it was kind, because Penny was estranged from her family and didn't seem to have anyone that she cared about or who cared much about her. Now she drained her cup and stood up, ramming her porter's cap on her dark curls.

'I'd better get back too,' she said, shooting Johnnie a cheeky look. 'Us working girls are winning the war as well, you know.'

11

Johnnie held up his hands in a mock gesture of surrender.

'Two against one, hardly fair,' he grinned. 'But go on, do your worst. I'll see you at home,' he added to Carrie. 'I've got news.'

Carrie's mother, Mary, had done her food shopping that morning, the usual wearying round of queues at the grocer, the butcher and the greengrocer, but when she regarded her haul she allowed herself a satisfied smile. She always made an extra effort when Johnnie was home, which she knew was ridiculous as the armed forces were better fed than anyone on the home front. But the mother in her just couldn't resist the urge to spoil her boy.

She was making a mutton stew. They grew potatoes and carrots on the roof of the air raid shelter in the yard, so those would be going in, plus a large scoop of pearl barley and a leek from the greengrocer's. Onions had become very scarce and there'd be no Seville oranges for marmalade this year – no oranges at all, in fact. But the housewives of Britain were doing their best, Mary Anderson among them.

She kept her eye on the clock: once the stew was in the oven, she'd take a cup of tea through to her husband in the shop. Anderson's Newsagent & Stationer was a third-generation business – fourth-generation now, thought Mary proudly, if you counted Carrie's venture. Since Carrie had branched out on her own, Norman managed the business alone, with help from fourteen-year-old Terry.

The time flew by, what with the cooking and the washing-up and putting up the blackout, and before Mary knew it there was the ring of boots and the sound of smaller feet down the side entry and she was taking off her apron and smoothing her hair to greet her children.

'Hello, Mum!' Johnnie, so tall and handsome in his air force uniform, swept her into a hug. 'Mmm . . . something's cooking!'

'He's good, isn't he?' Carrie raised her eyebrows. 'White-hot powers of observation.' She quickly closed the back door so that not even a pencil of light escaped.

Brockington was on the very outskirts of London. So far, it had never been a target for bombers. But the Andersons' home had still shuddered from explosions during the fifty-seven nights of relentless air raids on the capital in the autumn. Nights had been punctuated by the awful rise and fall of the siren, the panicked rush to the shelter, the juddering throb of planes overhead, the answering barrage of ack-ack guns, the scream of a bomb being dropped, the airless, hold-your-breath pause, then the crump of a distant explosion. The raids might have slackened off a bit, but they were still frequent enough and on a clear night like this you couldn't be too careful.

'Let's have a look at you.' Mary stood back and examined her son. 'We've hardly seen you since Christmas!'

But she seemed satisfied with what she saw. She worried less now that Johnnie wasn't actually flying.

'Move over, please,' Carrie chided her brother. 'I've got something to show Mum.'

'I'm off. I've admired it once,' grinned Johnnie. 'I'll go and say hello to Dad.'

He moved away and Carrie readied herself for her mother's delight at Mike's gift. Proud as she was of her bright, beautiful, golden-haired daughter, Mary had still worried that Mike, a junior officer, was 'too posh' and would break Carrie's heart. Instead, she'd come to see how much the two of them had in common and how deep-seated and genuine the feeling was on both sides. But Mary's own fiancé had been killed in the Great War. She knew that sometimes love wasn't enough, and nothing could be taken for granted. She pushed the thought away as Carrie held out her wrist.

'Oh, Carrie, it's lovely! But is that the time? I need to get the dumplings in the stew!'

Laughing, Carrie hugged her mum – always wanting to feed her family. Some things never changed.

'There's a drop of custard left . . .' Norman Anderson peered into the jug. 'Any takers?'

Carrie shook her head.

'You go ahead, Dad, I'm all done.'

'Nor for me,' said Johnnie. 'That was delicious, Mum.'

Mary beamed and Johnnie eased himself back from the table while his father set to scraping out the jug.

'What's this news of yours, then?' Carrie asked.

Johnnie had taken himself off to the cinema during the afternoon, then had come back to the station to walk home with her. But he'd refused to breathe a word, saying he wanted to tell the family together.

'You haven't been promoted, have you?' she went on. 'The RAF can't be that desperate!'

Carrie loved having her brother around. They'd always had a close, easy relationship; they'd never fought like some siblings, which was quite something, considering their very different interests. Johnnie had been plane-mad since boyhood, while all Carrie had ever wanted to do once she'd learned to read was lose herself in a book. As Johnnie said, reading for most people was a hobby; for Carrie it was more like a religion.

'Close, but no cigar,' Johnnie quipped back in a cod American accent.

'What then?' Carrie went on. 'A new girlfriend? Ooh, are you blushing?'

'Certainly not!' Johnnie took a deep breath. 'No. I wanted to tell you in person. I'm back on active service as of next week.'

'Oh, love!' It slipped out before Mary could help herself.

'I know, Mum, you don't like it. But they need me. The Blitz isn't over – far from it.'

'Too right, son.'

Norman was an ARP warden, and after Christmas he'd been drafted up to London to help out following a huge raid that had set off so many fires the papers had called it 'the second Great Fire of London'.

'Training up the new bods is all very well, and we need to do that too.' He didn't need to add why – so many pilots had been lost, and were still being lost, in fierce dogfights with the Luftwaffe. 'But we're desperate for experienced men.' He touched his mum's hand briefly. 'And I'm sorry if it's tough on you, but that means me.'

Carrie wasn't surprised by any of this. Johnnie had chafed against his training role since it had begun, but it wasn't just that. Carrie often had a sense, a sort of seventh sense, whenever there was a big shift in her brother's life, some change in his circumstances, and she'd had the feeling since Christmas. She thought of it as their twin telepathy.

Norman took charge. He knew Mary would be fretting late into the night, tonight and every night to come. The longer he could put it off, the better.

'Let's all have a nip of something to wish you luck.'

From the sideboard he retrieved the half-bottle of whisky that Alf Warburton, the local chief warden, had given him as a thank you after their gruelling time in London. It had come as a surprise, but a nice one, and Norman brought it to the table along with the rather sticky bottle of Christmas sherry.

'Finish your water, love, and have a drop of this,' he instructed Mary. He didn't say 'It'll settle your nerves,' but everyone knew that was what he meant. 'You too, Carrie.'

They held out their glasses while Johnnie poured himself and his dad two fingers of whisky.

Norman picked up his glass.

'Good luck, son, and . . .' He paused a moment, weighing up whether to say it or not. Would Mary say it was tempting fate? But Norman Anderson was a born optimist; he and Mary were living proof that opposites attract. He said it anyway. 'And happy landings!'

Next day, as soon as Brockington Junction's commuters, soldiers, airmen and sundry other passengers had boarded their trains with their copies of *The Times*, the *Mirror*, *Tit-Bits*, *Woman's Own* or a chosen Penguin, and Penny had finished unloading a stack of crates, Carrie beckoned her over. Penny seemed quite shocked at Johnnie's news.

'Flying again? He didn't say anything to me!'

Carrie frowned.

'No, well, he wouldn't, would he? He wanted to tell us first.'

'Yes, yes, of course.' Penny said quickly. 'Silly of me.'

'Anyhow, what are you doing on Friday?' Carrie straightened the newspapers and magazines laid out across the counter. 'I want to see *Waterloo Bridge*. They say Vivien Leigh and Robert Taylor are really good.'

'A bit soppy for Mike, is it?' asked Penny shrewdly.

'Probably! But in any case, he's at a send-off for some colonel who's leaving. So, are we on?'

'Sorry . . .' said Penny. 'I don't think I can.'

'Oh. OK.'

But Carrie frowned again. Penny never usually turned down a night at the cinema. For one thing, it was warmer than the room she rented in a shared house. Yet this was the third time in a fortnight. And with no real explanation.

'Another time!' Penny called over her shoulder, moving off. 'I'll have to go. There's a divorced bicycle wheel I've got to reunite with its owner, and a stack of parcels to get ready for the nine-fifty-two. See you!'

Carrie looked after her, puzzled. Penny had only revealed the truth about herself reluctantly: her real name wasn't plain Penny Edwards, it was the Honourable Penelope Eversleigh. She'd run away from home and taken her new identity and the porter's job to get away from her father, who was trying to bully her into a marriage she didn't want. She'd sworn Carrie to secrecy, and Carrie hadn't breathed a word.

17

Since that revelation, and the upsets of the war they'd been through together, Carrie had thought they'd become closer. Penny had spent Christmas with the Andersons, for goodness' sake, and they'd all had a lovely time. Now she seemed to be going all closed and clam-like again. But why?

Chapter Three

'I feel bad,' said Penny.

They were walking back from The Swan, a pub near her digs.

'What? Ill, d'you mean? I told you not to have those pork scratchings. The way they keep the beer in that place, they were probably . . . I don't know . . . elephants' toenails from the zoo!'

Penny looked up in exasperation at the tall, dark young man walking beside her, or what she could see of him in the blackout. He was guiding their steps by the light of a flickering torch.

'Not that sort of bad,' she insisted. 'A guilty sort of bad. When am I going to tell her?'

'Am I being dense?' Johnnie stopped and turned the torch on her raised face. 'Tell who? And tell her what?'

'You're being very dense! Your sister, of course. Tell her that we've been seeing each other.'

'Oh, that.' Johnnie laughed.

'Yes, that! Or do you want to keep me a secret, like some sort of madwoman in the attic?'

'Well,' grinned Johnnie. 'You are a bit of a madwoman, aren't you? Turning up in Brockington, nearly giving Mr

Puffy-Chest Bayliss a heart attack when he found out his new porter was – gasp! – a woman.'

'Johnnie, I'm serious,' Penny implored. 'Carrie's my best friend. I feel terrible fibbing to her. Well, not fibbing, exactly, but . . . not telling her the whole truth. She asked me to go to the pictures tonight and I just said I couldn't. Can't you see that it's hellish awkward?'

Johnnie smiled down at her expectant, elfin face and the dark curls escaping from under her little cherry-red hat. Cherry lips, too, he thought, and bent to kiss them. He drew her into a shop doorway so he could kiss them again, for longer.

'Stop it!' said Penny at last, releasing herself, albeit reluctantly. 'Stop trying to wear me down!'

'OK, OK. Say your piece.'

Johnnie leaned back against the tiled shop entrance.

'Look, it was fair enough when we first started seeing each other after Christmas,' Penny began. 'With Carrie and Mike so wrapped up in each other – not that they're not still, but . . . Anyway, the first few times, I felt we were . . . you know, just seeing how, or if, it would work out. Seeing if you liked me as more than Carrie's madcap friend. And if I liked you as more than her sometimes exasperating but somehow annoyingly attractive brother!'

'Oh, and you're convinced now, are you?'

Johnnie still had his arms around her waist and pulled her closer. Penny happily let him.

'Yes, all right, I'm convinced!' Eventually she pulled away, a smile in her voice. 'You don't have to make me keep on proving it.'

'But now you want a newsflash on the Home Service. And perhaps the Overseas Service as well?'

'Johnnie! Be serious just for one moment, please?'

'OK,' said Johnnie. 'I give in. But I'll tell you why I asked you not to say anything. I've been waiting for Carrie to work it out for herself.'

'What? How?'

'She hasn't told you, then? She's never said anything to me either, not in as many words. Maybe she thought I'd have laughed at her. And she'd have been right.' There was the teasing but affectionate tenderness in his voice that was always there when he was talking about Carrie. 'But from some of the things she has said, or hinted at with a kind of meaningful look, she reckons that because we're twins, she's got some sort of second sight. That she knows when something's up with me.'

The look Penny gave him – the little he could see of her face in the fitful moonlight – was doubtful but intrigued.

'I thought that was only supposed to happen with identical twins? And they're not even sure about that.'

Johnnie shrugged.

'I don't know, Pen. I don't know about any of it. It's a bit airy-fairy for me.'

'So you don't reckon you have it?'

'Oh, come on. What kind of ragging do you think I'd get in the mess at Biggin Hill if I told the others I could sense when Carrie's dropped a box of books on her toe or trapped her fingers in the roller shutter on the stall?'

'Don't be mean! From what you said, when Carrie feels it, it's a bit more serious than that.'

'Yes, all right,' Johnnie admitted. 'Look, maybe she's just more sensitive than I am. I'm perfectly willing to give her that. She's always been the thinker of us two, the dreamer. I'm more the doer. Wouldn't you agree?'

He made to pull Penny closer again, but this time she resisted.

'Stop it, you're sex-mad!'

'Can you blame me?'

But Penny was thinking. She'd first realised how much Johnnie meant to her when he'd gone AWOL after a punishing time in the Battle of Britain the previous summer. He'd hidden out in Brockington, and Carrie had seemed to know instinctively where to find him. There'd been a logical explanation for it – he'd been hiding in one of their old childhood haunts – but maybe there was more to it than that. Maybe Carrie did have some special connection to her twin.

'So,' she said. 'You want Carrie to work it out. To work us out.'

'Yup,' said Johnnie. 'And time's running out. I'm back flying next week, so her antennae should be twitching all over the place. So just . . . bear with me, OK?'

'Well, I'm not promising,' said Penny defiantly. 'If she challenges me directly, I shall have to say something.'

'Fair enough. But let's see, shall we?'

He switched the torch back on again.

'Now, shall we get back to your place? There's just time for you to invite me in for a nightcap before I have to get back to base. If I'm not being too exasperating, that is?'

'Well, you're pushing your luck,' said Penny. 'But the annoyingly attractive bit might just win.'

'I can't work it out, Mum.'

With Mike at his colonel's send-off and Penny seemingly 'otherwise engaged', Carrie was spending Friday night at home, helping her mum to sew gloves for sailors. At least these were mittens, so there weren't all the fiddly fingers to sew around, but they were in thick oiled wool. They might be welcome to the poor devils freezing on night watch as they ploughed through the waves, a target for U-boats and air attacks, but they were the devil's own job to sew up.

The task was made even more difficult because, to save electricity, they were working only by the light of the standard lamp. Norman was out on ARP duty, but so far, thankfully, the sirens had been quiet.

'You mean about Penny?' Mary replied when she'd finished rethreading her needle. 'Well, she doesn't have to tell you everything, does she? Even if you are friends.'

'No, but it's a bit odd.'

'Has she kept things secret in the past, do you know?' Mary asked, applying herself to her stitching.

Mary, of course, had no idea that Penny was one gigantic walking secret.

'Well, yes,' Carrie admitted. 'She has.'

'There you are, then,' said Mary. 'There could be any number of things she's doing tonight. Maybe she's doing an evening class. Maybe she's applied to join one of the services and she's swotting for some test or other. Anyone can see what a bright girl she is.'

'Yes, that's true.'

When Penny had first arrived, Carrie had been amazed that she hadn't chosen to join the forces, but Penny had explained that her wealthy father had 'connections' in high places and could have tracked her down. And that was the last thing she wanted.

'Although, of course, there is an even simpler explanation.' Mary put down her work and stood up, stretching her back. 'Oof! I'm going boss-eyed with this. I'll make us some cocoa, shall I?'

'I'll do it.' Carrie got up from the cushion she'd been sitting on at her mother's feet. 'What's your explanation, then?'

'Well, it's obvious. She's got herself a boyfriend, hasn't she?'

Carrie couldn't believe she'd been so dim.

'Of course! Why didn't I see it?'

'I'm surprised you didn't.' Mary sat down again. 'Though Penny's not the sort to go mooning about, all hearts, flowers and violins in the moonlight, is she?'

'No. But who is it?' mused Carrie. 'Someone she's met at the station? She's got plenty of backchat for anyone who gets fresh. But that doesn't mean she might not like them.'

'Well, maybe you should ask,' said Mary.

'I will,' Carrie declared. 'I wonder what he's like? He must be quite something to take Penny on. Oh, but that would be marvellous. We could go out as a foursome!'

*

Carrie was at work the next day, Saturday, but it was Penny's day off, and Mike had promised Carrie a day out on Sunday when the bookstall was closed. So, annoyingly, there'd be no chance to tackle Penny until the start of the working week.

She chatted to Mike about it, though, proudly wearing her new watch and consulting it regularly as they drove out to the countryside for a wintry walk. Mike had wangled an Austin Ten out of the army.

'Why wouldn't she tell me straight out?' Carrie puzzled.

'Penny doesn't need your approval!' Mike pointed out. 'Anyway, how can I put this . . . How well do you really know Penny? She's so . . . private. It might not be a man. She might prefer women.'

A bit taken aback – it hadn't occurred to her – Carrie thought quickly, but rejected the idea.

'Oh no, I don't think so, Mike. She was once . . . Look, don't say anything, but she did once let out that she was going to get married.'

'Penny? Well, well. She is a dark horse.'

'Yes, she is. But not for much longer. I want to hear it from the horse's mouth.'

'You do that,' said Mike, indicating as the half-timbered roadhouse where they were having lunch came into view. 'But I'm going to concentrate on what they've got on the menu. I did a five-mile run this morning with the men. And the only concession to my shoulder was no heavy kitbag.'

When Monday came, Carrie was poised to pounce on Penny, but first she had to deal with the usual early-morning passengers and a troop of children on a school trip who almost cleaned her out of her stock of Puffins.

The illustrated books – in colour, no less – were a new venture for Penguin. They'd launched four titles before Christmas, and Carrie was already on her third order. Three explained the war in a way children could understand – *War on Land*, *War at Sea* and *War in the Air* – and the fourth was simply called *On the Farm*.

Mr Parfitt, the Penguin rep, had told her that in future the titles would become more general – about nature, history, myths and legends, perhaps. Carrie thought it was a good thing – this generation of children had already had their childhood disrupted enough by the war. There'd be fiction, too, Mr Parfitt promised, with further adventures of Orlando the Marmalade Cat. Carrie was looking forward to that one. The original had charmed her when it was published a few years before; she was sorry Orlando hadn't been around when she was a child.

Even after the youngsters had waved their hot, sticky coins at her before boarding the train with their teachers, Carrie had no chance to buttonhole her friend. Penny was busy on the opposite platform helping a woman who seemed to be travelling with everything but the kitchen sink – she certainly had a very unwieldy lampshade. And on Carrie's platform, Uncle Charlie blew in, stamping his feet. There was a bitter wind.

'Cold enough to freeze the unmentionables!' he exclaimed. 'I'm not stopping, but I want to collect last quarter's accounts, if you've done them, love?'

Carrie triumphantly produced them from her tiny office. She'd laboured on them late into the night.

'December was well up on last year,' she told him, handing them over. 'Mind you, I'd only just opened then.'

'I knew I was backing a winner,' Uncle Charlie said smugly.

'I'd be nowhere without you,' Carrie replied. 'I'll give you this month's instalment on the loan as soon as a couple of credits from returns have cleared.'

'No hurry,' breezed Uncle Charlie. He turned to go, then turned back. 'I ran into your brother the other week, by the way. Up town.'

'Oh, did he have leave? He didn't bother to come and see us!'

'No, well, he was with some RAF mates. They'd gone up to collect a wedding present they'd clubbed together to buy some fellow who's getting married.'

'Oh, yes, he said something about that last time he came home,' said Carrie.

'There were the usual jokes about tying yourself down, henpecked husbands, the usual knockabout stuff, you know, but there was something about your brother that made me wonder . . .'

'What?'

'Well, if Johnnie hasn't got a girl himself.'

'Really? Johnnie? What made you think that?'

'Like I said,' shrugged Uncle Charlie, 'there was something about him. How can I put it . . . a spring in his step? A glint in his eye? A twinkle in his trousers?'

'I see.'

'Anyway, I'll leave you to ponder. I'm off to see some old boy's Humber with only a couple of hundred on the clock. Might be a tidy profit in it, even these days. Toodle-pip!'

'Bye,' said Carrie vaguely.

She looked across at the other platform again. Penny was crouching down now, offering a sweet to a fractious toddler whose pregnant mother was sinking down gratefully onto a bench. Penny had a man and Johnnie had a . . .

Suddenly, in a blinding flash, she got it. It couldn't be . . . could it? Was that why the family had seen less of Johnnie lately? Was that why Penny had been so very coy? Johnnie and Penny? Penny and Johnnie! It'd be too good to be true, but it might just explain everything.

When Penny finally sauntered up from the underpass between the platforms, Carrie was waiting.

'I know where you were on Friday night,' she cried triumphantly. 'I know why you wouldn't come to the cinema. You were seeing Johnnie!'

Penny's mouth almost dropped open.

'You know. You worked it out!'

'In a blinding flash,' said Carrie. 'It's true, then, is it? The two of you are seeing each other?'

'Yes,' admitted Penny. 'Yes, we are. You don't mind, do you? Oh, Carrie, I've so wanted to tell you, but—'

'Mind? Of course I don't mind!' said Carrie. 'I'm just so pleased. For both of you. For all of us!'

Chapter Four

'Your sister *has* worked it out, you know,' Penny told Johnnie when she next saw him. 'That we're seeing each other. She just came out with it.'

They were standing by the bar at an RAF dance, Penny having cast off her dark serge uniform for a coffee-coloured lace dress. Her shoes were gold with criss-cross straps and her dark curls were held back with diamante combs. If Mr Bayliss could have seen her now, his eyes would have popped like searchlights.

Johnnie looked disbelieving and took a swig of his drink.

'What, tuned in telepathically? Did she say so?'

'Well, I didn't like to ask. If you don't know officially, how am I supposed to? She just ... knew. And how else would she know?'

Johnnie shook his head, still sceptical.

'Well, all I can say is her famous second-sight specs must have been misted up lately. We've been seeing each other for weeks!'

'Maybe she has to tune into your ... your aura,' Penny retaliated.

'My what?' Johnnie almost choked on his pint.

'You shouldn't scorn things you can't disprove,' scolded Penny.

'Pah! It's all bunkum!' said Johnnie. 'She once hinted I had this "gift" of hers, all because I gave her a butterfly brooch on the day she happened to be told her poem about a butterfly had won some prize at school. I'd had the thing for ages! I was going to give it to her for her birthday. I just happened to find it in a matchbox I wanted to put a ladybird in and I needed to get rid of it.'

Penny tutted.

'Well, tackle Carrie about it if you must. She wants us to go out as a foursome.'

'I shan't say a word. I don't want to encourage her!' But Johnnie brightened. 'That's great, though. I haven't seen Mike for ages. I want to know his take on Greece now the Italians have invaded. We'll have to send our men in. And North Africa's a mess, the Luftwaffe are hammering the Med. It doesn't look good—'

'And they say romance is dead. Johnnie, please, not tonight!'

'Sorry, sorry.' Johnnie dipped his head and kissed her. 'No more war talk, OK?'

'I should think not,' said Penny. 'I haven't crammed my feet into these crippling shoes for nothing. So, are we going to dance or not?'

Johnnie took her hand and whirled her onto the dance floor, then held her close as the band struck up 'It Had To Be You'.

The next week, they did indeed go out as a foursome. Johnnie said nothing about Carrie's miraculous intuition, but she watched the pair of them closely.

She didn't need any psychic gift to detect that although Penny and Johnnie kept up their characteristic playfulness, they were really quite smitten with each other. She noticed how close to him Penny sat and how tenderly Johnnie helped her into her coat. And how the fiercely independent Penny let him do it with every appearance of pleasure.

Carrie and Mike were as much in love as ever, but as Mike said while they took a chilly walk in Brockington's denuded park one day, the new lovebirds made him feel as if he and Carrie were Darby and Joan.

'Which I'm very happy to be,' he assured her.

'I'll knit you a cardigan, shall I, next Christmas,' smiled Carrie. 'And get you some tartan slippers and a pipe?'

'Perfect!' grinned Mike. 'And we'll talk about bills and the children and what a worry they are. And on summer weekends I'll do the garden and mow the lawn and tinker with the car, and you can bring me cups of tea and home-made cake.'

And then, as if he'd gone too far, he laughed and changed the subject to the fact that jam was going on ration.

Carrie let him get away with it – she was sure he'd only said what he'd said in jest. But the merest glimmer of the thought that she and Mike might really have a future together, something more than just a wartime romance, made her feel quite off-kilter. To bring herself back to earth, she said:

'Talking of jam, Mum and I made some bramble jelly back in the autumn. Shall we go home and make toast and slather it on really thick?'

'You're on,' said Mike. 'Race you to the gate!'

There was no gate, of course – it had long since been

taken away and melted down for armaments; he meant the pillars where the gate had been. Carrie knew she had no hope of catching him, and after about fifty yards, she stopped and watched him run ahead, cap snatched off his head, dark hair ruffled by the wind, strong, lithe, long-limbed.

Those training runs he'd mentioned had paid off. So before she started getting visions of too many cosy firesides, either now or in the future, she'd better keep her feelings in check. Because they were at war.

Johnnie was back flying his beloved Spitfires and was busy with it, night after night, as the German bombers came over. London continued to be a target, but so too were other cities: Birmingham, Bristol, Plymouth and Swansea were enduring blitzes of their own. So far, thankfully, Johnnie had come back safely from all his sorties, though he spared them the details. But Mary worried, Carrie worried and now, Carrie knew, Penny must worry too, even though Johnnie insisted it was pointless, and he was right. He had to do what he had to do. His duty.

It was the same for Mike. He was a soldier, a junior officer. Since Italy had come into the war on Germany's side, the fighting had spread from Europe to North Africa, East Africa and Greece. The army needed all the men it could get and Mike wouldn't be on sick leave for ever.

He turned now and called to her.

'Come on, slowcoach!'

Carrie quickened her pace and he ran back to meet her, catching her in his arms and spinning her round, kissing her in mid-air as she squealed.

He couldn't have done that a few weeks ago, she thought

as he put her down. His shoulder was definitely very much better. Feet on the ground, she told herself again. Feet on the ground. But she seized his hand to bring it to her lips. Darby and Joan, indeed – she'd show him!

All was going smoothly, but there was one bump in the road.

'What did Johnnie say when you told him your real name and your . . . your family set-up?' Carrie asked.

She and Penny were having a quick bite to eat at Lyons and then, just like old times, they were going to the pictures. Penny made a big play of cutting the remaining half of her fishcake into perfect quarters.

'I haven't told him,' she said, her eyes on her plate.

'What? Why ever not?'

'For goodness' sake, Carrie!' Penny snapped, lifting her head, her dark eyes defiant. 'Why d'you think?'

'I've no idea.' Carrie was genuinely amazed. 'You like him, he likes you—'

'Yes, he likes me as Penny Edwards. Who knows what he'd feel about Penelope Eversleigh? And all her trappings.'

'He'd feel exactly the same, you dope,' said Carrie. 'It's not going to make any difference.'

'You don't know that,' Penny protested. 'He might feel . . . You must see, he might feel completely different about me. He – I hate to say this, Carrie, but he might feel he's . . . he's not good enough. Which would be ridiculous. And quite wrong!'

'Not as ridiculous and wrong as you keeping the truth from him and assuming something you don't know. For goodness' sake, Johnnie's mixing with all sorts of upper-class

33

types in the RAF – I know he doesn't behave any differently around them.'

'That's completely different,' snapped Penny. 'All boys together, brothers in arms and all that—'

'It certainly is completely different – he's not going out with them!'

'Keep your voice down, will you?' The man at the table across the aisle had put down his newspaper and was listening avidly. 'They'll throw us out.'

Carrie lowered her voice.

'What have you told him, exactly?'

'I haven't lied,' Penny insisted. 'He knows my mother is dead and I don't get on with my father.'

'That's the least of it! Johnnie doesn't know your father's a . . .' Carrie's voice had risen and she lowered it again. 'That he's titled.'

'And he's not going to. I've changed my name by deed poll. I feel like Penny Edwards now. I think like Penny Edwards, I act like Penny Edwards, I *am* Penny Edwards. My identity card says I am, my ration book says I am. There's no need to complicate things with your brother unnecessarily. Not yet, anyway.'

'Well, I still think he'd be very hurt that you haven't told him the truth.'

'That's your opinion and you're entitled to it. But it's my decision, and I want to leave things as they are.'

'So when are you going to tell him?'

Penny put her head in her hands.

'Can we just drop it? Please don't make this difficult for me, Carrie. I know you've kept my secret all these months and not breathed a word, not to Bette, not even to your mum or Mike, and I'm so grateful.'

'I'd never say anything. I promised you I wouldn't. I've been waiting for Johnnie to come out with it, assuming you'd have told him.'

'Well, now you know why he hasn't. So, please, go on keeping it quiet. Please?'

Carrie shrugged.

'It's your story to tell, Penny, but I still think you're doing Johnnie a disservice.'

Penny stretched across the table and grasped Carrie's hands tight.

'Please don't say anything, and please don't let it be an issue between us. Just respect my wishes. Of course I'll tell him, but in my own good time. I just – you must understand, the way you are with Mike ... I'm loving how things are between me and Johnnie at the moment. I don't want to do anything to threaten that.'

Carrie shook her head in exasperation.

'You're a stubborn devil, aren't you?' she said, though kindly.

'I know my own mind, that's all,' Penny sallied back, and attacked her food again. 'Now can we change the subject? Who's the better writer, Jane Austen or Thomas Hardy?'

'Oh, don't be daft. That's like comparing ... Laurence Olivier with Laurel and Hardy!'

'Ah, but who's who?' Penny teased. And then she changed the subject again. 'Gosh, this fishcake's horrible. Bleugh. I'm going to have to have a pudding to take the taste away. Pass the menu!'

Chapter Five

The middle of March, the middle of the day, and still freezing. Snow, fog, frost, the lot.

'Here, sweetheart, can't you get a bit more heat out of this stove? It's colder in here than outside!'

Ruby, the waitress-cum-kitchen-help who worked with Bette in the tearoom, gave the soldier at the corner table her chilliest stare. He was exaggerating, but it was true that the winter of 1941 had been just as cold as the previous one. It made the shortages and the rationing harder to bear, but that was no excuse.

'Don't you know there's a war on?' she parroted, which was what everyone said if you complained or asked for a bit more of anything.

'You'd better get yourself some specs, darling,' the cheeky Tommy retorted. 'See this uniform? And the stripe? Don't that tell you anything about what I know?'

'Excuse me. Is this person bothering you, miss?'

Ruby spun round to the voice at her shoulder. She saw a solidly built, fair-haired young man in shabby civilian clothes. He had unusually pale blue eyes and spoke with a slightly foreign accent.

'And who asked you to stick your oar in?' sneered the soldier.

'I don't like to hear impoliteness,' replied the other man coolly. 'Especially to a lady.'

A lady! No one had ever called Ruby that before. She favoured the stranger with a grateful smile and pushed back the lock of mid-brown hair that had fallen over her forehead.

'Oh, don't ya?' The soldier stood up. 'Well, I don't like to see foreigners over here scrounging off us, scoffing our rations and doing sweet Fanny Adams to help win this war. And don't give me no excuses about what a hard time you've had of it or about being hounded out of your country. If you didn't like what was happening there, why not stay and fight for it? Eh?'

'Look, let's not let this get out of hand . . .' Ruby began, panicking slightly.

She looked round to see if Bette – Mrs Saunders to her – was watching. But Bette was at the counter serving a woman whose child was making a right palaver of choosing a cake.

The young man, though, seemed quite in control of the situation and perfectly able to answer for himself, even if his English was a bit stilted.

'If you want a discussion about the atrocities which took place in my homeland of Holland, I am very willing to engage with you,' he said with a stiff little nod of the head. 'But I can tell you, if you saw what I have seen, then you would know that the best chance you have of fighting for your country, and ultimately to rebuild it, is to save your own life by fleeing. And then, when the tide has turned against the enemy, as it surely will, to return and fight them when your presence might make a real difference.'

'Look, matey,' said the soldier, squaring his shoulders. He was a puny specimen, and Ruby was surprised he'd even made it into the army. 'I don't need no lectures from you, whoever you are and wherever you've come from. I've seen things too. And I still say you're nothing but a shirker and a yellow-bellied coward!'

Ruby gasped. She was a regular at Brockington's Rialto cinema and had recently seen a Western where a saloon-bar brawl had ended up with all the tables and chairs smashed to matchwood and the bottles behind the bar shot to smithereens. She dreaded to think what Bette would say if something similar happened in her refreshment room.

Just then a bell rang and the adenoidal voice of Mr Bayliss intoned:

'The next train at platform two is for HM troops only. All other passengers, please await the next train, the scheduled two-fifty-two, which is running approximately thirty-two – thirty-two – minutes late. The next train at platform two is for HM troops only. Thank you.'

A groan went up from a couple of tables as passengers for the two-fifty-two settled down to a longer wait.

The stranger smiled.

'Your train, perhaps? You should go.'

'Yeah, well, some of us know what duty is. Saved by the bell or what?' Shouldering his kitbag, the soldier turned to Ruby. 'See ya, darling. Next time I'm passing through, I'll bring a hot brick for me feet.'

He stamped out. When the door had closed and the bell had stopped jangling, Ruby turned to the young man.

'Thank you,' she said. And then, tentatively: 'Don't I

recognise you? You've been in here before. Last year? A few times.'

The young man inclined his head.

'How observant you are! Yes, I was, how do you say it, quite a regular for a time.'

'And now you're back. Been away, have you?'

'Yes, that's right.'

'You were living in Orpington, I remember,' said Ruby, blushing.

It was a bit embarrassing. Back then, she'd been desperate for a boyfriend and had sort of hinted to this bloke that as he was all alone in a strange country, they might meet up. But he'd never followed it up – and anyway, that was all in the past. Things were different now. She had a boyfriend – Bette's son, Eric.

She didn't exactly *have* Eric, strictly speaking, because he'd been captured at Dunkirk and was in a POW camp in occupied Poland. But Ruby was writing to him once a week and he was writing back, had been for months. Strictly speaking again, he wasn't really her boyfriend because they hadn't even been going out before his call-up. But Ruby had always liked Eric, even if he hadn't seemed to notice her. Once she'd started writing to him 'as a friend', though, and he'd written back, and enthusiastically, it was a small step to think of herself as 'Eric's girl'. It had been a bigger one to convince Bette that Ruby was entitled to write in the first place.

Eric was Bette's only child. His father was dead and to say Bette was a possessive mother was like saying you supposed Clark Gable was an OK looker, if you liked that sort of thing. Bette had made quite a fuss, in fact, when she'd

39

found out that Eric and Ruby were corresponding, but Carrie had had a word with her and Bette had come round in the end.

Then, at last, six months on – no wonder he'd never realised that Ruby liked him when he was still in Brockington – Eric had actually asked if, when he got back, they might start walking out together. He'd also asked Ruby to send a photograph, and Ruby had been in raptures. She'd rushed off to have her picture taken at the studio in the High Street (hair set, best dress, becoming smile) and sent it off as soon as it was developed with a letter gladly accepting his request. She longed for a photograph of Eric to keep in her handbag, or by her bed, but he was hardly in a place where he could get one taken, so Ruby had to make do with gazing at the portrait-sized one that Bette had hung on the tearoom wall alongside the ones of the King and Mr Churchill.

Still, Eric had asked her to be his girl, and Ruby was keen to oblige. The shops had had a pathetic selection of Valentine cards this year, some of them clearly last year's, from the brownish tinge to the envelopes, but she'd bought the best she could find and fired that off with a big question mark on it, and two kisses. Lord knew when Eric would get it – sometimes the post took weeks and Valentine's Day was well past. But if that didn't make Eric realise how she felt and take it for another big 'Yes, yes, yes – and more!', then nothing would.

But the fair young man was speaking again, and Ruby's thoughts swam back to the present.

'I am living once more in Orpington, yes,' he said. 'But I mustn't keep you from your work.'

He gave that formal little bow again. He was so . . . Ruby searched for the word . . . so . . . continental! And so polite with it. It was a nice change from the usual – dealing with half-cut Tommies and grumpy passengers who barely raised their eyes when she put their sardines on toast in front of them.

'I should probably get on,' she admitted, taking her wiping-round cloth from her apron pocket to show willing.

But she didn't move. The mother and child were at a table now, but Bette was occupied chatting to a woman who was showing her a bolt of material and they were clucking about the poor quality and shocking price. Ruby liked a chat as much as anyone and as this fellow seemed to be moving from one place to another, he probably still didn't know many people. He must be lonely.

'You're Dutch, then, are you?' she asked. 'I don't know much about Holland. Except that you grow tulips.'

'Ah . . .' A faraway look came into his eyes. 'The bulb fields. In the springtime, they stretch as far as the eye can see, huge blocks of colour – red, yellow, pink . . .' His face darkened. 'Of course, the invaders ran their tanks across them like . . . what do you call it? . . . bulldozers, yah? They didn't care.'

'It must have been awful,' Ruby sympathised, her eyes widening. 'You were lucky to get out.'

'Indeed so,' said the young man. Then he checked himself. 'But I should introduce myself.' He held out his hand. 'Hendrick van Roon.'

Ruby wiped her hand on her apron and held it out too.

'Ruby Yateman,' she said. 'Pleased to meet you.'

41

Hendrick smiled. He had very even teeth, better than Eric's, which were rather gappy and a bit goofy, Ruby had to admit. He wasn't as skinny either – and that had been before Eric was on prison-camp rations. But Eric was nice and tall and he had deep, dark brown eyes. Ruby was Eric's girl, and for all she knew, this Hendrick bloke had a sweetheart back in Holland, or even in this country. She mustn't get carried away.

'So,' he said, 'when I next pass in Brockington I shall make sure to have my cup of tea here. And your cakes are very good too.' He smacked his lips. 'We like our cakes in Holland.'

'You do that,' said Ruby warmly. Poor fellow. Where was the harm?

She could see out of the corner of her eye that the woman was putting her bolt of cloth back in her basket and the conflab with Bette was coming to an end. With a meaningful look at Hendrick, Ruby made a big play of collecting a couple of cups from a nearby table and sweeping her wiping cloth over it. Hendrick took the hint and sat back down.

Ruby took the crocks to the counter.

'Don't think I didn't see you,' said Bette at once. 'Isn't that the same feller that was in here last year, that you were setting your cap at?'

'It is, and I didn't then and I'm not now, Mrs Saunders,' Ruby replied with dignity. 'He's a refugee, that's all. Dutch.' And in a masterpiece of improvisation, she added, 'He wanted to practise his English.'

'That's what it's called now, is it?' retorted Bette. 'I'm watching you, my girl. Any hanky-panky and I'll be making sure my Eric knows about it.'

Ruby wanted to say 'He's not just your Eric any more!' but she knew when to keep quiet. Eric had written to his mum and explained that his relationship with Ruby had moved up a notch – he'd told Ruby so. And if she didn't like it, Mrs Saunders would just have to lump it!

Chapter Six

Later that afternoon, between trains, Carrie was browsing through a selection of recently arrived Penguins when a theatrical cough made her look up.

'What does a bloke have to do to get served around here?'

'Mike! I wasn't expecting you! Where did you spring from?'

'Hitched a lift on a lorry,' he said. He smiled, but he seemed to be holding himself rather tensely inside his greatcoat, Carrie noticed, though maybe that was simply because of the wind that was scything down the platform. 'I . . . er . . . I don't suppose you can get off, can you?'

'Now?' Carrie consulted her watch. 'No . . . There's over an hour to go, and you know I'm always busy with the evening commuters.'

'Yes, I know. I hoped your uncle might be here.'

'Not today. Mike, is something wrong? You haven't – it's not bad news from home?'

His sister Jane had been poorly with food poisoning – a bad batch of potted meat – and at one point they'd thought she'd have to go to hospital.

'No, no, they're fine. Jane's very much on the mend. I've said I'll go up and see them soon.'

'Good. Well . . .'. look, I'm sorry if you've come on the off chance, but I won't be free till six.'

'No problem,' said Mike. 'I'll while away the time in the tearoom.'

'All right.' Carrie smiled. 'It was a lovely thought, Mike. And take one of these. It'll help you to pass the time.'

'Buying me off with a book, are you?'

But he brightened. Mike loved to read almost as much as Carrie did.

His eyes passed quickly over the new titles. *Aircraft Recognition*, *Europe at War* and *Britain Gathers Strength*. ('No thanks, I get enough of that sort of stuff on duty.') He quickly dismissed *Fall Over Cliff* ('I'm not in the mood for murder') before settling on *Sunshine Sketches of a Little Town* by a Canadian author who was new to Carrie.

'Something cheery, I think,' he said, fishing in his pocket for sixpence.

'Don't insult me by paying,' said Carrie. 'It's a present to make up for the fact that you're being deprived of my company. Think you can survive?'

'It'll be tough, but I have my endurance training,' Mike grinned. 'Just make sure you account for the book. I don't want Uncle Charlie chasing me for unpaid debts.'

And with that, he swung away down the platform. He still seemed to be walking rather stiffly, though, Carrie thought, watching him. She knew the army had upped his exercise regime to involve upper body strength; he'd even been doing target practice earlier in the week. Maybe it had hurt his shoulder. The last thing she wanted was for Mike to be in pain, but it could only be good news for her. The longer he was around, the better.

'A bit of a frosty atmosphere in the tearoom, I thought,' Mike said as he helped Carrie to close up later. He tidied the bookshelves as she tied string around the unsold newspapers.

'Don't tell me Bette and Ruby have had words.'

'There weren't many words being exchanged between them.'

Carrie sighed. Bette and Ruby had had their ups and downs, but she'd hoped all that was in the past.

'Oh, well. I expect it'll blow over. Bette knows she's not going to get a better worker than Ruby, with everyone joining the forces or the factories.'

Women weren't being conscripted – yet – but every other poster trumpeted 'JOIN THE WRENS – AND FREE A MAN FOR THE FLEET' or reminded them that 'WOMEN WITH A WILL TO WIN JOIN THE ATS!'

Carrie occasionally felt a pang. When Johnnie had volunteered, she'd thought she might join the WAAF, but Mary was a worrier and Carrie had realised she couldn't put her mum through the anguish of both children being away in the forces. But she'd had the brainwave of opening the station bookshop and now she only had to look around it and hear the praise and the gratitude of her customers, both troops and civilians, that she was there at all to know that she, too, was providing a service. It was a service that was vital for morale and gave her a swell of pride. But tonight she was glad to lock the door and walk away, arm in arm, with Mike.

'Where are we going?' she asked him.

'I thought the Station Hotel,' Mike replied.

'You sentimental old thing!'

It was where they'd had their first date.

Mike bought the drinks as Carrie settled at a table and slipped off her coat. It was a new one for the spring that had to come eventually, a light tweed, sage green with an overcheck in white. She had a dear little sage-green hat to go with it.

Mike came back and sat down beside her. He chinked his glass against hers and said 'Cheers,' his eyes meeting hers – it was bad luck, he said, to chink glasses without making eye contact. He took a sip; so did she. And then he said:

'I've got something to tell you.' There was something in his voice that told her she wasn't going to like it. He angled his body towards hers, his face serious. 'I've been posted away again.'

Carrie swallowed hard. She'd known it would come, and this was it. This was the test.

'I see. Where? When?'

'Early May. I only found out today and I wanted to tell you straight away. I want us to have time to get used to the idea.'

What had she told herself that day in the park? Feet on the ground, feet on the ground.

'So, what is the idea?'

'It's not as bad as it could be,' Mike said quickly, then kept his voice low and gave her a warning look to do the same. 'They're sending me to Washington.'

'Washington?' It was a good job he'd warned her to keep

her voice down, because nothing he could have said would have surprised her more. 'Why?'

'You know Churchill's desperate to get America into the war. Has been since he took over, since Dunkirk, really.'

'They're not budging, though, are they?'

'Not at the moment, no. So, we're sending a few more people to the States, to beef up the diplomatic effort. And I'm to be part of it, a very junior part. Liaison, it's called.'

America . . . Carrie tried to take in the implications – for both of them. At least he'd be a long, long way from the fighting. It was away from the front line, and not even in London, at the War Office, a sure target for the bombers.

'Well, that's exciting.'

'I'm sorry?'

'To go to Washington!'

'Hang on, I'm going away and you're excited?'

'I didn't say that, silly! I'm excited for you. That's quite a feather in your cap, isn't it? Surely it's an honour to be selected for something like that?'

Mike had the grace to look modestly pleased.

'Yes, yes, I suppose it is.'

'Of course it is!'

'I'm not going as military attaché or anything, you know, Carrie.' Mike smiled. 'I'm attached to the British Embassy as one of two assistants – the junior one – to the ADC to the military attaché.'

'Yes, whatever, I'm not bothered by how many strips of braid you've got on your uniform. I'm just proud of you. And look, Mike, it could have been a lot worse. At least you'll be safe there. Safer than me!'

Mike seized her hand.

'You are brilliant to take it like this, Carrie. You know I hoped to be around for longer. I would have been if they'd wanted me to go back on active service. I'm not ready for that yet, which is why this posting is a very sensible move. It'll give my shoulder time to get properly better.'

'I can see all that.'

She'd said she was proud of Mike, and she was, but Carrie spared herself a bit of praise for her own award-winning performance. Inside she was churning at the thought of them being apart again – but she wasn't going to be that clinging ivy of a creature she saw so many times at the station, making her husband or boyfriend's departure that much more painful.

Mike squeezed her hand.

'And it's only for three months, so that's good, isn't it?'

'What? Why didn't you say? That's nothing!' Carrie flung her arms around his neck, almost sending her drink flying. 'You'll be back by the summer.'

'With the swallows,' grinned Mike. 'Well, not quite, but, yes, by the summer.'

Carrie settled back down.

'Can I ask you one thing?' she said. 'One thing you could do for me. Apart from write to me once you're there, of course.'

'Ask away.' Mike had visibly relaxed – it was the thought of telling her, she realised, that had been making him tense.

'Can we not do so many nights out with Penny and Johnnie now? It may be selfish, but I'd like you to myself till you go.'

'I was going to say the same! I'm all yours – do with me what you will.' Mike gave her a mischievous smile and muttered under his breath, 'I wish.'

Carrie snuggled in close and he put his arm around her with a sigh.

Their kisses had become more and more passionate of late, and they could both feel how much they wanted each other. It was becoming increasingly difficult to leave the secluded darkness of the back row of the cinema; sometimes they were still there when the lights went up and the usherettes and cleaners came round collecting people's forgotten umbrellas and sweeping up the cigarette packets and sweet wrappers.

As for parting on the doorstep, Carrie was having to gently peel Mike's hands away from where he couldn't help them from straying. But neither of them had anywhere private to go, Carrie living at home and Mike at Caterham Barracks. Oh, other couples might carry on in the backs of cars or outside dance halls – it was everywhere. For all she knew, Penny and Johnnie were going further, but Carrie knew Mike would never expect that of her. And among everything else she loved about him, she valued that as well.

In all their evenings as a foursome, Carrie had kept faith with Penny. She hadn't so much as hinted at her posh – well, aristocratic – background. So when Johnnie brought up the subject of Penny during a weekend leave, Carrie was on her guard.

Mike was up in Leamington seeing his parents. Johnnie

and Carrie were doing the veg for Sunday lunch; Penny was joining them later.

'You know how Penny rattles on,' said Johnnie, scraping a carrot, 'but there's one thing I can't get her to talk about, and that's her family. Do you know anything about them?'

'Not much,' said Carrie cautiously. She was on carrot-slicing duty. 'What's she told you?'

'Only that her mother died and she doesn't get on with her dad. If I try to ask a bit more, she just closes down.'

'Yes, she does that.' Carrie had seen it herself before she'd been taken into Penny's confidence. She concentrated on cutting the carrots into even circles. 'I can't be much help, I'm afraid. I know her dad can be difficult. And very old-fashioned. Tried to control her.'

'Good luck with that, with Penny!'

'I know. But he's, well, let's just say he's got his own ideas about who she should go out with.'

'That goes for a lot of fathers. I'm not such a bad catch, am I?'

Carrie knew her tall, good-looking brother, cheeky yet courteous, wearing his intelligence and skills as a pilot lightly, was the sort of boyfriend most parents would welcome with open arms. But that wasn't the way with Penny's father. He'd wanted her to marry an equally posh and wealthy neighbour – a complete drip, in Penny's view. But their own ancestral home was entailed, meaning Penny couldn't inherit it in her own right, and this might have been one way to secure its future.

Carrie gave Johnnie a playful nudge.

'You're fishing for compliments now, but, no, I suppose

you're not.' And then, fishing herself, she asked: 'You really like her, then? You mean you'd like to meet her father?'

'Not particularly,' Johnnie replied quickly. 'But, well . . . just to know a bit more about her background. She's practically one of the family here – it seems a bit one-sided.'

'Hmm.' Carrie scraped the carrots from the cutting board into a saucepan and covered them with cold water. 'The thing with Penny is, I've never known her do anything she didn't want to do. She'll tell you more if and when she feels like it. But for now, I'm afraid, you're going to have to take her as you find her.'

'Oh, well.' Johnnie picked up the tin plate of carrot peelings and carried them to the pig bin. 'I suppose what I find isn't so bad.'

'Come off it, I think you really like her,' Carrie probed. 'Well, we all do. And you know Mum's always got her ears cocked for the sound of wedding bells . . .'

Mary and Norman, who'd already taken her to their hearts as Carrie's friend, had been delighted when they'd realised that Penny and Johnnie had paired off.

'Oh, no, no, no!' Johnnie replaced the lid of the pig bin and wagged a finger at her. 'You're not catching me out like that. Penny and I get on, we like each other's company, we're having fun.' Then he sobered. 'Yes, OK, I do really like her. I like her a lot. More than a lot. Don't look at me like that!'

'Like what?'

'In that, I don't know, arch sort of way.' He sighed. 'For God's sake, Carrie, do you seriously think I'd ask a girl to tie herself to me when I could be blown out of the sky at any minute? We've lost four from the squadron this month alone, one of them married with a six-month-old baby. It was only his third-ever flight.'

'Oh, Johnnie. I'm sorry,' said Carrie quickly. 'I don't know how you keep it all together, any of you, I really don't.'

'Work hard, play hard, make the most of every moment,' said Johnnie. 'It's the only way.'

Carrie nodded. 'Seize the day' – just like she'd sworn to do with Mike.

Chapter Seven

Bette was shrouded in a cloud of steam: the urn was reheating.

'This thing'll be the death of me,' she muttered to Ruby, who was hanging up glasses near the optics.

They both looked across as they heard the bell jangle and Hendrick van Roon came in.

'I see your Dutch friend is back,' said Bette with a heavy emphasis on the word 'friend'.

Eric's confession to his mum that he'd asked Ruby to be more than just a pen pal and how pleased he was that she'd agreed hadn't exactly gone down well with Bette. Eric was still firmly attached to her apron strings as far as she was concerned, for all that he was cooped up behind barbed wire in Stalag XXA. But 'what can't be cured must be endured', as Bette had said to Carrie, and in her heart of hearts she knew that anything or anyone that brightened her precious Eric's days while he was stuck in that place had to be a good thing.

Ruby turned from the back wall as Hendrick crossed the room.

'What's he done to his face?' she wondered out loud. He was sporting a black eye and cuts to his cheek and lip.

'Walked into a lamp post in the blackout, I dare say, or

fallen over a pile of sandbags. I nearly did it myself the other day. Blooming lethal they are,' tutted Bette.

Hendrick came up and gave his now-familiar little bow.

'Good afternoon, ladies.'

'Tea, is it?' Bette enquired crisply, lifting the huge metal pot.

'And a cake, I expect,' smiled Ruby. 'There's no apple turnovers today, I'm afraid. I know they're your favourite. But we've got some iced buns.'

Hendrick wagged his finger. 'Ah, you are tempting me now!'

'Go on,' said Ruby, opening the glass cabinet, tongs poised. 'You know you want to.'

'Don't force the customers, Ruby,' tutted Bette. But, not wanting to lose a sale, she added to Hendrick: 'Will you be having a cake?'

'How can I resist!' he grinned, showing his very white teeth – amazing for someone with such a sweet tooth.

'Then that'll be fourpence,' said Bette. 'We've had to put the prices up – more shortages, thanks to those blooming U-boats.'

Hendrick nodded.

'I heard about the losses of the ships.'

He felt in his pocket for the money.

'What's happened to you?' said Ruby, unable to contain herself any longer as she passed him his cake, eyes wide. 'You're all bashed about.'

Hendrick looked at the floor.

'I was set upon,' he said. 'I went into a pub to buy some cigarettes. A couple of drinkers heard my accent. They assumed I was German and followed me out. They dragged me into an alleyway and gave me, I think you call it, "a good kicking".'

'Oh no!' Ruby was horrified. 'That's awful!'

'Well . . .' He spread his hands in another continental gesture. 'Feelings are running high. It's not easy to be a foreigner in a strange land at this time. Everyone is very nervous.'

Bette pursed her lips. Whatever she thought about Adolf Hitler and his doings, this Hendrick wasn't even a German, let alone a Nazi, and this sort of thing didn't show her fellow countrymen in a very good light.

'Even so. I don't hold with unprovoked violence,' she said. 'I'm sorry to hear that.' She sniffed. 'I'll take tuppence for the tea, but you can have the cake on the house.'

'Oh! But that is more than kind.' Hendrick handed over two pennies. 'I think I will sit down now. My head still aches rather. And my . . .' His English failing him, he indicated his ribs.

'You take a seat by the stove, dear,' Bette counselled. 'This cold weather seems to be going on for ever.'

Ruby looked at her boss in amazement as Hendrick moved off. What a turnaround! Still, if it meant Mrs Saunders would stop jibing at her every time he came in, that could only be a good thing. Next she'd be giving her and Eric her blessing! Well, maybe that was too much to hope for. But Ruby shot Bette a grateful look.

'That was very kind, Mrs Saunders,' she said. 'And he really is only a friend – not even that, just a customer to me, 'cos of Eric. I hope you know that.'

'Well . . .' Bette dismissed the compliment, and the

reference to Ruby's ongoing relationship with her son, and justified her generosity. 'Time's getting on, and those iced buns are never the same next day.' But she looked over at Hendrick and frowned. 'What a carry-on! What do the police think they're doing, letting things like that happen? I don't know . . .'

And she bustled off into the kitchen to refill the milk jug. Ruby turned back to her task with the glasses, but not before she'd flashed Hendrick a smile. If she could establish whether he had a regular day to come in, she could make sure apple turnovers were on the menu. It didn't seem too much to ask.

Easter was going to be a strange affair this year. Carrie didn't sell sweets or chocolate: people had the refreshment room if they wanted sustenance, and there was a chocolate machine, though that was less popular now that it only offered ration chocolate, made with dried milk, less sugar and vegetable fat instead of cocoa butter. In the family shop, though, Norman offered a range of sweets and had always had a decent display of Easter eggs. Not any more.

'Carrot lollies, I ask you,' he moaned, citing the latest desperate suggestion from the Ministry of Food. 'As if any kiddie's going to be fooled by those when what they want is to stuff their face with a nice chocolate egg!'

Mary was determined to make her usual effort for the occasion, though. She'd stinted on meals and saved up the family's coupons so she could lay on a decent lunch. Johnnie didn't have leave, but Penny was invited, and Mike too, naturally.

Carrie couldn't wait. After his visit to his parents, he'd had to go straight on to a course at Staff College to prepare for his stint in America.

The Carrie of a year ago would have said it had been the longest two weeks of her life, but she'd endured months without Mike, and was about to have three months without him again. She knew now that, in the scheme of things, she was lucky. Not that it had made their parting any easier, and Mike had held her very tight when they'd said goodbye. Before that, though, he'd had a new photograph done in his lieutenant's uniform with the extra pip on the shoulder tab. Carrie had put it in a lovely walnut frame she'd spotted in a box of oddments in a sort of Old Curiosity Shop in town.

Foolish as it seemed, she'd been gazing at the photo every night before she went to sleep, willing it to come to life and give her a goodnight kiss. Even in black and white, Mike looked so handsome, a lock of his dark hair brushed to one side beneath his cap, his eyes frank and amused as he stared at the camera. So much for spending all the time they had left together! But they still had a few weeks before he'd be packing his bags for America.

Norman had disappeared on some mysterious errand – ARP-related, Mary and Carrie assumed. Mary was in the kitchen and Carrie was setting the table when Mike arrived, almost hidden behind a massive cardboard box and looking extremely pleased with himself.

Carrie flung down the knives and forks with a clatter, and would have thrown herself at him but for the box he was carrying.

'Hello, stranger,' he said, kissing Carrie over the top of it. 'Let me put this down.'

'What is it?' asked Carrie, as Mike placed the box on a chair. 'You haven't brought us a turkey, have you? Mum's got a rolled shoulder of lamb in the oven!'

'I know,' said Mike. 'I smelled it as I came through. Delicious. Just like you look.' And as he drew her close, he added: 'And smell.'

Carrie folded herself into his arms, melting against him and lifting her head to be kissed again. And again. Finally, they drew apart.

'I've missed you,' she said.

'Missed you too, in case you hadn't guessed.'

And then, because she'd resolved not to be feeble in the face of him going away, since he had no choice, she said, as brightly as she could: 'But I suppose it was a rehearsal, of sorts.'

Mike nodded, knowing how hard she was trying and grateful that she wasn't making things any more difficult than they were.

'Yes, good practice,' he smiled. Then he indicated the box and said: 'This is for you.'

'What?' exclaimed Carrie. 'We don't do presents at Easter, do we? If so, I'm sorry, but I haven't got you anything.'

'I don't want anything,' Mike grinned. 'I've got all I need.' He kissed her again. 'Now, are you going to open it, or am I?'

Carrie picked up the box and gave it a gentle shake. There was no sound from inside and it was very light.

'Is it a giant Easter egg?' she asked. 'Did you win it in a raffle?'

How on earth could he have come by one otherwise?

'You won't know, will you, till you open it,' he said annoyingly.

Obediently, Carrie untied the string and lifted the flaps. Inside, all she could see was a mass of crumpled newspaper.

'Thanks very much,' she said. 'As if I don't see enough newspaper every day!'

'Keep going,' chided Mike.

Slowly, Carrie started pulling bits of paper out.

'Oh, come on! Hurry up,' Mike urged. 'Oh, let me. But first close your eyes.'

'You're such a fool sometimes,' she said affectionately. 'Like a little boy.'

But she closed her eyes.

There was a pause, a lot of rustling, then another pause.

'Can I open them yet?'

'No!' said Mike sternly. 'Not till I tell you.' There was another pause. Then he said: 'All right, you can open them now.'

Carrie opened her eyes – and looked down. Mike was on one knee in front of her, holding up a small leather box. He looked up at her, his eyes full of feeling. Carrie felt her own eyes begin to brim. Mike took her hand in his free one.

'Carrie,' he said, 'I tried to think of a hundred ways to surprise you. I'd like to have done this on a deserted beach in the moonlight, but the beaches are all covered in barbed wire and mines. I thought about getting hold of a car again and driving us out to the countryside ... to find a little stream running clear over pebbles, and a stone bridge over it, and us leaning on the parapet. But what about the roadblocks and the Home Guard charging through on an exercise? It'd rather ruin the moment, don't you think?'

'Mike—' Carrie smiled.

'But in the end, you know . . .' Mike looked around him at the moquette armchairs, the standard lamp with its parchment shade, the *Light of the World* aquatint, the table spread with the best cloth, the fire irons on the tiled hearth, the family photos and the pair of matching china dogs on the mantelpiece, '. . . here, where you've grown up, all the happy times you've had with your family, all the happy times we've had here too, well, it's as romantic a spot as any. I think so, anyway, and I hope you do too. And what I want to say is: wherever we are, wherever you are and wherever I am, I love you, and when this wretched war's over, I want us to be together for ever.'

'Mike—' Carrie said again, almost choked. 'Do you really mean it?'

'Yes, of course I mean it. I'm asking you to marry me. What d'you say?'

Carrie found her voice. 'What do I say? Well, yes, of course I will! Oh yes, yes!'

And then they were both laughing and she was in his arms and he was kissing her again, with the table half laid and next door's cat watching them unblinkingly from the window sill.

He released her and flipped open the lid of the box. Inside was a beautiful three-stone diamond.

'Would you like to put it on?'

Without waiting for an answer, he took the ring from the box and slid it onto her finger.

61

'Oh,' she breathed. 'I never expected any of this! And the ring . . . it's just . . . stunning!'

'I'm glad you like it,' Mike said. 'It was my grand-mother's.'

'What?'

'I told my folks I was going to propose, and my mother went upstairs and came back with this. And I took one look at it and thought it was perfect.'

'It is!'

Mike took her hand and studied the ring.

'I've just realised something else. Three stones,' he smiled. 'One for each: our past, our present – and our future.'

Chapter Eight

The rest of the day was a blur of happiness and congratulations from her parents and Penny, who had arrived for lunch.

'And Carrie says I'm a dark horse!' Penny joked as she kissed Mike on the cheek. 'Had you got any idea this was coming, Carrie?'

'Not a clue!' Carrie replied, her arm wrapped around Mike's waist.

'Well, I had an advance warning, anyway.' Norman turned from the sideboard, where he was getting out the best glasses. Mike had called at the mess bar and had brought a bottle of champagne to celebrate. 'That little errand I had to see to this morning? It was Mike tipping me the wink.'

'I thought I'd better do it properly,' Mike explained to an open-mouthed Carrie. 'Ask your father for your hand, and all that.'

'How very quaint!' Penny raised her eyebrows.

Carrie wondered how Penny would wriggle out of it if a future husband – maybe even Johnnie – wanted to do the right thing and ask her father the same question. Then Norman unpeeled the foil and eased the cork out of the bottle with a gentle pop. The bottle seemed to smoke, but not a drop was spilled.

'Where did you learn to do that?' asked Carrie in amazement. She'd seen it in films, but to her knowledge this was the first bottle of champagne ever consumed in the Anderson household.

'Aha!' grinned Norman, tilting the glasses as he poured. 'The First War wasn't all trench foot and bullets, you know. We did get leave . . . Ah, some of the times we had when we were off the leash in this little bar in Amiens . . .'

'That's enough of your war stories, thank you,' said Mary primly, accepting a glass from Mike, who was handing them round. When Norman met up with his old comrades, he was liable to roll in well oiled. From what Mary could hear of their raucous laughter when he brought a few of them back, what they'd got up to with some of the French mademoiselles was nobody's business.

When everyone had a glass, they chinked and raised them to Carrie and Mike.

Norman cleared his throat.

'It's not a speech, don't worry,' he said as Carrie pretended to look alarmed. 'I'm not going to mention any embarrassing incidents from your childhood – I'll save those for the wedding!' As everyone laughed and Carrie protested, he went on. 'No, I just want to say, what a happy day this is. We were proud enough when you set up on your own at the station bookshop, Carrie – we could see how happy you were to be running your own show. And to think it introduced you to this fine young man who's had the gumption to see you're a terrific girl – well, me and your mum couldn't be more delighted, could we, love?'

Mary, overcome by the fizzy wine and the way her Easter

64

Sunday lunch had suddenly turned into something even more momentous, could only nod and smile.

'Hear! Hear!' said Penny, raising her glass again.

Carrie looked around the room with almost all her favourite people gathered in it. It was a shame Johnnie couldn't be there, but they'd phone him later, she and Mike together.

This homely living room, where Carrie had eaten her meals, done her homework at the table, played snap with Johnnie and, more recently, listened to every news bulletin and knitted and sewn till her eyeballs felt as if they'd been rolled in sand, had never looked so vivid or so lovely. Mike was right. It was romantic because it contained everything she held dear. She wouldn't have wanted to be proposed to anywhere else.

When lunch was over and they'd phoned Johnnie and received his delighted congratulations, Penny tactfully excused herself. Carrie and Mike headed off for a walk, Carrie refusing to wear her gloves so that she could admire her ring twinkling in the sun. After months of dismal skies, it had finally made an appearance.

'The ring, the champagne ... you even managed to ask Dad for my hand! You thought of everything.'

'Strategy,' smiled Mike. 'You don't think I'd lead my men into any kind of situation without a bit of advance planning? Well, it was the same here.'

'Oh, so I'm just another battle plan? Thanks very much!'

'You know that's not what I mean.'

Carrie did know, of course she did. She stopped, Mike stopped too, and she slid her arms round his waist. 'I love you so much. I can't believe you've planned all this for me. Thank you. I just – I love you.'

Mike smiled down at her. The sun was glinting on the lighter tones in her hair, making them gleam like gold. Her blue eyes were turned trustingly to his, her lips parted in a way he found most exciting.

'I love you too,' he said. 'And I meant every word. I can't wait till we're together for ever. As soon as I come back from America, we're getting married.'

Carrie breathed a blissful sigh and snuggled in closer.

'Oh, yes please!' she said.

But as he held her close, knowing how much he wanted her, and she him, could they wait that long?

Next time she saw Mike, it was Carrie who had something to announce. They were walking to the cinema, but they weren't sure if they'd actually go in. Thanks to Double Summer Time, the evening was still light. The air was almost warm and the sky a translucent blue – far too nice to go and sit in the dark.

'Mike,' she began, 'I don't want you to go away—'

Mike stopped and turned to her.

'Oh, Carrie, I thought you'd taken it too well.'

'No, silly, wait till you hear the rest.' Carrie drew him aside to sit on the low stone wall that spanned the memorial garden in front of the Town Hall. She took a deep breath. 'I don't want you to go away without us spending the night together.'

Mike looked at her and gave a tiny shake of his head, as if he hadn't heard right.

'You do? Are you sure?'

'Absolutely.'

Since the ecstatic day of their engagement, Carrie had thought about nothing else. Through all the heady congratulations from Bette and Ruby and her regular customers who noticed her ring, she'd imagined the future with Mike – going to bed together, waking up together, and all the blissful togetherness, the ultimate togetherness, in between. If things had been different, if they hadn't had such a lengthy separation after Dunkirk and had to get to know each other all over again, they might have slept together long ago. And now they were going to be married! Carrie knew Mike's intentions were honourable – she'd never had any doubt. And she certainly had no doubt about her feelings for him. Or her desires.

Mike grabbed her hands.

'You know how much I want to. But I don't want you to feel you have to. I hope you don't think I expect it just because we're engaged.'

'I know you don't! I really want us to do this.'

'You're sure?'

'Stop asking me that!' Carrie stopped his questions with a kiss. 'Just book us a room.'

'Bye, love, have a nice time, and stay safe!'

It was four thirty on a Saturday afternoon in April. Carrie had closed up early so that they could get off in good time. Mary waved the Austin Ten, which Mike had once more managed to wangle from the army, away from the kerb. She turned to Norman, standing in the doorway of the shop.

'I hope she knows what she's doing.'

'Oh, Mary, don't you know our Carrie at all?' scolded Norman. 'She's a grown woman! She's been running her own business for a year and half – she's got her head screwed on right. A few months and they'll be married anyway.'

'You reckon it's a double room he's booked, then?'

'I'd be surprised if it's not. But we could hardly ask.'

Carrie had had to tell them she and Mike were going away overnight; she wasn't going to fib and pretend she was staying at Penny's. To her relief, her parents had been both circumspect and helpful. Mary had carefully ironed Carrie's latest rummage-sale find, a delicate silk crêpe de Chine blouse with pintucks and an embroidered collar, not an easy task even under a damp cloth. Norman had pressed a ten-bob note into her hand 'for emergencies'.

Now he added to his wife:

'There's plenty of girls Carrie's age that are married with a kiddie or two by now – don't look at me like that, I know that's what you're worried about! Carrie's a sensible girl. She's more interested in books than babies. And I'm sure we can trust Mike to . . . you know, take care of things. Take care of her.'

Mary sighed, but had to agree.

'That's true. Mike's a lovely lad.'

'He is. He'll look after her.'

'Yes,' agreed Mary. 'All right.' Then she added: 'It'll be funny, won't it, just the two of us with the house to ourselves all night. We haven't had that since the twins were born.'

'Ooh, you're not suggesting a bit of how's your father for us, are you? You cheeky madam!'

Norman gave his wife's waist a squeeze and planted a smacking kiss on her lips.

'Norman Anderson!' said Mary, shocked. 'Out in the street as well. What about my reputation!'

And, smiling together, they went inside.

In the car, Mike and Carrie were laughing too. Mike was refusing to tell her where they were going.

'But I don't doubt you've planned it out,' said Carrie. 'Strategic thinking again?'

She was trying to keep things light to cover her nervousness now they were actually embarking on this experience – the biggest experience of her life so far.

And lo and behold, Mike *had* planned it. The fact that all the signposts had been taken down in case of invasion played into his hands. Periodically, he stopped the car and glanced at a hand-drawn diagram – there were no maps any more – turning away theatrically to consult it ('No peeping!'). Occasionally, Carrie fed him a sweet ('Fruit bonbon? Peppermint?'), her dad having thoughtfully provided her with a selection from his stock. But the rest of the time, she stared out of the window, enthralled, as they bowled along through the spring countryside. Her senses heightened by excitement, the trees had never looked so vividly green, the birds had never chirped so loudly, the primroses and violets had never studded the verges so voluptuously.

After a while, they turned off what had seemed to be a main-ish road. Carrie turned to Mike.

'I've got it,' she said. 'We're going to a little country pub in the middle of nowhere. I just hope there isn't a ghost!'

'Wrong!' sang Mike, keeping his eyes on the road as he negotiated a corner. They drove on down a succession of winding lanes until he pulled into a farm gateway and stopped the car.

'Come on,' he said, easing his shoulders back. 'We're going for a walk.'

'Really?'

'Really.'

They got out and Mike took her hand. Carrie followed him, mystified, until, round another bend, she saw it. A little river – more of a wide stream, really – set between lush green banks where willows dipped their boughs to the water. Over it stretched an old stone bridge with a parapet.

'You're not serious?' smiled Carrie. 'You're not really going to propose again?'

'Come on!'

Mike pulled her along, and, just as he'd promised on Easter Sunday, they leaned on the parapet in the soft evening light and stared down, mesmerised, at the ceaseless progress of the water over the pebbly riverbed.

'So,' he said eventually. 'Shall we have Take Two?'

'Oh, no!' warned Carrie. 'You can propose all over again if you like, but I'm not taking my ring off – I'm not risking it going in the water! And anyway, my answer's the same.'

'That's good,' said Mike. 'Just checking. But I'm going to ask anyway, because sometimes I can't believe my luck.'

He dropped to one knee and looked up at her. Carrie met his eyes, her love for him coursing through her from her fingertips to her toes and warming her inside and out.

'*Your* luck? Are you sure you've got that right?'

70

'Absolutely certain,' Mike replied with a grin. 'So for the second time of asking, will you marry me?'

Carrie didn't hesitate. She pulled him to his feet and into her arms. The sunlight trembled through the fretwork of leaves, finally slanting onto the bridge and warming Carrie even more as Mike laced his fingers through her hair for a long and delicious kiss. As she emerged, a shimmer of blue caught her eye and she whirled Mike around.

'Look! A kingfisher!'

Mike turned just in time to see a vivid flash as the bird disappeared into its perfectly spherical tunnel in the bank.

'Look at that,' said Mike. 'Someone knows how to keep safe!'

They leaned there happily for another few minutes as the water tumbled lazily on its way, as it had for centuries, oblivious to whoever stood on the bridge above it, their joys or sorrows, triumphs or disasters. Some things never changed and never would. With the world as it was, it was good to be reminded of that.

Chapter Nine

Finally, Mike led her back to the car. They had, he said, some way to go yet. After another hour or so, with Carrie having little sense of where they were going, except that it seemed to be due south, she sat forward.

'Is that . . . Can I see the sea?'

'Yes,' said Mike. 'Well spotted.'

Soon they were winding through narrow cobbled streets lined with ancient-looking houses.

'Where are we?' Carrie asked, entranced. 'It looks like something out of, I don't know, Dickens, or even . . . Shakespeare, or Chaucer!'

'It's Rye,' Mike grinned. 'Where the river leads to the sea. You're right about Dickens, by the way. He popped down here for the flower and veg show in 1852, I believe. Oh, and it was the inspiration for Tilling in the Mapp and Lucia books.'

'Of course!'

'I thought you'd want some kind of literary connection,' Mike smiled, 'and getting up to Yorkshire for a Brontë sisters pilgrimage was a step too far.'

He turned the car into the courtyard of a half-timbered inn and they got out, stretching and shaking their limbs. He got their bags out of the boot and took her hand.

'Ready?'

Carrie's insides were churning, but she nodded.

'Of course.'

The reception desk was in a small, red-carpeted lobby. A kindly-looking woman bustled from the office at the rear to give them their key. Mike signed them in as 'Mr and Mrs Hudson'.

'Now,' the woman said coyly, 'you didn't say, sir, when you booked, but from the look of you young people, I think I've done the right thing. We had a cancellation, so I've been able to put you in the honeymoon suite.'

'Goodness! How lovely,' Carrie managed.

She hadn't said a word until then, and was keeping her gloves on to cover the whole business of rings. She'd baulked at buying a curtain ring from Woolworths.

'Dinner's served till nine o'clock,' the woman said. 'Yours is the table in the window.'

'Thank you.'

Mike took their bags and the key and the woman pointed them upstairs. Carrie followed him in silence as he led the way. The corridor was long, narrow and low-ceilinged – Mike had to stoop. The door to the room was old, oak and heavy. Mike opened it and stood aside to let her in. Then he closed the door and leaned against it, exploding with laughter.

'Honeymoon suite! Look at it! I honestly didn't plan this bit.'

'Even you couldn't have anticipated this,' agreed Carrie.

The room was large and very, very pink. The four-poster bed with its carved frame had a pink brocade cover to match the curtains. The sofa and little armchair were pink, and so were the shades on the bedside lamps.

When Mike returned from investigating the bathroom down the corridor ('At least that's not pink!'), Carrie crossed to the window. The sun, dipping now, slanted rosily on the latticed panes, which looked out on the cobbled street and the houses and shops opposite. When she turned her head, she could see water in the distance, flat and calm like a silvered mirror.

'Can we explore before we eat?'

He smiled at her excitement.

'Just what I was going to suggest.'

Hand in hand, they strolled down past houses that leant this way and that, past a huge fortress, well guarded, that Mike said was called the Ypres Tower and was nearly seven hundred years old.

'It's seen off plenty of would-be attackers,' he said. 'Everyone from smugglers to Napoleon.'

They walked on towards the river and then along it as far as they were allowed. This whole strip of coast, like all the south coast of England, was heavily fortified against invasion. Nearby Camber Castle was an observation point; there were machine-gun posts in concrete pillboxes strung out across the marshes. In the distance was the soft shimmer of the sea and the cries of the wheeling seagulls.

'It's not moonlight, and we can't quite get to the beach, such as it is.' Mike stopped walking. 'But if you want me to go down on one knee for that other proposal you didn't get . . .'

'I've a good mind to make you do it,' laughed Carrie. 'Stop teasing. I've had my proposal, thank you very much. Two of them, in fact!'

They walked a little further, then turned back to wash and brush up for dinner. Suddenly shy, Carrie changed her everyday blouse for the cream silk while Mike was in the bathroom. She was brushing her hair at the dressing table when he came back.

'Have I seen that before?' he asked.

He always noticed her clothes.

'No, you haven't.'

Mike ran his hands down her arms.

'Feels nice. You feel nice.'

Carrie got up and he put his arms around her. They stood for a while, each leaning into the embrace.

'I'd better let you go, or we'll never get our dinner,' said Mike after a long while.

Carrie had thought the same thing.

They had a wonderful evening. There were only a few other diners in the restaurant by the time they got there, and they sat on happily in the twilight, talking about their plans for the future – when, not if, the war was won. Until now, they'd been so intent on living in the moment, this far-distant future hadn't really come up.

Carrie knew Mike had never intended to take over his parents' shop in Leamington, which sold sewing machines and fabric and haberdashery, and there were no expectations that he would. She was relieved. She couldn't see herself swapping books for measuring curtain material with a yardstick and counting out duck-shaped buttons for children's cardigans.

'What do you see yourself doing?'

'Well, I don't want a stuffy job in the City,' declared Mike. 'I could stay in the army, of course, but I suspect I'll have had plenty of soldiering by the time we get through this war. And more than enough of being away from you.'

'So?'

'I always thought I wouldn't mind teaching,' he reflected. 'History, English ... But now I've seen what fun you're having in the bookshop, well, if you like the idea, maybe we could expand on that.'

'Really?' Naturally Carrie had had her dreams, but she'd dismissed them as impossible. 'More bookstalls? In stations that aren't big enough for a W.H. Smith?'

Mike wrinkled his nose.

'I was thinking more of a proper dedicated bookshop. There isn't a decent one in Brockington at the moment. Not newspapers or magazines or stationery, just books. And we'd run it together.' He looked at her, quizzical, amused. 'If you think you could bear working with me.'

'Oh, it'd be dreadful – that would never work!' teased Carrie. 'Don't be silly, it'd be wonderful!'

'I suppose you'd insist on being the senior partner,' Mike challenged.

'Naturally!' Carrie shot back. 'Stop teasing. We'd be equal partners – a joint enterprise.'

At the end of the meal, the young waitress, who reminded Carrie of Ruby in both looks and attitude, swept the crumbs from their table into a little pan.

'Coffee's in the lounge,' she announced cheerily. 'You serve yourselves. I'm off now.'

It was pretty clear what the rest of her evening had in

store. Before the blackout curtains had been drawn, a young man in a sailor's cap had appeared outside the window, cheekily signalling to her and tapping his watch.

'Have fun,' Mike smiled at her, grinning at Carrie too.

'Ta! Will do!'

She sashayed off, depositing the crumb tray on a sideboard and untying the strings of her apron before she'd even reached the swing door of the kitchen. Very like Ruby, bless her! After the evening they'd had, Carrie was filled with warm feelings towards everyone. And the evening so far was just the start.

'Would you like coffee?' asked Mike.

'I don't think so, thanks.'

Mike looked at her meaningfully.

'Shall we go up then?'

'Yes. Let's.'

Carrie's heart and stomach tumbled again – nervousness mixed with excitement – as he took her hand and led her to the stairs. Up in the room, Mike followed her as she moved to draw the curtains.

'Leave them for now,' he said.

There was enough light from the moon to see his face as he pulled her against him.

'Well, we've got the moonlight,' he said. 'But no roses, and no violins. No nightingales either. Sorry about that. A big failure on my part not to organise those.'

'You've planned it beautifully,' she said, meaning it. 'It couldn't be lovelier or more romantic. It's all . . . magical.'

She meant it. It was as if a benevolent being had cast a spell. The drive, the stop by the stream, the walk before dinner, the meal itself, and their plans for the future. And now they were here in their room and the moment had come.

They were touching all the way down their bodies, closer than they'd ever been before. She could feel his heart beating against her breast and she was sure he must be able to feel hers beating in the same way. She wanted him so badly, and she knew he felt the same. But at the same time . . . Oh, she knew he'd be kind and tender; he loved her and she loved him—

'Carrie . . .' he said, as in the same moment she said, 'Mike . . .'

'I don't think we should do this,' he said, his voice tight. 'I want you, so much, but despite everything, it doesn't feel quite right somehow. That is, I don't think it's right for us. Not now, not yet. I'm sorry, but I think we should wait.'

'Oh, so do I!' she burst out. 'I think so too! Oh, I'm so glad you said that. I didn't like to because coming away together was my suggestion, and I meant it at the time, I really did—'

'I know you did—'

'And it's all been so perfect – it *is* perfect, and maybe that's why. I want to remember this evening like this. It's enough. It's more than enough. If it's enough for you.'

'We've waited this long,' said Mike. 'And the minute I get back from America, we're getting married. Three months – that's not much more to wait, is it, to do it right?'

'It's nothing,' said Carrie, thinking of the ten months they'd been apart the year before. 'It's the blink of an eye.'

'Come on,' Mike said. 'Let's lie down. We may as well test out the bed anyway.'

So they took off their shoes and Mike shrugged off his

jacket and loosened his tie, and they lay down together on the bed.

'Even this,' said Carrie as she snuggled into the crook of his arm, 'even this is so much more time and privacy together than we've ever been able to have before. It's ... it's delicious!'

Mike kissed her hair.

'You are funny,' he said. 'Funny and bright, and never ever dull.'

'If I am, it's because you make me that way,' smiled Carrie. 'I – well, I've come out of myself since I met you. Though I suppose running the bookstall has helped as well.'

'I might have known I'd have to vie with your beloved bookshop! Can you see now why I have to go into partner-ship with you in every sense of the word? I wouldn't get a look-in otherwise!'

Comfortable, cuddled together and plotting their future – a chain of bookshops covering the whole country, they'd decided by the time they finished – they finally fell asleep in each other's arms.

Chapter Ten

Carrie was the first to wake the next day. No one had told Tudor glaziers when they fitted their lopsided windows that there might one day be a world war, or indeed aeroplanes, let alone the Luftwaffe, so light was filtering through around the edges of the blackout curtains. But it couldn't have done much harm anyway: the night had been siren-free.

She looked at Mike's sleeping face. His head was half turned towards her and she marvelled at things she'd not seen up close before – the length of his eyelashes and the stubble on his cheeks. She longed to reach out and touch it, but face to face with him, didn't want to wake him. She must have moved, though, because his face twitched, he wrinkled his nose and stirred. Carrie lay still, but he stretched, yawned and frowned. He opened his eyes.

'Oh, it's you!' he said, smiling. 'I wondered what this dead weight was on my arm.'

Carrie was lying against his left side: she was still conscious of trying to spare his right shoulder.

'Good morning to you too,' she smiled. 'Sleep well?'

Mike turned on his side and put his other arm around her.

'Surprisingly well,' he replied. 'You?'

Carrie nodded. 'Are you still glad we, you know ... waited?'

It wasn't too late for a change of heart. And lying close to him was very tempting.

'Don't start all that again,' said Mike.

He sat up, put on the light and reached for his jacket. From the inside pocket he took out a small diary and began to flick through the pages.

'I go in the first week of May,' he mused. 'So three months on is . . . How does an early August wedding sound?'

'If you can get leave – any time!' said Carrie.

'You say that, but you've forgotten one thing. You'll have to close the bookshop for a day, maybe two or more.' Mike drew in an exaggerated breath. 'A big sacrifice, I know . . .'

'You!' Carrie sat up and made as if to grab her pillow. 'You're in trouble now!'

But Mike pulled her down and kissed her, and that was the end of that.

Carrie hadn't told Penny, let alone Bette, that she and Mike were going away, and when she got back to the station on Monday she still didn't want to say anything. She'd never asked about Penny and Johnnie's sex life, and she doubted Penny, the ultimate secret-keeper, would have told her if she had. Why should she? Such things were better kept private. But there was one thing she could report, leaning out over the counter as Penny swept the platform – something else she and Mike had decided.

'I'm going up to meet Mike's family before he goes away.'

'Oh, are you now? On trial?' Penny pushed a collection of discarded cigarette butts, ticket stubs and general detritus into a heap. 'Looking forward to it?'

'Terrified!'

Although she had no reason to be, really. Carrie ran through what she knew about Mike's parents – Clara and Geoffrey. Their shop in Leamington was, like Anderson's Newsagent & Stationer, an old family business, and though Mike played it down, it sounded a slightly more prosperous one. Even so, it had taken a rich auntie to put him through a good school and army college. If his fifteen-year-old sister, Jane, who was animal-mad, remained set on becoming a vet, Mike had implied his aunt's help would be needed again to fund that.

'Oh, rubbish,' said Penny, tipping the contents of her pan into the bin. 'They'll love you.'

'It's all right for you,' Carrie retorted. 'We all knew you long before you started seeing Johnnie romantically.'

'And yet that still didn't put him off,' said Penny smugly. Then she asked: 'What are you wearing? Want to borrow anything?'

It was kind of Penny to offer – she had some lovely clothes, well cut and in good fabrics, from her previous life. She hadn't baulked at bringing those with her for her new start. But Carrie had already decided what she'd wear: she had a pretty spring dress of pale green, scattered with mauve and white flowers.

So she was wearing that, together with her new spring coat, when the next Sunday morning she was for once a traveller on one of the trains whose passengers she served every day. Carrie and Mike changed trains in London and boarded another train to Leamington. Carrie had done her homework. As a spa town, it might not have the reputation of Bath or

82

Buxton, but its waters had brought wealthy Georgians there and it still had a lot of elegant Regency architecture. It had escaped significant war damage so far, despite its nearness to poor old Coventry, devastated the previous autumn thanks to its aircraft and armaments industries.

The platforms at Leamington Spa looked comfortingly like Brockington Junction – iron pillars supporting a pitched roof with a decorative wooden trim. But the station building itself was startlingly modern – a huge art deco affair almost the size of Brockington's Rialto cinema. A massive clock, 'presented by the Corporation', had been installed in 1939 – just in time.

Carrie would have loved a peek at the bookstall to check out the competition, but Mike hustled her into a taxi ('Mum will have rushed back from church to get lunch on the table at one!') and before Carrie knew it, they were drawing up in a street of Edwardian semi-detached villas. Unlike her own family, Mike's didn't live 'over the shop'.

Even so, she was relieved to see that the house was a modest two storeys with a small square of garden at the front. She took in the privet hedge, the chequerboard-tiled path edged in blue brick, and the lace café curtains in the front window. Mary had demanded a full report.

Once inside, Carrie felt all her nerves disappear. Mike's parents could not have been more welcoming, his mother kissing her on the cheek and his father shaking her hand. They ushered her into the front room. Again for her mother's delectation, Carrie noted its cast-iron fireplace and a bergère suite, the canework and arms rather battered, with olive-green velvet cushions. The curtains were beautiful, as you'd expect with their business – it looked like a William Morris design, big open lilies on a dark green background. Carrie was even more pleased with what she'd worn; she felt she toned in rather well. Mike's sister, his mother explained, was out – she'd got herself a job mucking out at a local stables.

'She'll come in stinking to high heaven, I warn you!' Mike's father told Carrie. He was tall, like his son, but with lighter brown hair that was turning grey, and bright blue eyes behind glasses. His mother was tall, too, and carefully but not flashily dressed in a tweed skirt and pink twinset. Carrie noticed that her stockings, like Carrie's own, had a darn at the heel.

When they'd had coffee, Mrs Hudson murmured something about seeing to the lunch. Carrie quickly offered to help, half expecting to be brushed aside, but Mrs Hudson said that would be lovely, so Carrie followed her mother-in-law-to-be out to the kitchen. Like the kitchen in Carrie's home, it had been converted from what had been the scullery at the back of the house, and though the stove was a bigger model than Mary's Baby Belling, the cabinets and the small deal table looked well used.

Mrs Hudson bent to check the oven.

'I managed to get a chicken,' she said. 'We're lucky here, the farmers come round with rabbits and game and vegetables. I don't suppose you have that so much in London?'

Carrie didn't point out that Brockington wasn't really London, not by a long way, but she didn't want to disagree.

'Not at all. It'll be a treat!'

She thought of the meat loaf, the not-much-cheese-and-lots-of-potato pie and the thing called 'lentil bake' that were staples on the table at home. A ruddy-cheeked farmer with a cartload of produce would have been very welcome.

Just then, the back door crashed open and a young girl, tousle-headed, in filthy dungarees and giving off a strong smell of horse, stepped inside.

'Boots!' cried Mrs Hudson at once. 'Jane, really, how many times—'

'OK, I know!' muttered the recipient of this reprimand, easing off her boots on the back step. Mrs Hudson raised her eyebrows at Carrie.

'Are you sure you want this creature for a bridesmaid?'

Mike had already told his parents this was Carrie's suggestion.

'Of course. Maybe not with the muddy boots, though!'

Jane said nothing, just closed the door and stood by it in her socks, looking Carrie up and down. Carrie held out her hand.

'Hello.'

Jane sniffed.

'Better not. I need to wash them first. Excuse me.'

Carrie stepped aside, puzzled, as Jane pushed past and ran upstairs.

'I'm so sorry about that.' Mrs Hudson's cheeks were pink. 'It was very rude. I don't know what's got into her lately. But I suppose she's at a difficult age.'

'Don't worry about it.'

But Carrie was puzzled: she was used to people liking

her on sight. This felt like more than just a fifteen-year-old's moodiness. What could she possibly have done without even meeting the girl to prompt such animosity?

Jane didn't appear downstairs again before lunch. Her mother called her several times from the bottom of the stairs, but in the end, flustered and obviously embarrassed, she sent Jane's father up to winkle her out.

'Sorry about this,' Mike said when his parents were out of earshot. He seemed embarrassed too. 'It's not the Jane I know.'

'She's taken against me,' Carrie said simply. 'You should have seen the look she gave me when she came in. Thunderous.'

'Mum did say on the telephone she'd seemed rather difficult lately – not like herself. She put it down to her not quite being over that food poisoning.'

'It's more than that. Do you think – do you think she doesn't want to be a bridesmaid? I mean, I don't want to force her.'

Mike shrugged. 'Search me.'

Jane finally appeared at five past one, still rather casually dressed in a corduroy skirt and a flannel blouse.

'Oh, Jane!' said her mother. 'I ironed your best frock – it's on the back of your door!'

'I didn't see it,' said Jane unconvincingly, taking her place.

'Do sit down, Carrie,' said Mr Hudson. 'Here, on my right, with Mike beside you.'

Carrie took her place as Mrs Hudson brought the chicken

86

to the table and placed it in front of her husband to carve. Mike carried in a dish of roast potatoes, followed by stuffing and gravy. Mrs Hudson brought in dishes of vegetables.

'What a feast!' said Carrie. 'It all looks delicious.'

And it was. As they ate, Mike, Carrie and his parents kept up a bright, initially over-bright, conversation: the war, the weather, Carrie's work. Then they moved on to more serious things – the difficulties of running a business with all the shortages, and the torrent of ever-changing requirements from various government ministries to be complied with. They spoke about the fearful battering nearby Coventry had taken. The two further raids it had endured before Easter seemed extra cruel when the cathedral and so much of the medieval centre had been wiped out already in the early part of the Blitz. They even touched on how hard it must have been for Carrie, as it had been for them, when Mike was missing for so long. Jane spoke when she was spoken to, and then in not much more than monosyllables. Even Mike could get nothing out of her.

Mrs Hudson produced a trifle for pudding, and when Jane had demolished an enormous helping, though everyone else had barely put down their spoons, she excused herself, saying she'd start the washing-up.

'You can leave that, dear. Mike and Carrie will have to go soon—' Mrs Hudson began.

But Jane had already gone.

Mike threw down his napkin and stood up.

'I'm not having this. Excuse me.'

He followed his sister out.

In the kitchen, Jane was running water into the sink.

'What do you think you're playing at?' Mike demanded. 'You're being so vile in front of Carrie! What's she going to think of you?'

Without replying, Jane held the packet of soda crystals high in the air and shook them in a snowstorm over the water. Mike grabbed the box from her.

'Stop wasting the stuff. Why are you being so annoying? And damn rude!'

Still Jane said nothing.

Mike reached past her to turn off the taps, took her by the shoulders and turned her round.

'Jane! Talk to me!'

Face to face with her brother, Jane burst into tears.

They were all back in the sitting room, Jane still dabbing her eyes with Mike's handkerchief.

'You mean this is all to do with Granny's ring?' her mother asked.

Jane blew her nose loudly.

'I always thought it would come to me. On my eighteenth!'

'Oh, Jane,' said her mother affectionately. 'You are a silly girl. Or maybe we're the silly ones, for not explaining to you. Granny said in her will that her engagement ring should go to Mike's intended. She left you her pearl necklace!'

Jane looked up.

'I didn't know Granny had a pearl necklace.'

'Well, why would you, Mum's mum died before you were born!' Mike butted in. He was obviously still cross with his sister. 'I didn't know about the ring till Mum produced it when I was last home. You were away on that orienteering course. And it's completely unfair to take it out on Carrie. She had nothing to do with any of it!'

'It seems to me there've been a lot of assumptions made,' Mr Hudson chipped in. 'A lot of wrong assumptions.'

He was standing by the fire, filling his pipe from a tobacco jar. Carrie was pleased about the pipe – something else, apart from the tribulations of keeping a shop going in these hard times, he shared with her own father.

Jane had the grace to look a little abashed.

'And let's be honest, Jane, what use would a diamond ring be to you?' Mike's tone was warmer now. 'If you carry on with this veterinary idea, you'll have your hand up a cow's backside half the time!'

That broke the ice once and for all. Everyone laughed. Jane flicked the handkerchief at her brother, he ducked away, and Carrie, who'd been silent while this little drama played out, said:

'I wonder . . . if you think it's a good idea, Mrs Hudson, and if you do want to be a bridesmaid, Jane – there's no obligation, honestly, but if you do – well, maybe you could wear the pearls on the day?'

'That is a good idea!' said Mrs Hudson at once.

'I don't know . . .' said Mike doubtfully as Carrie shot him a puzzled glance. 'How are they going to look with her wellies?'

Chapter Eleven

Carrie and Mike had one final Sunday together – this time deliberately by themselves. Carrie knew his last week in the country would be full of final briefings and that she wouldn't see him again before he boarded his special flight the following Friday.

The weather was still chilly, if sunny, so they wrapped up warmly and went for a bracing walk in Petts Wood, one of their favourite places. Late frosts had been death to the tender plants in Brockington's gardens, but out in the woods, spring had sprung as it had done for hundreds of years and would a hundred years hence. The beech leaves quivered a vivid green, and succeeding the wild garlic and primroses, there was the faintest suggestion of the blue haze that would turn the forest floor into a sea of bluebells.

They walked and chatted and stopped and kissed, knowing that in the scheme of things, they'd had a good run – Mike had been home for a full four months. They'd have a short separation and then they'd be married, and then ... well, who could tell? He'd be posted again, of course, but Carrie couldn't help hoping, and she felt Mike was too, that the job in Washington meant he was being marked out for some kind of organisational role in the future, which might keep him in London for the rest of the war. Though he loved army life and had never shirked active service, nor ever would, 'Together for ever' had become a fervent if unspoken hope between them.

Mike telephoned the evening before his flight.

'I love you,' he said, as if Carrie needed telling. 'Don't forget to write.'

'Do you really have to remind me?'

She watched the clock for all of Friday, knowing that Mike's long flight was due to take off at half past three. As the hand of the station clock ticked round, she sent up a silent prayer for a safe journey and a safe landing. He'd promised to let her know as soon as he could that he'd arrived, and Carrie planned to write her first letter that very evening.

But Penny wasn't having any of it: she turned up at the Andersons' and told Carrie firmly there was to be no 'mooning about'.

'I'm fine,' Carrie told her. 'Look, dry eyes! I'm not going to spend tonight crying into my pillow.'

'Maybe not,' said Penny wryly. 'But I ask you, writing this evening! Let him get there, the poor thing.' She held out Carrie's gas mask and handbag. 'Fetch your coat and come on. You're coming to the pub with me and Johnnie.'

Carrie gave in, not entirely unwillingly. She saw Penny every day, but she felt as though she hadn't seen Johnnie for ages. At her own request, they'd dropped their evenings as a foursome and he'd taken to calling in at home to say hello to their mum and dad before Carrie had made it back from the station. Most of his leaves or evening passes were spent with Penny, which Carrie understood completely.

On their way to the Rose and Crown, she worked out

that it was almost a month since she'd seen her brother properly, not since he'd come home for a rest after there'd been a bad raid on London just after Easter. They were due for a decent catch-up. When they got to the pub, she spotted Johnnie instantly across the smoke-filled bar, tall and trim in his uniform – and he wasn't alone.

'Oh, great!' cried Penny, beginning to elbow her way through the mass of drinkers. Carrie had hardly ever seen the place so full. A couple of the town's other pubs must be out of beer. 'The gang's all here!'

Carrie followed in her wake. She'd be interested to meet Johnnie's RAF crowd, but at the same time she was a bit disappointed. So much for their catch-up. Johnnie kissed Penny and greeted Carrie with a huge hug, then introduced her round the group. All the men were in uniform, as was one of the women. The other two girls were in regular clothes.

'Meet my sister,' Johnnie said. 'The elder by five minutes, and never lets me forget it . . . Carrie, this is Heather and Peter, Sue and Derek, Sally and Martin. I take no responsibility for their behaviour, they're a reprobate crew—'

This was met with jeers of 'Speak for yourself!' and 'You've never complained!' from the other men.

Carrie nodded and smiled and shook hands. Johnnie asked the new arrivals what they'd like to drink and there was another immediate chorus from the pilots of 'Oh, well, if you're in the chair . . .', 'Ah, your round is it, Anderson? Watch the moths fly out of his wallet!' and 'Mine's a double!'

This was all taken in good part, and Johnnie came back at them with a few friendly jibes of his own. Penny looked on indulgently; she was obviously used to this kind of banter.

For Carrie it was a rare and precious glimpse of Johnnie's other life – the kind of camaraderie he'd mentioned in passing. Otherwise, he kept his home and RAF life separate.

With Johnnie disappeared to the bar and the others engaged in a game of darts, the girls started chatting. Sally, blonde and perpetually smiling, was in the WAAF, a clerk at Biggin Hill.

'Escaped from my boring job at the council as soon as I could,' she explained. 'I will say, you're never bored with this lot!'

Sue echoed the sentiment. She was a teacher who'd been evacuated from Hackney with her pupils at the start of the war. Though it had clearly been a sensible move, given the pounding the East End had taken, it hadn't been plain sailing.

'We're better off here, don't get me wrong,' she told Carrie, 'but it's been tough on the children – and some of the families who took them in. They're from pretty poor homes. Some had never had a proper meal – just chips or bread and scrape. There was bedwetting. A couple ran away from their billets. Some were so unhappy, they begged their mums to come and take them back. So they did – just in time for the Blitz.'

This wasn't news to Carrie. She'd seen the little groups of evacuees passing through the station from the moment war had been declared, luggage labels tied to their coats and with their pitiful bundles of belongings, their dolls, their grubby teddies, their brown paper bags of sandwiches, their child-sized gas masks. Her heart had ached for them.

'So how did you meet up with this crew?' asked Carrie. 'At a dance?'

Heather chipped in. She was a nurse and had met Peter after he'd been shot down. He'd managed to land, and had been lucky to emerge with only superficial injuries.

'I knew Sue from church,' she said. 'And I have the dubious honour of having introduced her to Derek.'

Sue looked at her boyfriend lovingly.

'Never regretted it for a minute,' she said.

Carrie would have liked to ask them how they coped with the constant danger their boyfriends put themselves in, but with Johnnie back with the drinks, the men were getting jollier and jollier, and louder too. The women peeled slightly away, partly to make themselves heard, but Carrie withdrew from them and listened in to the other group.

She started off fascinated; before long, she understood. From the quick downing of pints and the lighting of cigarettes, one from another, to the quick-fire jokes and what seemed like a competition for the most hair-raising anecdote, Carrie got an impression of life lived at a breakneck pace. Even off duty, the pilots spent their time reliving their working lives – their own exploits and those of others.

They talked a language only other pilots could understand. How their machines worked and what could go right – and wrong – in the split-second decisions they had to make. As Carrie listened, she realised why Johnnie didn't bring his working life home. What lay beneath but was never acknowledged – that would have been 'yellow'– was the bowel-clenching terror they must feel on every mission. In the retelling, the near misses became one more big adventure – they had to. How else could they get into those cockpits time after time?

Every time the noses of their Spitfires lifted into the air, they saw the green fields of England, its towns and cities, disappear beneath them, possibly for the last time. They climbed higher and higher into the atmosphere, powered by the impossible miracle of flight, in a fighting machine that, however strongly reinforced, was not much more than a tin can. They never knew what they'd encounter, let alone if they'd come back alive. Even if they did, they'd see unimaginable things – their comrades trying to control a crippled plane, or a man bailing out, burning as he descended. No wonder that when they were finally back on the ground together they couldn't snap back into anything like normal life. Every moment had to be seized by the scruff of the neck and lived to the full: it might not come again. Laughter was one way through; drink was another.

After a while, the other women drifted back and listened in too.

'And what about Dougie Douglas?' Martin grinned. 'Back from a sortie, got to the pub just before closing with a few others, landlord swung them a bit of extra time, then up to the fleshpots in London, back to base about two, absolutely hammered. On call at zero four hundred hours, so he sobered up by walking the perimeter – told the CO who was out for a predawn run he was inspecting the guard!'

'Back in his kite by six,' added Peter. 'Up on a scramble, got back safely despite his condition. What a legend!'

Derek, who seemed the most sober, in every sense, of the merry band, added quietly, 'That was the day McIntosh bought it.'

For a moment, everyone went quiet.

'It was awful,' Penny whispered to Carrie. 'The boys had just bought his wedding present.'

'Poor old Haggis,' said Johnnie, raising his glass. 'He was a great bloke. RIP.'

Everyone raised their glasses in a toast.

Carrie watched her brother as he drank. He never talked like this at home; he never drank like this either. He'd been joking and laughing with the rest, but in this unguarded moment she saw a faraway look come into his eyes. He sensed her scrutiny and flashed her an automatic, but somehow empty, smile.

In a particularly brutal period in the Battle of Britain – not that it hadn't all been brutal – the tally of losses in Johnnie's squadron had mounted and mounted. Despite, or perhaps because of, seeing a friend spiral to his death in front of him, Johnnie had insisted to his superiors that he was capable of flying night after night – and, desperately short of pilots, they'd let him. The result was predictable: Johnnie had eventually cracked and gone AWOL. That was when Carrie and Penny had found him, thanks to Carrie's instinct about where in Brockington he'd be hiding out.

Johnnie had gone back to his squadron after a couple of weeks, to that nice, safe training role, but that wasn't enough for him, of course. Now he was back on active service, but that one fleeting moment and hollow smile had told Carrie that the 'work hard, play hard' ethic was taking its toll. Had Penny noticed? If so, why hadn't she said?

Sally was in the middle of a story about the modesty panel under her desk being attacked by mice, or maybe rats, but Carrie took Penny by the elbow and pulled her to one side.

'The Ladies, please.'

Penny looked perplexed.

'You know the way. This is your local!'

'Then let me show you.'

Penny still looked puzzled, but shrugged and followed her. The toilets were across a brick yard, but Carrie headed to where empty crates and barrels were stacked up against a side wall. She turned to her friend.

'Is it always like this? Do they always behave like this when they get together?'

'Well, yes. You must realise it's how they let off steam.'

'Yes, I know that, of course I do, they're celebrating being alive. But . . .' She trailed off. 'The drinking, the smoking, the making light of things . . . it's all a front, isn't it? A cover, for how scary and awful it is. And they're all rota'd to fly tomorrow, I heard Peter say. Surely, if they're hungover it puts them at even more risk.'

'Maybe. But perhaps it helps.' Penny grimaced. 'Look, I'm sorry if it's come as a bit of a shock. I didn't know the others would be here. I thought it'd just be the three of us. I know Johnnie reins it in in front of the family. But he . . .' she shrugged '. . . he doesn't want you to worry. And he is taking his rest days, I promise you.'

'And what does he do on them? He doesn't come home, and he can't see you in the day, you're at work.'

'He sleeps. Sometimes at mine, sometimes on the base.'

'And he drinks.'

97

'They all do!' Penny retaliated. 'You heard the story about Dougie Douglas.' And then: 'You've never seen Mike in the company of his army mates, have you? I bet they're the same.'

'I suppose you're right,' Carrie agreed reluctantly. Mike had explained the drinking culture in the military, how it was a sort of defence mechanism. 'Before he went to France last year, well, we just wanted to be together. And when he came back . . .'

'You wanted to be together even more,' Penny agreed. 'Of course you did, apart from the odd evening with us.'

She sat down on one of the empty barrels and drew Carrie down onto another.

'I have tried to talk to Johnnie about it,' she said. 'I don't want to lose him any more than you do. I asked him to ease up, calm down, not volunteer for anything he didn't have to. I reminded him about what happened last year.' She seized Carrie's hand impulsively. 'I did try, Carrie. I worry too, but he got cross and barked at me. Said had I not noticed cities were still being smashed to pieces here? That people were being killed, dreadfully injured, and losing their homes? That the war was getting more intense, not less? He closed himself off and refused to talk about it any more. He told me not to dare say anything to you. And I . . . I'm sorry, I should have pressed him, or ignored him and said something to you anyway, or to your mum and dad, or, I don't know, to his commanding officer, but I knew he'd be furious and I . . . I really like Johnnie. I mean, I really, really like him – all right, I love him – and I . . . I just don't want to jeopardise that!'

'Oh, Penny.'

Her friend looked so agonised, she had to sympathise. She couldn't blame Penny. Carrie knew how stubborn Johnnie could be when he didn't want to talk about something. He'd done it often enough with her when they were growing up – not wanting to tell her where he'd found his 'world-beating' prize conker, or which girl in their class had left him a love note inside his desk. But this was infinitely more serious. Above all, Carrie felt cross with herself – and guilty.

Where had her special connection been, the one that had always helped her sense when he was troubled? She could only think she'd been so wrapped up in her own affairs – Mike's posting, their night away, meeting his family, their final farewell – that she'd blocked everything else out. Add to this the fact that Johnnie had definitely been avoiding the family, her specifically, and deliberately didn't talk about his air force life at home anyway, and that Carrie and her mum and dad knew they couldn't, or shouldn't, ask, it was no wonder he'd been able to get away with it. You had to see him with his friends to realise. But now Carrie knew things weren't right. The question was, what was she going to do about it?

In other circumstances, the headlong, almost sheepish declaration from the independent, fiercely private Penny that she loved Johnnie would have been cause for celebration. After all, hadn't he already told Carrie how much he really liked her? But there was no time to dwell on that. Penny might be afraid of losing him as a boyfriend, but Carrie was family. Johnnie would be furious and think his sister was interfering, but she loved him so much too – she couldn't let it lie. If Penny felt she couldn't contact his commanding officer and ask him to give Johnnie some extended leave to rest and recharge, well, Carrie would have to do it herself.

Chapter Twelve

The next day was Saturday, so there was less of a commuter rush, but it meant that business was more spread out through the morning. Trying to serve the customers was like trying to cross a busy road when the traffic came first from one direction and then another. Carrie would normally have been pleased – she liked to be busy, and it was all money in the cash box – but today it was simply frustrating.

It was almost one o'clock by the time she could ask Penny to mind the shop while she slipped to the telephone box outside the station. Her plan was to put in a call to the only contact she had at Johnnie's base.

Squadron Leader Sheridan was the officer who'd been so understanding when Johnnie had gone AWOL. Carrie didn't want to split on her brother, or in any way make him sound weak. Nor did she want him transferred to the sort of back-room role he'd hated. But she could a least try to secure him a proper break.

Squadron Leader Sheridan had given the Andersons his card last year. Now, Carrie fed her coins into the slot and dialled the number. A young woman who sounded about her own age answered in a clipped, almost upper-class accent.

'Wing Co's office.'

'Oh!'

Squadron Leader Sheridan must have had a promotion – she should have realised.

'Hello?' said the voice at the other end briskly. 'Are you there? Can I help you?'

'Yes, sorry,' Carrie replied quickly. 'I was hoping . . . is it possible to speak to Wing Commander Sheridan, please?'

'Who? This is Wing Commander Fraser's office.'

This wasn't going well.

'I'm sorry. Let's start again,' said Carrie. 'I'm trying to contact an officer who was based there in September last year. Squadron Leader Sheridan.'

'Look, I'm fairly new,' said the other girl. 'But I know the names of all the officers. And there's no one of that name here.'

This was going even less well.

'All right, I see.' said Carrie. Squadron Leader Sheridan must have been moved. 'But I was trying to contact him, or someone, because—Hang on, don't go!'

The pips were sounding and Carrie frantically fed coins into the slot.

'Are you still there?' she asked when the money had clattered down into the box.

'I'm here.'

'My name's Carrie Anderson, and it's about my brother,' Carrie said urgently. 'Please help me. I need to speak to Pilot Officer Anderson's immediate CO, whoever that is.'

'Well, I don't know . . . It's rather irregular—'

'Please,' begged Carrie. 'I'm . . . I'm concerned about him.'

The young woman sighed. She could tell Carrie wasn't going to give up.

'Let me see.'

'Thank you!'

Carrie waited impatiently, drumming her fingers on the top of the coin box while there was the sound of pages being turned at the other end of the line. The girl's voice came back on.

'Very well,' she said. 'We've got two Andersons. Are the initials J.B. or R.H.—'

'That's him! J.B. – Johnnie!' cried Carrie.

Just then, a bell rang deafeningly in the background.

'I'm sorry, you'll have to call again,' said the young woman hurriedly. 'Looks as though there's a flap on.'

The phone went down.

In frustration, Carrie pressed button B for the return of her unspent coins, but the two pennies that rattled into the slot were no compensation.

She'd have to try again later. At that point, the sirens sounded in Brockington.

If she was at work when the sirens sounded, Carrie had two choices. Once she'd quickly pulled down the shutter on the shop and locked the door, she could hurry with the rest of the station staff and passengers to the underpass between the platforms, or she could head for the shelter at the end of the road. Sometimes the wardens came round and insisted they went to the public shelter. This was one of those times.

The raid went on for hours. The shelter was packed with all sorts of people: factory workers, travellers, shoppers, the young and the old, men and woman, mothers and children. Much was made on the newsreels of the grit, resolve and even cheerfulness shown by the British public in the face of the Blitz, but there wasn't much in evidence here. People were resigned, frustrated, weary with it all. Carrie wasn't infected by the general mood; she was too much on edge.

She was acutely aware that the same bell she'd heard at the end of the phone would have summoned Johnnie from the mess with the others. She could imagine the scene all too well. They'd have put down their cards and their billiard cues, their books and newspapers. Leaving the radio still playing, they'd have shrugged into their flying jackets and raced across the airfield to the waiting riggers, who'd hand them their parachutes, goggles and helmets. They'd climb up into the cockpit, connect the oxygen, check and recheck that the tyres were pumped, the release catch was working smoothly, the machine gun calibrated correctly. Then, on the signal, they'd taxi off, up, up into the blue, to face the Luftwaffe's Messerschmitts and Focke-Wulfs.

Having seen Johnnie and his fellow pilots just the night before, Carrie didn't need her special bond with her twin to know what they'd be feeling – that mix she'd identified of nerves stretched taut as piano wire and yet somehow, once they were up there, the determination to do their job and do it well. She marvelled that after so many months of war, they could still steel themselves to do what they did. She understood as she never had before that it was more than patriotism: they did it not to let their country down, but also not to let each other, or themselves, down. And she knew her brother, sensitive as he was beneath all the bluster, would feel it particularly acutely.

Late in the afternoon, the all-clear sounded and everyone

stumbled out into the daylight. Carrie had been separated from Penny in the scramble for the shelter and she didn't have the heart to go back to the station. All the trains would have been disrupted, the regular timetable, such as it was, thrown out. She and Penny had said all they could say about Johnnie the previous evening. There was no point in overlaying Penny's worries with her own. If Johnnie had been in action that day, with any luck he'd call and tell them he was OK. And the place he'd call would be home.

Her mother was surveying the little veg garden on top of their own air raid shelter when Carrie got back. She was surprised, but pleasantly so, to see her daughter. Mary, too, had spent the afternoon in a communal shelter, caught out when she'd made a foray to the butcher.

'I waited that long in the queue,' she began, 'that when a woman came out and said he had some reasonable mince, I thought, I'm going to get a decent amount for once and make us a nice cottage pie. I could almost smell it – a nice thatch of potato on top, criss-crossed with a fork and all brown and crispy—'

'Stop it, Mum,' cried Carrie, 'you're making my mouth water!'

'I'd got us a full six ounces,' she went on. 'I'd have had to stretch it out even so, make it last two meals maybe, but then the siren went and I had to leave it on the butcher's counter!'

'Oh, Mum. I hope you hadn't paid!'

'No, that's one good thing,' Mary agreed. 'But now it'll have to be that leftover cheese pie your dad didn't like first time round.' She hacked off a head of spring cabbage. 'He had to shut the shop. That's another afternoon's profits gone, such as they are, and a load of evening papers not delivered!'

Mary straightened and handed over the knife.

'Cut some sticks of rhubarb, love. We can stew it for afters.'

Carrie pulled a face. There was no sugar to spare for sweetening; she could feel the enamel being stripped off her teeth at the thought.

'I know,' her mother sympathised. 'But if we swamp it with custard . . .'

How often, thought Carrie, had they had conversations like this? Neither wanted to voice what was uppermost in their minds: how involved had Johnnie been in defending the skies? And if the bombers came back tonight, would that be another call to action for him?

They were in the middle of the rather dense cheese pie – no butter or marge for the potatoes, a meagre two ounces of cheese and a thick crust of breadcrumbs with a few dried herbs on the top – when, sure enough, the sirens started up again, that mournful rise and fall which sounded like someone heaving their guts up.

Without a word, Norman put down his knife and fork and went off to fetch his gas mask and steel helmet and to don the blue boiler suit that had been newly issued to air raid wardens. Carrie and Mary stopped eating too, not entirely reluctantly, and began to collect their own air raid survival kit: gas masks, blankets, coats, hats, gloves, torches. Mary gathered up her knitting; Carrie took her book from the arm of the chair. Norman came back through the kitchen as they were collecting the flask of tea Mary kept topped up and a packet of biscuits. He kissed his wife and daughter.

'Come back safe,' said Mary, as she always did.

'Bye, Dad. Love you,' said Carrie.

'Roger that,' said Norman, affecting cheeriness. But he muttered under his breath: 'Will the silly b's never give up?'

Then he was gone.

For Carrie and her mother, so began another night in the shelter. It was dank, dark and thoroughly unpleasant, but at least it was their own space. There was no heat, of course, but there was light – a storm lantern hanging from the ceiling, shaking with every reverberation.

Mary, swaddled in a rug, had the canvas deckchair. She knitted resolutely, her mouth set, as the bombers droned over, chased by the searchlights, then anti-aircraft fire from the big guns. Her head drooped as she dozed, then jerked up as she was awakened by another huge bang.

It was a bad raid, one of the worst Carrie could remember. The storm lantern swayed in the aftershocks of massive explosions; the ack-ack guns never seemed to cease firing. Carrie lay on her back on damp cushions on the bench, listening to every far-off blast, ears straining for the sound of fighters screaming overhead in pursuit. Her eyes were wide open and she was possessed by the sickest feeling she had ever had. It was nothing to do with the cheese pie, or even the bombing. Her intuition, her twin telepathy, had switched itself back on, or she had willed it back on, and it was working overtime. Johnnie was up there in the skies and she was up there with him in all the chaos and the terror. She lay awake all night.

*

When Carrie and her mother finally staggered up from the shelter and fumbled their way indoors, dawn was breaking. Craning out of her bedroom window, Carrie could see a pall of smoke – this was no early-morning mist – over London. Below it was a sinister orange glow: fires still burning.

The station bookshop wasn't open on a Sunday. It was Carrie's one day of rest, but the family shop opened until lunchtime for the Sunday papers and their essential accompaniments – an ounce of tobacco, a quarter of liquorice allsorts or a Fry's Chocolate Cream, according to your age and taste.

Mary occasionally helped in the shop, but a broken hip a few years back and a poor recovery meant that she wasn't able to stand for long. The daily queuing that was a necessity of life was already taking it out of her, so Carrie knew she'd have to hold the fort while her dad's young assistant, Terry, did the deliveries.

'You go to bed, Mum,' she ordered. 'See if you can get a couple of hours' rest at least.'

Mary didn't need telling twice and headed gratefully to bed while Carrie turned on the wireless in the living room. The news bulletins always tried not to alarm, or to give the German propaganda machine an easy headline. But the serious tone of the newsreader as he admitted that there had been another extensive raid on the capital told Carrie – as if she hadn't realised – all she needed to know. She jumped when the phone rang and raced to the little hall. It was her father.

'Dad! Where are you? You're all right, are you?'

Norman had popped his head into the shelter at about

midnight to say that he and a few of the other Brockington wardens had volunteered to go up to London to help out where the damage was greatest.

'I'm all right, just knackered,' he replied. He did sound weary. 'And I'm sorry, but I won't be back to open up the shop today.'

'That's fine, don't worry about it. Mum's gone to bed, but I'll do it. And Terry'll be in to deliver the papers.'

'I can't think there'll be any,' said Norman. 'I can't tell you what a mess the place is in. It breaks my heart. God knows how many killed – they must have dropped thousands of bombs. Thousands! And the incendiaries! The fires are still burning.'

There was a terrific 'whoomph' in the background and Carrie felt, rather than saw, her father duck. And heard him swear.

'Hell's bells,' he said more mildly, when he came back on the line. 'That's a gas main gone up. I'll have to go, love. See you later, I hope. I'll let you know if I have to stay up here.'

'Oh, Dad – take care. How much longer can they go on like this?'

What she really meant was 'How much longer can we go on?'

'If I knew the answer to that . . .' Norman trailed off. 'But we've got no choice, love. We've all just got to get on with it. And stick it, and stick it, and stick it.'

It could have been a maxim for the whole country. Yet the thought of her father and everyone else, the wardens, ambulance drivers, firemen, heavy lifting squads, searching the rubble for bodies, hailing ambulances for the injured, trying to reunite distraught families, consoling people who, though alive, had lost everything, made Carrie seriously wonder how much more the country could take.

And then there was Johnnie . . . Carrie's sick feeling had not dispersed and every nerve ending was alive. Something wasn't right, she knew that much, she could sense it. Things had gone beyond her desire to get his superiors to force him to take a well-earned rest. If only she'd been able to speak to someone yesterday! She needed to find out where he was, how he was, and get him signed off any further duties before it was too late, if it wasn't already. But a phone call to Biggin Hill would be even less favourably received today than it had been yesterday. That didn't mean she wouldn't try, but it was too early yet. They'd still be debriefing after last night's raid.

If only she and Mike hadn't been so wrapped up in each other, overriding her connection with her brother. If she'd realised sooner the toll the endless raids were taking on Johnnie, perhaps she could have asked Mike to talk to him, man to man, and who knows, Johnnie might even have taken some notice. But then again, what Penny had said was right: with his fellow soldiers, Mike was probably just the same – work hard, play hard, pretend the bad things never happened, or turn them into an anecdote. Look how Mike had played down the danger he'd been in and the fear he must have felt during and after Dunkirk – and he'd admitted there'd been some pretty raucous nights of celebration at the barracks on his return.

Even so, Carrie would have given anything to hear Mike's voice reassuring her now. Had he really only been gone less than forty-eight hours? It seemed like a lifetime.

She was still standing there, lost in thought, when the telephone bell shrilled again.

'Hello?' she said desperately, grabbing the receiver. 'Johnnie?'

There were the usual clicks as the line connected.

'No, it's me,' said Penny shortly. 'You haven't heard from him, then?'

'No, we haven't.'

'Nor me. I'm coming round.'

'All right—'

But Penny had already slammed down the receiver.

Carrie knew she wouldn't be long. Penny had acquired a bike and rode it like a demon. Johnnie had often told her off, convinced she'd have an accident – talk about pot and kettle!

Carrie trailed back into the living room as Mary came down the stairs.

'I heard the telephone. Was it . . . ?'

'No. First it was Dad, then Penny.' Carrie mentally edited all her father had said to make it palatable. 'Dad's fine, but he won't be back till later, maybe much later. And Penny's coming round.'

Mary nodded.

'I'll make some tea. I can't get off to sleep anyway.'

They were in the kitchen, waiting for the kettle to boil – it made a change from willing the telephone to ring – when they heard Penny rattling her bike down the side entry. She came through the back gate and tossed her bike against the coalhouse wall, flinging open the back door and leaving it swinging on its hinges. Her hair was tousled and her cheeks were pink from the ride, but the dark shadows under her eyes looked anything but healthy. She clearly hadn't slept a wink.

'Still nothing?' she asked.

Carrie shook her head. Penny's lip trembled.

'Come here, love.' Mary opened her arms and wrapped them around the other girl. 'You did the right thing to come. You shouldn't be on your own. Much better that we're together.'

The kettle began to sigh and steam. Carrie reached for the tea caddy with its familiar pattern of pagodas and trees in blossom. It was a wonder the pattern hadn't worn off with handling since the start of the war.

'You go on through,' she said. 'I'll make the tea.'

Chapter Thirteen

Beyond sending Terry out to do the deliveries, Carrie had given up any thought of opening the shop. It would hardly have been worth it – only a fraction of the usual newspapers had arrived anyway, their print runs and distribution systems thrown into disarray by the night's catastrophic bombing.

By nine o'clock, the three women had fallen silent – what was there to say? – and were seated at the table, their third cups of increasingly watery tea untasted in front of them. Mary had got out her scrapbook of verses by Patience Strong, which she snipped out of the *Daily Mirror*; she found them a great comfort in moments like these. Carrie wasn't sure they were Penny's sort of thing – a bit sentimental for her, probably – but Penny, perhaps grateful for any distraction, seemed quite absorbed. There was a frozen moment as the telephone bell, never louder, shrilled throughout the house, then all three rose as one, before Penny sank down. It wasn't her place to answer it.

Carrie looked at her mother. Mary gave the slightest inclination of her head to indicate that Carrie should take the call. Ice-cold, though the sun was already probing through the window and the day promised to be warm, she went through to the little hall. In its Bakelite blackness and with its twisted brown cord, the telephone looked like some malevolent creature, crouched and ready to pounce. Carrie had never been so reluctant yet so desperate to answer it. Was it Johnnie himself? Or was he missing, injured or – God forbid – dead?

She took a deep breath and lifted the receiver. Throat dry, she gave the number.

'Is that the Anderson household?'

Carrie nodded, then realised she would have to speak. 'Yes.'

'This is RAF Biggin Hill.' Of course it was. 'May I speak to Mr Anderson, please?'

'He's not here,' said Carrie urgently, wishing they could just get on with it. 'And my mother's—' She broke off. Surely she recognised the voice at the other end. That same rather clipped tone? 'This is Carrie Anderson,' she said. 'I'm – did we speak yesterday?'

'Miss Anderson – Carrie. I thought it was you. Yes, we did. And that's why – well, why I asked if I could make the call. This is Aircraftwoman Radford from the Wing Co's office.'

'Just tell me!' Carrie burst out. 'Johnnie. What's happened to him?'

'He's all right. He made it back.'

'Oh, thank God!' Carrie was suddenly aware that Mary and Penny had crowded into the little hall and she turned to them. 'He's all right, Mum, Penny, he's all right!'

Carrie saw her mother and her best friend turn and embrace one another as the voice in her ear said, 'If I could just finish—'

114

'Sorry.' Carrie turned her attention back to the phone. Whatever came next, it was not the worst. 'So – you said he's all right.'

'Yes, but . . .'

Carrie went cold again. She'd been so reassured by Aircraftwoman Radford ringing in person, she'd let herself believe for a moment that all was well, that this was simply a continuation of their call yesterday and she would be told that after all he'd done till now, her appeal and the heroic part he'd played in the raid, they'd decided that Johnnie deserved a decent rest. Now she knew that her feeling of dread had not been misplaced.

'Tell me. Please.'

Behind her, she sensed Penny and Mary bracing themselves.

'His plane sustained some pretty serious damage, but he managed to land it.'

'*Crash*-land it? So he's injured?' Carrie heard the intake of two breaths behind her. 'How? Badly? Oh no, please, it didn't catch fire, did it?'

Another intake of breaths, and Carrie sensed Mary and Penny clutch one another harder.

'I'm sorry, but I don't have those details. All I know is that he's been taken to hospital. A civilian hospital, at least for now.' She named it, and Carrie did a quick calculation. It would take about forty-five minutes to get there – by car, if they had one. Without one, it could be a couple of hours at best, more like half a day, probably, with the inevitable disruption to transport after the raid. There was no time to lose.

'Thank you,' she said quickly. 'Thank you for calling.'

'I'm sorry,' said the girl on the other end. 'I'm sorry I wasn't more help yesterday—'

'Never mind.' Carrie just wanted to get her off the phone. Her attention was already on to the next thing – getting to see Johnnie. And finding out how bad his injuries were.

It was Uncle Charlie who came to the rescue. Carrie rang him, apologising for disturbing his Sunday morning lie-in.

'I'll throw on some clothes and be right there,' he said on hearing her plea. 'Don't you worry, darling, he'll be all right!'

In the absence of her own father – and with no way of contacting him – it was so reassuring to hear his voice.

Penny and Mary busied themselves getting together everything they imagined a recovering invalid might need. Penny went to select some magazines from the shop, while Mary, tutting at the paucity of her offering, put together a basket of the most tempting things she could muster: a packet of digestive biscuits, all four ounces of cheese in the house, a handful of radishes from the garden, a pot of jam and a basin of rice pudding.

Carrie, having left the selection of reading material to Penny, wandered into the yard. It was a ridiculously beautiful day, if she'd been able to enjoy it. Instead, she wondered how many other families had been waiting for the call all through the night and into the early morning; how many other homes in the land had had bad news, or the news that no one ever wanted to hear. She looked up at the huge dome of sky and wondered, not for the first time, how it could rain down so much terror and destruction on innocent people who'd never asked to be involved in a war, people on both sides of the conflict. But the sky had no answers. She already had a headache from a night of no sleep; squinting into the sun was making it worse. She was about to go back in when she heard a car draw up in the street. Uncle Charlie.

Carrie went down the side entry to meet him. He opened his arms to give her a huge hug.

She shuddered with the relief of having him there, someone to take charge when she'd been trying so hard to hold it together for her mother and Penny. She'd allowed them their conviction that Johnnie's injuries wouldn't be so bad. Penny cited Johnnie's friend Peter's experience. Airmen had walked away from crashes before, so somehow they'd convinced themselves that Johnnie would be one of them. They believed he'd soon be sitting up, eating rice pudding with jam and reading *The Illustrated Carpenter and Builder*. Maybe they only half believed it, but if it helped them, Carrie certainly wasn't going to share her fears.

Aircraftwoman Radford had been nothing if not professional, and maybe she genuinely didn't have all the details, but Carrie had detected some reticence in her tone that was more than her usual clipped manner of speaking. It only added to the dread Carrie had been feeling since Friday night: she knew she wouldn't feel better until she'd seen Johnnie for herself.

The hospital was a huge, sprawling complex with a main building constructed, the date over the door informed them, in 1907. Other, more modern blocks had mushroomed in the grounds, some of them rather makeshift and presumably added since the start of the war. Stopping the car in front of the entrance, Uncle Charlie said he'd park up and wait outside.

'It's you three he'll want to see,' he said. 'I've got my smokes and my paper, it's a lovely day and there's a bench under that tree . . .' He gestured to a large cedar on a patch of lawn. 'I'll wait there. I don't suppose they'll let you see him for long – you may have to go in one at a time as it is. Give him my best, and tell him I'll see him when he's home.'

In the once grand hall, with its imposing staircase, a glass-panelled booth had been added, marked 'Reception'. Nurses, doctors and other staff criss-crossed the echoing space, passing to corridors on the left and right, carrying clipboards, issuing instructions, pushing trolleys with patients on them. Trying to ignore the hubbub and the temptation to rush and see if one of the patients was her brother, Carrie approached the booth. The receptionist slid back the glass. Mary and Penny stood to one side, watching the comings and goings, Mary with her basket of treats, Penny with her armful of magazines.

Carrie gave Johnnie's name and explained who they were. The woman pushed aside a half-drunk cup of tea and reached for a sheaf of papers. 'Anderson . . .' she repeated. 'A pilot . . . Can you give me his squadron, rank and number?'

Carrie knew all these by heart and rattled them off.

The woman found Johnnie's name. She seemed to stare at it for an inordinate amount of time before raising her eyes and saying to Carrie:

'Right. I've got him. Brought in at four o'clock this morning. But you can't see him, I'm afraid. He's in surgery.'

Carrie gripped the wooden shelf in front of her.

'We can't go away,' she said. 'We've come miles. We'll wait.'

'I'm afraid that's impossible. We don't have any waiting facilities for relatives.' The woman drew a notepad towards her and scribbled something on it.

'Here's our telephone number. I suggest you go home and telephone later to check on his progress and find out when you can visit,' she said firmly.

So firmly that Carrie replied meekly: 'I understand. Thank you.'

Moving away from the booth, she gestured to the far wall and explained the situation to the others. Mary started to panic at the thought of Johnnie needing an operation, and Penny protested at being turned away, but Carrie shushed them.

'It's all right,' she said. 'We're not going anywhere.'

One of the skills she'd developed from running the bookstall, where the magazines and newspapers were laid face out to the customers, was the ability to read print upside down. She'd seen on the list the name of the ward where Johnnie would be transferred once he was out of the operating theatre.

'The wards are all named after birds – which is kind of appropriate, I suppose,' she told the others. 'Johnnie's going to be in Goldfinch Ward.'

On the wall behind them was a large plan showing the layout of the hospital. The corridors to the left and right were just the start of it and formed one side of an open square. All the wards were marked. Penny glanced over her shoulder to see if the receptionist was watching, but she was dealing with a messenger delivering something.

'Look,' said Penny, pointing quickly up at the map. 'There's a side door near Goldfinch. We can get in there.'

The messenger had gone and the receptionist was watching them again. They filed obediently out of the main entrance, stopping only to tell Uncle Charlie what they were up to.

'You go, girls!' he said, giving them a thumbs-up.

Round the side of the building, the door stood open, letting in some fresh air. Goldfinch Ward was the first on the right. As they paused outside the double doors to the ward, they heard the rattle of a trolley. An orderly was pushing it and a nurse walked alongside, holding a drip. The patient on the trolley was covered with a sheet, prone and still, but Carrie felt she knew at once who it had to be.

'Johnnie!' she cried.

Chapter Fourteen

All three of them ran to meet the trolley. They crowded round it as the orderly, slowing, cried, 'Whoa, whoa, what do you think you're doing?' and the nurse began: 'Please let this patient through!'

'I'm his mother!'

'I'm his sister!

'I'm his girlfriend – oh, Johnnie, what have you done to yourself?'

Penny might well ask. Johnnie's eyes were closed, his face cut and bruised. His head and his hands, which lay on the sheet, were swathed in bandages and there was a cradle over his legs.

'What is going on here?'

A woman's voice with a mild Scottish accent cut through the hubbub. Carrie spun round to see a nursing sister who was probably, she guessed, in her mid- to late thirties. She had the classic Scottish colouring of pale auburn hair with milky skin so fine it was almost translucent. Her accent might have been gentle, but she looked crisp and competent in her belted navy-blue uniform with its starched cap and cuffs.

'I'm sorry, Sister Munro,' babbled the nurse. 'This is Pilot Officer Anderson's family.'

'I don't care if they're the royal family of Ruritania,' said Sister Munro, calm but firm. She obviously never needed to raise her voice. 'Get this patient into the ward immediately. The doctor's there with Staff Nurse to cast an eye over him.'

'Yes, Sister. Sorry, Sister.'

'But—' Carrie began, only to be quelled by a look from Sister Munro.

She, Penny and Mary had no option but to press themselves against the wall as the nurse, the orderly and Johnnie disappeared through the double doors into Goldfinch Ward. Sister Munro turned to the trio.

'So, tell me. How exactly did you get in?' she enquired.

The soft accent couldn't disguise the steeliness.

Carrie indicated the side door.

'I'm sorry,' she said. 'But we had to see him.'

'Well, now you have. So will you please leave us to get on with our work.'

Carrie and Penny opened their mouths to protest, but it was Mary who spoke first. Carrie looked on in astonishment as her usually quiet and unassuming mother said passionately: 'Oh, no, I'm not going anywhere until I know what his injuries are. That's my boy, my baby, lying there, out cold, hurt in God knows what way. I'm not budging till you tell us how he is and what we're to expect. As a mother, that's the least I deserve!'

Jean Munro looked Mary up and down. She took in the pleading and pain in her eyes, the white knuckles where Mary clutched the handle of her basket. She saw, peeking out from under a tea cloth, the humble offerings inside, put together with such love. She looked at Carrie, all youth and hope, biting her lip with anxiety, and at Penny, with her dark curls and desperate eyes. Three against one? It was hardly fair. And if she'd been a mother, wouldn't she have felt the same? Then a man's voice spoke behind her.

'Well? What's the story? Have you found our Johnnie?'

Sister Munro blinked as Uncle Charlie, in his cream interlock sports shirt and flannels, loomed up beside her. Four against one! Marvellous!

'Ah!' she said. 'And you're the father, I suppose?'

'Good heavens, no, I'm the uncle,' said Uncle Charlie swiftly. 'Johnnie's dad's an air raid warden. He's been doing his bit up in the city since last night.'

'He doesn't even know our boy's injured!' Mary's lip had started to tremble and Carrie put her arm protectively around her mother. 'He'll be beside himself that he wasn't here. Please, just tell us so we can tell him how bad it is.'

Sister Munro seemed momentarily thrown and Uncle Charlie seized the advantage.

'I know you're very busy, but please, in two minutes – how bad is it?'

Sister Munro sighed. She'd met determined relatives before, but these were in a league of their own.

'I can tell you in thirty seconds,' she said. Carrie could see Penny was about to say 'Why have we wasted all this time then?' and she put a hand on her arm to restrain her. 'Pilot Officer Anderson has a broken tibia and fibula, two broken ribs, injuries to the face, hands and chest – largely superficial—'

'But . . . his head! It was bandaged! What about the head injury?' Carrie asked.

That was what had been worrying her most.

'Scalp wound, not deep,' said Sister Munro dismissively. 'Nothing to worry about. Now, if that answers all your questions – and even if it doesn't – I have to get on.'

'Thank you,' said Uncle Charlie, quelling the questions he could see half forming on Penny's and Mary's lips. 'One more thing. I take it it's not possible now, but when can we see him? We won't come mob-handed like today.'

Sister Munro gave him a look that said 'Sense at last!'

'We'll bring him round in a wee while, but he'll be too groggy to take anything in and we'll sedate him again, for the pain and the shock. So I suggest you come back tomorrow. Visiting is from two till three and seven till eight.'

Uncle Charlie held out his hand and briefly grasped hers.

'Thank you,' he said, shepherding the three women away. He added over his shoulder, 'We'll be back. You can be sure of that.'

Uncle Charlie drove them home. It was by now well past midday. Mary put together a scratch lunch – half a loaf, a small tin of corned beef and the cheese and radishes that had been destined for Johnnie.

'I'm sorry, Charlie, it's the best I can do—' she began.

She was always conscious that her husband's brother lived in a flashier style than they did. The garage business seemed to be doing well. Despite restrictions on private motoring and petrol, it had what Charlie called 'contract work' and he'd recently moved from his former digs into a serviced flat.

'Don't be daft.' Uncle Charlie helped himself to a dollop

of Mary's tomato and apple chutney. 'You always feed me fit for a king!'

Penny agreed.

'This is perfect, Mrs Anderson. If it was cinders, it'd still be a celebration lunch. Johnnie's alive!'

'Hear! Hear! And pretty soon he'll be turning his little escapade into a funny story, I bet,' said Uncle Charlie. 'And lapping up the attention from all those nurses!' He turned to Penny. 'Not that it'll alter his feelings for you, sweetheart, I'm sure.'

'It had better not!'

Carrie refused the pickle dish Penny was passing her and concentrated on cutting a slice of bread.

The natural optimists among them were off. It wasn't that Carrie or her mother were pessimists, but with no disrespect to her uncle or her friend, she and her mum did have stronger bonds with Johnnie. He was Carrie's twin; they'd shared the same space since before birth. And for their mother, the visceral umbilical link meant that she'd rather take any amount of pain on herself than think that one of her children might suffer.

But, as Penny had said, Johnnie was alive, Carrie reminded herself. The optimists were right – he would and could get over this. And in time, no doubt, his crash would become another tale of derring-do like those Carrie had heard in the pub and the cause for another round of drinks. Because that was what pilots did – the ones that survived. But for now at least, Johnnie would have to have the properly extended break from flying that Carrie had wanted for him, and she gave heartfelt thanks for that.

All that remained was to try to get hold of her father and tell him what had happened. And neither of those things would be easy.

'Blimey, family gathering or what?'

Carrie leapt up and everyone else turned as Norman, his face streaked with dirt and his overalls stained with dust, mud and Lord only knew what else, came in from the kitchen. He dropped his tin hat and knapsack on the floor and sank into a chair. He put his head in his hands.

'Dear God, the sights I've seen! Hell on earth.' He raised his eyes. 'What are you doing here, Charlie? To what do we owe the honour?'

Penny looked at Carrie. Carrie looked at her mother; they both looked at Uncle Charlie.

'Not been bombed out, have you?' Norman went on.

Their silence spoke volumes and he realised that it was the wrong question.

'Oh, no, not that, please. Not Johnnie. What's happened?'

Carrie had never seen her father cry, but the shock of hearing the news and the guilt that while he'd been comforting strangers, he'd not been there to comfort his family or go with them to see his son – on top of his sheer exhaustion from the horrors he'd seen in the night – were all too much.

'I'm sorry, I'm sorry,' he kept saying, as tears smeared the dirt on his face.

'Oh, Dad, don't be.'

Penny and Uncle Charlie were standing by. Carrie was seated on the arm of her dad's chair and Mary was kneeling beside her husband. She was holding his poor, filthy hands, nails torn, skin cut and bruised from tearing at bricks and rubble, wood and masonry, to try to free people buried in the wrecked remains of their homes.

'Shall I go?' Penny mouthed.

Carrie shook her head.

'Stay. You can sleep in Johnnie's room tonight,' she mouthed back.

She wanted her friend there. It was better that they all stayed together, for whatever came next.

What came next was something Carrie hadn't even considered. The telephone rang, as did alarm bells in the room.

'Do you want me to take it?' Uncle Charlie made as if to move.

'No. I'll go.'

Fear making her legs like lead, Carrie moved to the phone. They'd only seen him a few hours ago – surely Johnnie hadn't taken a turn for the worse?

Her throat was dry as she answered.

'Hello?' she gulped.

There was an agonising pause as the line connected.

'Carrie?'

It was a woman's voice, but it wasn't Sister Munro.

'Yes.'

'This is Heather. We met on Friday?'

'Oh! Heather. Hello.'

'Look, I'm sorry to disturb you. We weren't sure if you'd be there. We're all so sorry about Johnnie. We know he's been taken to hospital, and we wondered … Have you managed to see him?'

'Yes,' said Carrie, relieved it wasn't bad news and touched

that Heather had rung. 'Yes, we have. Not to speak to, though. He hadn't come round. His leg's broken in two places.'

'Just his leg?'

'Yes. I mean, there's some other injuries – two ribs broken, and he's pretty bashed about, but that's largely superficial, they said.'

Heather let out a breath.

'Oh, that's good to hear. We've been so worried.'

'Do you know what happened? We don't have any details.'

'Ah,' said Heather, and what she didn't say said it all.

'It was a bad crash?'

'Mmm.' Now Carrie knew for certain that it had been. But at the other end of the phone, Heather brightened. 'But his injuries don't sound too bad at all, considering. Well, that's a relief!'

Suddenly Carrie began to feel much more cheerful. Heather was a nurse, after all, and if she didn't think things sounded too bad . . . It was a huge relief and a blessing, and by the sound of it, something of a miracle. She slumped against the wall, and at last the tears came, all the dammed-up tension released in a flood of tears mixed with laughter and an overwhelming love for her brother. He'd defied them all, the bombers, the bullets, her own anxieties. The little hall was dark, but it seemed suffused with light and the lightness she now felt coursing through her body.

'Are you still there?' Heather asked tentatively.

Carrie sniffed and wiped her eyes.

'Yes. Sorry. It came over me all at once.'

'Of course. Look, we had a think after church, Sue and I,

Sally too. The boys were all flying last night, so they're due some rest days. So, we – they – can help you with lifts to the hospital if you need them. And we can all visit in shifts if you can't get there. Let me give you a couple of telephone numbers where you should be able to get hold of one of us.'

'Oh! That would be so kind!'

Carrie had already been wondering how much time Uncle Charlie would be able to sacrifice from his business to keep driving them over. She grasped the little pencil that hung on a string near the telephone and jotted down the numbers that Heather dictated.

'Thank you,' she said, over and over.

'No thanks needed,' said Heather. 'We all love Johnnie. We'll be praying for him. And all of you.'

Carrie put the receiver down with new hope in her heart. It had been another dark day and night for the country. Johnnie certainly wasn't the only airman injured; there'd be those who'd not come back at all. And, of course, there were many people – thousands, possibly – who'd been killed, injured or bombed out last night in London itself.

Families all over the country – all over the world – had faced and would go on facing unimaginable hardships and pain. But as Mr Churchill had said after the evacuation from Dunkirk the previous year: 'We shall go on to the end.' Or, to put it another way, as her father had said to her early that morning – that morning! It seemed like a lifetime ago – 'We've all just got to get on with it. And stick it, and stick it, and stick it.'

And stick it they would.

Chapter Fifteen

The next day, Monday, was a beautiful morning at Brockington Junction, although the stationmaster's mood was anything but sunny.

Lucius Bayliss had never exactly been a sunny character: his life had been blighted from an early age by his mother's flight of fancy. At school he'd been mercilessly bullied and called 'Lucy' or even 'Lucifer'. To this day, he didn't know which was worse. He'd suffered it then, but in later life he paid it back to anyone he felt was beneath him.

Married to an equally mean-spirited wife, he made the most of his position of power at the station, the only place he could throw his not inconsiderable weight around. He'd been sceptical that Carrie, a mere 'slip of a thing', could make a success of the bookshop; he was appalled when his regular porter, Eric, was replaced by a girl. At the same time, he fawned clumsily over any attractive young women travellers, carrying their cases himself and handing them up into trains – hoping for a glimpse of their stocking tops, no doubt. He'd even tried it on with Ruby once. Carrie, Penny and Bette had faced him down over that and had threatened to report him to his superiors. It had not endeared them to him.

So he was tutting as he erected a hastily chalked A-board at the station entrance, following a telephone call from Penny:

Then he moved down to the bookstall to tape a notice to the closed roller shutter. Penny had dictated it to read:

CLOSED UNTIL FURTHER NOTICE DUE
TO FAMILY EMERGENCY

Mr Bayliss sighed. The newspapers and the wireless had commented since the start of the Blitz how amazing and impressive it was that cities all over the land had somehow carried on. Shop assistants stepped through shattered plate-glass windows and over decapitated shop dummies to get to their posts. There was little hope of serving customers, but the sooner the mess was cleared up, the sooner they'd be back in business. Clerks and typists swept up glass from blown-out windows and cleared plaster dust from their typewriters and filing cabinets. Bosses rolled up their sleeves and mucked in with the rest.

Buses, diverted around road closures, ran where they could, but if central stations had been bombed or the rails had buckled in the heat of fires, the railways were harder hit. Saturday night had been horrendous, but Sunday night had been mercifully quiet. Brockington Junction's regular commuters would be doing their best to get to work on whatever trains might still be running, though the station would inevitably be quieter than normal.

In that sense, the absence of Carrie and Penny didn't matter that much, but Mr Bayliss's inflated sense of importance had been punctured. He caught sight of Ruby shaking out her wiping-round cloth on the platform and hurried down to tick her off.

'I thought I told you not to do that!' he barked. 'Do it round the back, by the dustbins. If you must attract rats and mice, let's keep them where the passengers can't see them.'

'Sorry, Mr Bayliss,' Ruby stuttered. 'I'm not thinking straight. Oh, isn't it awful about Carrie's brother! Thank the Lord he's all right, but what must they have been through, that poor family, and Penny, waiting to hear something!'

Sympathy, let alone empathy, was not something that came readily to Lucius Bayliss: all he could see was the inconvenience to himself.

He wrinkled his nose.

'I'll have a pot of tea in my office,' he said in reply. 'With extra hot water. Which is what you'll find yourself in, my girl, if I catch you doing that again out front here. You mark my words.'

'Ruby, what is it?' Arriving mid-afternoon, Hendrick van Roon fixed his pale eyes on her. 'Have you been crying?'

Ruby almost dissolved again at the concern in his voice. She was a sucker for anyone who showed her a bit of kindness. It was in short supply at home, with a bad-tempered father working all hours as a labourer and a mother stretched to the limit, even though five of the nine children in the family had now left home. Ruby glanced over her shoulder, but voices from the kitchen told her that Bette was occupied: the gas had been playing up and at last a man had come to fix it. Ruby blinked back tears, which had been coming unprompted all day, ever since she'd heard what had happened to Johnnie.

'It's Carrie,' she blurted out. 'The girl that owns the bookshop. Her brother, you know, the one that's a Spitfire pilot? He got shot down!'

'Really? When?'

'That awful raid on Saturday night!'

Hendrick's eyes popped. 'Ah, that is terrible. Much destruction and so many fires. So, how did it happen? Is he dead? And is the plane a – what do you call it? – a . . . a wreck?'

'Oh, no!' Ruby contradicted him. 'Well, I dunno about the plane, I 'spect that is a write-off, but Johnnie, he got out!' Then she added more disconsolately: 'He's in hospital, though. He's got broken ribs and a smashed-up leg, and he had to be operated on! That's why the bookstall's closed, and Penny's not here either to do the portering – she goes out with Johnnie, you see.'

'Ah,' Hendrick replied. 'Now I understand. I saw the signs on the platform. But where did he crash? In the sea? On land? Did he make it back to base? Where is Johnnie based?'

Ruby shook her head, unable to cope with the succession of so many questions.

'He was at Biggin Hill, the last I heard. I dunno exactly where he crashed. I've only had it third-hand from Mrs Saunders, and she got it from Mr Bayliss 'cos Penny rang him. But I can't get it out of my head, imagining what her and Carrie and his mum and dad have been through.'

'And Johnnie himself, in the moments before he crashed,' Hendrick pointed out. 'A battle in the skies, man against man, machine against machine. Side by side, eye to eye, maybe, with the enemy. And maybe face to face with his death.'

'Oh, don't!' Ruby covered her eyes. 'It don't bear thinking about!'

Hendrick reached across the counter and touched her hand briefly.

'I'm sorry, I shouldn't have . . . You're a very kind girl, Ruby, to worry for your friends.' He withdrew his hand. 'I have been meaning to ask you . . . You have a sweetheart, I know – of course you do, a pretty girl like you.'

Ruby blushed the same vivid colour she went when she'd been standing over the stove. She looked up from under her eyelashes in what she hoped was a modest fashion.

'Well, I dunno about that—'

'Nonsense. But I wondered if maybe one Sunday we could do something together,' he suggested. 'As you don't work that day? Something simple, only – a walk in the park, or to take tea somewhere. I ask as a friend, if I may call myself that. My intentions would be entirely honourable, but I would be most flattered if you would agree.'

'Well, I dunno about that . . .' said Ruby again.

But she did know. In the weeks since Hendrick van Roon had become a regular, Ruby's usual fantasies about Clark Gable or Humphrey Bogart making a picture in England and their paths somehow crossing with Ruby's had been replaced by something, or someone, at least a little more realistic. Ever since the day he'd turned up battered and bruised and elicited even Bette's sympathy, Bette had tolerated Ruby's little chats with Hendrick, and Ruby had to confess they brightened her day.

Oh, she loved Eric, but it was hard keeping up a correspondence when she was the only one with anything to say. Eric was a lovely feller and tried his best, but he didn't have much to impart. Camp routine was the same every week: roll call, drill, reading, playing cards, whittling a bit of wood – one of the other men was making a model of Nelson's *Victory* and Eric was helping. Chivvied by their hut sergeant, he also helped tend the little garden they'd set up with seedlings, and he played football and did keep-fit exercises . . . It sounded like a holiday to Ruby, but Eric said it was dead boring. Though in his last letter but two, Eric had said he'd put his name down to be in a work party. The censor had crossed out exactly what, but Eric said it was 'OK' and at least helped stave off what he called 'barbed-wire-itis'. Ruby wondered if he'd got the phrase off someone else – it was rather witty for Eric – and had immediately felt so mean she'd had a fresh photograph done in her new summery frock – home-made in royal-blue gingham with a square neck that was only a bit wonky, edged in white rickrack braid – and sent it off. Gratifyingly, Eric had replied saying she was beautiful and he longed to see her and give her a kiss. But it still it wasn't the same as having a real flesh-and-blood person by your side. Not that she'd be kissing Hendrick van Roon, certainly not! Though she might take his arm if he offered it on a walk, as he almost certainly would. He was always the gentleman.

He was waiting for her to finish her sentence.

'Well,' said Ruby again. 'As I say, I don't know, but . . . I suppose it can't do any harm.'

She could have a think about whether to tell Eric or not.

And when the worry about Johnnie was over and Carrie came back to work, no doubt she would have some good advice on that score.

'Very good!' Hendrick smiled, showing those even white teeth. 'Maybe not next Sunday – I have to see my pupils.' He did a bit of coaching, he'd told her, teaching English to refugees, all for nothing, which was good of him. Ruby was sure he'd be good at it, too. Better than an English person, probably, because his English was very correct. He smiled again. 'But soon. We will make the arrangements next time I come.'

'Lovely!' Ruby heard the back door slam: the gasman had gone. 'Tea, is it?' she said pointedly as Bette came through.

He got the message. He gave his funny little continental bow.

'Mrs Saunders.'

'Good afternoon,' said Bette graciously.

Hendrick cast his eyes over the cakes.

'Today only flapjacks and fruit cake?' he asked. 'None of your delicious apple pies?'

'Apple turnovers? I'm afraid not,' Bette replied. 'The gas has been off, you see. I've only got what was made on Saturday.'

'In that case, I will take tea, thank you, and a shortbread biscuit.'

He placed the correct change on the counter. Bette poured the tea and Ruby placed the biscuit on a plate, choosing the largest on offer.

'Usual table?' said Bette, ringing up the till. 'Ruby'll bring it over.'

'Thank you. I go first to the conveniences, but I will return.'

136

Hendrick crossed to his favourite table, put his jacket on the chair and went out. Bette swept off 'to test the stove' and Ruby carried his plate and cup to the table. On an impulse she quickly scribbled something on the back of a sheet from her order pad and tucked it into one of his jacket's inside pockets.

A walk one Sunday! Or tea out! Well, why not? There really could be no harm in it. Suddenly she remembered Johnnie and his family and felt guilty. But Carrie wouldn't begrudge her, she knew, just because she was having a hard time of it herself. In all the doom and gloom, thought Ruby, didn't a soul deserve something to look forward to?

Ruby spent the rest of the afternoon dreamily drying teaspoons and pondering her outfit for the proposed jaunt – the gingham dress, of course, but regretfully she had no decent summer shoes. She'd have to ask her sister Pat for a loan of her white sandals, if she promised not to scuff them and to give them a good going-over with Blanco before she gave them back. Pat's feet were half a size smaller, so they'd cripple her, but there was nothing else for it. Ruby sighed. What she'd give for a few, or even one or two, nice things of her own, or the money to buy them. Maybe, if she stayed on good terms with Hendrick (friendly terms, that is, no funny business, she was Eric's girl and she wasn't about to forget that), maybe – as a friend – Hendrick might buy her something nice. Even a pretty handkerchief or a little bottle of Devon Violets would be something.

Chapter Sixteen

Uncle Charlie had stayed at the Andersons' for all of Sunday and had nobly driven all the way back to the hospital so that Mary and Norman – Norman in particular – could sit with Johnnie at evening visiting. Johnnie was still out cold, but at least Mary had got close enough to touch his hand this time, and Norman had been able to see for himself that his son was alive.

On Monday morning, Carrie had telephoned the hospital and was told that Johnnie's condition was 'stable', that he'd had a 'reasonably comfortable' night and briefly been awake. But he'd been in a lot of pain and the staff nurse who answered the telephone – presumably even the indomitable Sister Munro had to have some time off – said they'd given him another shot of morphine.

Now, at afternoon visiting, both Carrie and Penny were seated beside his bed, each holding one of his hands. His leg was protected by a cradle and his black eyes from the bang on the head were developing nicely. But he was alive, he was breathing by himself, he was right there in front of them. He was still deeply asleep, but if the girls had their way, not for much longer. If sheer force of will and the power of concentration could have made Johnnie wake up, he'd have shot up in bed as if he'd been electrocuted.

'Come on, Johnnie,' Carrie whispered in her head. 'Please!'

'Come on,' Penny urged him in hers, characteristically more impatient. 'We've only got another forty minutes!'

Johnnie certainly tested their resolve. It was a quarter to three before he stirred, moving his head on the pillow with a slight frown, then wincing. His eyes flickered open briefly. Penny and Carrie sat forward and tightened their grip on his hands.

'Johnnie!' they said together, but his eyes closed again.

'Johnnie, we're here. It's me, Carrie!'

'And me!' Penny cried, so desperately that the visitors at the next bed turned around, startled, and on the other side of the ward a nurse dropped a medicine spoon.

Johnnie frowned again and moved his hands in theirs. Then he opened his poor, swollen eyes a crack.

'Water,' he whispered.

On the locker on Penny's side of the bed, a glass was already poured and in it was a sort of lolly stick with a bit of bandage wrapped around the end. Penny pressed it against the side of the glass to squeeze out some of the water and held it tenderly to his lips. Carrie's throat throbbed with trying not to cry; she knew she mustn't give in to it for Johnnie's sake. Johnnie sucked on the water and Penny gave him some more. Then he closed his eyes again.

Carrie and Penny looked at each other in despair. Was that it? To have seen him awake for a moment was better than nothing, obviously – but then he spoke, or rather, croaked:

'Where am I? And when am I? What day . . . ?'

'It's Monday, Johnnie,' Carrie said. 'You're in hospital. You crashed, do you remember?'

'I'm hardly likely to forget.'

Carrie could have jumped up and danced a jig. That was so Johnnie! He was still there! He might be physically battered, but mentally he was intact. And very much still himself. Penny grinned and Carrie knew she was thinking the same thing. Still the same old Johnnie!

Johnnie shifted sightly in the bed and his face creased with pain.

'Go on, then,' he said slowly. 'I don't feel too dandy. My leg feels like I've got a ton of concrete on it. My head hurts, my side hurts, I can't bear to open my eyes . . . what have I done?'

'The feeling is you got off pretty lightly,' said Penny matter-of-factly. 'As far as your leg goes, both bones are broken below the knee, plus you've two broken ribs and a bit of concussion. As for the rest – well, I wouldn't look in a mirror for a bit.'

'Thanks.' But Johnnie managed the ghost of a smile. 'Kind words from my adoring girlfriend.'

'It's true, Johnnie, you've had a lucky escape.' Carrie was remembering her conversation with Heather. 'It could have been much worse.'

'I know.' Then, presumably remembering and not wanting to talk about it any more, he said, still taking it in: 'Hang on, if it's Monday, why aren't you two at work? You've never closed the bookshop?'

'Oh, you!' Tears sprang into Carrie's eyes from the sheer Johnnie-ness of what he was saying and she had to blink them back. 'Don't worry, it'll be the first and last time, if that's all the thanks I get!'

'Yes,' Penny chipped in, 'same for me! People are giving themselves hernias lugging their own bags, and I'll be getting it in the neck tomorrow from Bayliss. He must have had to clean the pigeon droppings off the front windows himself. And water his own pelargoniums!'

'Well, thank you for coming. Seriously.' Johnnie yawned. 'Sorry not to be more lively, but I'm really quite tired.'

'They're about to ring the bell anyway.' Carrie squeezed his hand. She leaned down and dropped a kiss on the least bruised part of his face. He still winced. 'But it's so good to see you. And hear you.'

'Don't write me off yet.'

'Bye, darling.' Penny leaned in and kissed him softly on the mouth. 'We'll soon be tripping the light fantastic again.'

Johnnie, bless him, tried to smile.

'You bet. My Lindyhopping'll win us the spot prize at the next RAF do, you'll see.'

'Huh!' smirked Penny. 'Hop being the operative word. We don't want you running, or dancing, before you can walk.'

'And you thought I was bossy!' smiled Carrie. 'But she's quite right.'

The nurse came down the ward, ringing a bell. Johnnie flinched: the sound must have gone right through his head.

'Bye,' he said, with another yawn. 'Tell Mum and Dad I'm fine.'

'They'll come this evening,' Carrie assured him as she stood up. 'You get some rest.'

141

Outside the ward, the friends turned to one another for what Carrie thought would be a hug of sheer triumph. But to her astonishment, Penny sagged against her and wept.

'He's all right, he's all right!' Penny kept repeating. 'Oh, I'm so happy! I just – I love him so much! I love him to bits, Carrie, I've never felt anything like it before. I don't know what I'd have done if he hadn't come through this.'

'Shh, shh,' Carrie soothed.

She didn't know what she'd have done either, or her mum and dad. They hadn't had to face the worst and she'd be eternally grateful, every single day of her life. She was deeply moved by Penny's heartfelt love for her brother, but her mind was seething with feelings of her own.

Relief, joy and relief again . . . These past couple of days had been another test of her courage and resilience, not the first she'd been asked for in this war, and probably not the last. But she'd face every one square on, armed with the same resolve that had led her to opening the bookshop and making a success of it, which had seen her refuse to give up on Mike in all the long months of his absence and which would see her through supporting Johnnie in his recovery and coping with Mike being away again. She would fight to the end. She would stick it, and stick it, and stick it.

Carrie and Penny were back at work the next day. Bette and Ruby greeted them with such rapture it was as if they were the ones who'd survived a plane crash, Bette wiping away tears with the corner of her apron and Ruby openly blubbing when they heard Johnnie had come round and spoken to them. Mr Bayliss managed a gruff 'So he's all right, is he?'

before reverting to his usual self. He strutted off to inform a pair of soldiers lounging against the wall that they were a disgrace to their regiment, demanding that they pick up their cigarette butts and stand up straight.

Carrie's regular customers had missed her and were sorry to hear the reason she'd been away. Miss Cattermole, who knitted comforts for the troops, declared that she'd knit Johnnie 'a nice muffler', and not in the standard-issue wool either, but with some special three-ply she'd got put by. Professor Mason, who taught English literature and had a sideline setting crosswords for the *Brockington Post*, promised to compose one especially for Johnnie consisting entirely of aircraft-related terms.

'I'm so glad you're back,' he said. 'Quite apart from Bayliss bellyaching yesterday about your and Penny's absence as if it were the Peasants' Revolt, I spent half an hour trying to explain to Ruby that the three-letter answer to my clue of "Selfishly keep pig" was, of course, "hog". And as for the answer to "Nothing going on" – two words, one of eight letters, then one of four – being "birthday suit" . . .' He tapped his forehead. 'Nothing going on upstairs, or not much, I'm afraid, in that girl, sweet-natured though she is.'

Carrie smiled – her first smile of amusement in days.

'I don't think I'd have got that one, to be fair,' she said. 'And isn't it rather risqué for the *Post*?'

'Ha!' trumpeted Professor Mason. 'If this war doesn't broaden a few people's minds about all sorts of things, nothing will!'

Then, raising his hat, he moved off as his train pulled in.

Carrie straightened her display of magazines and

wondered if she'd ever felt happier. She knew that Johnnie had a long, long way to go until he was back on his feet, but she also knew how determined her brother could be. Even so, it would be a while before he was behind the controls of a Spitfire again, and for that she could only give thanks. The strange thing was that for a second successive night, there'd been no air raid. How ironic if Johnnie had got himself shot down on the very last day of the Blitz.

Gradually, day by day, hour by hour, Johnnie got better. Soon he was sitting out of bed with his leg on a stool. Sister Munro didn't believe in patients lying around and getting bedsores.

'What a harridan!' Johnnie told Carrie, but with affection. 'We're all terrified of her. Talk about an iron fist in a silken glove.'

'She needs it with you lot!' Carrie replied.

Carrie and Penny had taken to visiting in the evenings, alternating with Norman, Mary and Uncle Charlie. Johnnie's RAF friends came in the daytime when they were off duty, and he'd made plenty of friends on the ward. They'd set up a card school, and read to the ones who, poor souls, had their eyes bandaged.

'Plenty are far worse off than me,' Johnnie reflected.

Uncle Charlie had predicted that Johnnie would turn his crash into a funny story. It was hardly that, not by a long shot, but bit by bit the tale emerged. Most of it came out one evening when Carrie and Penny pushed him in a wheelchair to the little garden in the quadrangle formed by the four wings of the hospital.

'Oi, watch it!' he complained as a wheel caught the edge of a flower bed. 'Are you trying to finish me off? I've had smoother rides at twenty thousand feet in a thunderstorm!'

'Oh shut up!' Carrie retorted.

Their normal jokey brother-and-sister relationship was back, but nonetheless she and Penny steered more carefully after that. They parked themselves in a corner whose bench was catching the last beams of the sun. Johnnie raised his face gratefully to the sky.

'Gosh, I miss being up there,' he said.

Carrie and Penny looked at each other over his head.

'Even after what happened?' Carrie ventured.

'Is that your way of asking me to tell you?' He smiled kindly at them. 'I suppose you've been waiting for it. But I didn't want to say much till I'd got it all straight in my mind. I keep seeing it, of course, like a film, but I couldn't put it into words.'

Penny had been lighting two cigarettes and she handed him one. Johnnie took a long draw on it.

'All right, here goes,' he began.

Chapter Seventeen

'We'd seen them coming on the radar, and we know there's a lot of them, so we start with six of us going up—'

'Six? Is that all?' squeaked Penny.

Johnnie gave her an under-the-eyebrows look.

'If you're going to keep interrupting, you're never going to hear this.'

'Sorry,' said Penny, chastened. 'Carry on.'

'Thank you,' said Johnnie with dignity. 'So we spot them halfway over the Channel, tucked in the cloud cover – V-formations, groups of six, and a whole lot of them, maybe sixty, seventy in all, bombers and fighters.'

Carrie looked at Penny and gave a warning shake of the head: no more interruptions, however much they might want to.

'So the leading pilot – Tim – comes over the radio, but we knew what to do anyway.' He smiled. 'We climbed high above the cloud – above them – turned and got in front of their leading formation. Then, of course, they realised we were there. They massed into one huge swarm and their 109s screamed out to circle the bombers. But that's the thing about the Spit, you see – the speed of the dive.' He gave a secret sort of smile, thinking of his beloved plane. 'Three of us dived straight into their leading bombers, and the other three – I was one of them – got to . . . to tease their fighters a bit, lead them astray.'

'Tease them . . . I see,' repeated Penny sardonically, while Carrie rolled her eyes. She knew from the night in the pub how the pilots played things down, but when it was Johnnie in the thick of the fighting, the deadpanning was hard to take.

'Yeah, well, it's the job.' Johnnie shrugged and took another drag on his cigarette. 'We were doing fine. I was doing fine, and more of our boys arrived, but . . . anyway, the next thing is, I'm hit, my port engine's on fire. The Spit began to play up. I was losing height. And I really didn't want to ditch in the Channel.'

Carrie knew that a landing on water could be a harder landing, in every sense, than on the ground.

'So, long story short, somehow – don't ask me how, I don't know. Self-preservation? Luck? – I got away and started to limp back. One of theirs was following me, but, thank God, got taken out by one of ours. I've never been so glad to see the coastline, but I was starting to spin down by now, and fast. I could see roofs, houses . . . I was desperate not to land smack on someone's home. And then, thank you, Lord, trees and a field. I was too low to jump – I'd have broken more than a leg and a couple of ribs. I had to pitch the kite as best I could, half-stuck in the field, which is why, I suppose, I'm smashed up more on one side than the other. The local Home Guard and ARP came running. I was out cold – they pulled me out and brought me round. I owe them a lot, because my poor old kite went up like a rocket.'

Penny threw down her cigarette and ground it out

abruptly. Carrie closed her eyes. Johnnie might not have wanted to drown, but surely, being trapped in a burning plane . . .

Johnnie's own cigarette had burned right down while he was talking. Penny took it from him and stubbed it out, then leaned down and kissed him.

'What are we going to do with you?' she said, sounding choked. 'All that, but the minute you can, you'll be back in the cockpit, won't you?'

It wasn't often that Penny showed her emotions. Johnnie turned to her and took her hand.

'Not for a while. So make the most of me while you can. Even in this state.' He turned to Carrie. 'You too, sis. Once I can get about, I can come and help in your little shop while I recuperate, if you'll have me.'

'Less of the little!' joked Carrie.

Partly she was covering her own emotions about Johnnie's narrow escape, but his quip made her think about the plans she and Mike had made for a whole chain of bookshops. Mike . . . Their time together seemed so long ago.

Back at the beginning, once Johnnie had come round, Carrie had asked her father's permission to place an international call to the number in Washington that Mike had given her. Lord knew what it would cost – a week's wages, probably – but Carrie judged that it would be worth it. Mike had said the number was for emergencies only, but if this wasn't an emergency, what was?

When she was finally connected, an American voice, male, had answered. Carrie gave her name and asked for Mike.

'Lieutenant Hudson?' (He'd pronounced it 'loo-tenant', not 'lef-tenant', with the emphasis on the 'loo', and if the reason for the call hadn't been so serious, Carrie would have giggled.) 'Just one moment, please, ma'am. I'll see if he's available.'

Crikey, Mike must be important if he didn't even answer his own phone! Carrie waited, breath bated, and when he came on the line, Mike already sounded worried. He knew she wouldn't be telephoning long-distance for nothing.

'Oh no,' he said when she'd told him what had happened. 'When we heard about the raid, I did wonder . . . You poor love – poor all of you. I'm so sorry I'm not there.'

'You can't help it,' Carrie had said, knowing that being so far away wasn't his choice.

'I wish I—Sorry, I nearly swore. I wish I could,' he said.

'Johnnie's in the best place,' Carrie reassured him. Simply hearing Mike's voice was making her feel stronger. 'He's getting all the care he needs. We've just got to get him back on his feet. Literally.'

'Yes, of course. What timing, though! I've only been gone five minutes.'

'How are you getting on, anyway?' Carrie asked; she'd been dying to know. 'Have you had a T-bone steak yet? Or a Harvey Wallbanger? Walked along a sidewalk and been into a drugstore or a soda fountain?' They'd joked about such things before he'd left. 'Oh, and by the way, before all this happened, Johnnie wanted to know if you'd be going to a baseball game?'

Mike laughed. 'I'm here to work, you know.'

'You've got to have some time off. I hope you will!'

149

Mike had telephoned again, twice, since then and it had been wonderful to hear his voice – even better than the letters that had begun to arrive, describing the wide boulevards, the shops stuffed with goods, and the crazy traffic. Carrie treasured them and read them over and over, writing back at once. She told him about her customers – the man with a dog exactly like the one on the His Master's Voice record label, and the woman whose summer hat was like a melted strawberry ice cream. She kept him up to date with Johnnie's progress, and told him about the books she was putting aside for him: anything and everything, from *The Natural History of Selborne* to the new Penguin biography of Tennyson.

But every day, Mike's three-month stretch in America was getting shorter. He'd be back soon, and they'd be married. Johnnie would be better, and everything – everything – would be right again.

May slid into June, and after the long winter and the cold spring, the weather finally bucked up its ideas.

In the past few weeks, Ruby and Hendrick van Roon had got into quite a regular routine: they'd meet on a Sunday at two o'clock by the 'bandstand' – or what passed for a bandstand these days. The council still put out deckchairs once a month, when the Brockington Silver Band gave a concert on the circular stone platform, but the fancy Victorian wedding-cake structure had gone the way of all decorative ironwork and was now less decorative but more useful as gun turrets or tanks.

'Ha, it is the same in Holland, I am sure,' Hendrick told

her sadly when Ruby bemoaned the loss. 'The Nazis will take everything that is necessary to win the war!'

'It's a blooming shame, that's all I can say.' Ruby licked the ice cream Hendrick had bought for her. He really was very kind. 'The bandstand looks so bare without it. I wonder when, or if, we'll ever get things back.'

'After the war, many things will be different. There will be no going back to the old ways for many people.' Hendrick's face was set and Ruby touched his arm. She was in her gingham dress again and he was in shirtsleeves. The sun was lovely and warm.

'You must miss home a lot.'

Hendrick seemed to snap out of his low mood and flashed her his sudden smile.

'You are a great help in making me feel at home in England, Ruby,' he said. 'But tell me, I still know so little about how things work here. Brockington Junction, it's a busy place. There must be how many trains in a day?'

'Goodness, I ain't never counted! I 'spect Mrs Saunders would know. Or Mr Bayliss, of course.'

'He is very important, that one? He keeps all the times in his head?'

'Well, some,' said Ruby grudgingly. She had her own good reason for disliking Mr Bayliss, but she wasn't going to go into all that with Hendrick. 'But in his office, it's all written down on big charts – I've seen 'em. Not just the regular timetable, all the extra trains too, and what they've got on 'em. Extra troop trains and that.'

'Yes, of course. And the trains continue all night, even when the tearoom is closed and he is not there?'

'Oh yeah, they rattle through at all hours, wake me up sometimes, they do. The cutting's at the end of our street, see. Goods trains, mostly. Coal and that.'

'Ah, goods trains. And the – you call it the mail train, I think? The Post Office.'

'That's right, the mail train. You got such a good head on you, Hendrick. I don't suppose I could manage for five minutes if I had to pitch up in another country not speaking the language. Imagine me in Holland trying to get by! I wouldn't know where to start.'

'Oh, I think you would do very well anywhere, Ruby, a charming person like yourself.'

Ruby simpered. It was true what they said about continentals – they did have a way with words.

In her tidy cottage near the station, Bette was writing her weekly letter to Eric. She'd filled half the regulation page – all that was allowed – with snippets about the neighbours. Now it was time to answer the question Eric had asked in his last letter: was 'that Dutchman' still coming in the tea-room? Short of anything to say, Bette had told Eric about the time Hendrick had been beaten up, and to be fair to Ruby, the girl had told her she'd mentioned the incident to Eric too. But somehow, something had communicated itself to Eric, stuck where he was with not much to do except read and reread his letters. And something about Hendrick van Roon had bothered him.

When Ruby had started working at the refreshment room, she'd tried to make the most of herself. But copious applications of makeup, drenching herself in cheap scent and perming and peroxiding her hair to a brittle frizz had created anything but the desired effect. Gradually, under Carrie's influence and, it had to be said, once she'd begun this long-distance relationship with Eric, she'd settled down. She'd toned down the makeup and let her hair revert to its natural colour, which suited her far better. It might only have been a mousy brown, but it had a nice natural wave. More importantly, for Ruby' s own reputation and that of the tearoom, she'd stopped her rather obvious flirting with 'anything in trousers', as Bette tartly put it.

Even so, Bette always observed Ruby and Hendrick van Roon's exchanges closely. Ruby was a good worker and a useful little baker, Bette had to give her that, and she'd grown accustomed to the girl. She'd warmed to Hendrick, too, since his encounter with the two no-goods who'd beaten him up. All in all, Bette felt she could reassure her son. She took another sip of tea as she considered how best to put it to Eric.

'You needn't worry about Ruby,' she wrote. 'I keep an eye on her when he's in, but I haven't seen any funny business. He does just seem keen to improve his English. He still speaks a bit formal, but if you heard some of the language from our lot, you'd be glad of it. I know I am.'

Then in smaller writing – she was running out of space – she added: 'I hope they're treating you right on whatever work it is you're doing. At least it'll keep you occupied till you're home which I hope will be very soon. All my love, Mum.'

Bette laid down her pen. That should do it.

Chapter Eighteen

'Well, that's all my news,' said Mary.

Once debriefed, Johnnie had been moved to an RAF hospital and then an RAF rehabilitation unit to complete his recovery.

'Let out for good behaviour,' he'd joked. 'Parole instead of prison!' Whatever, it was closer to home, thankfully, and the family were able to get there more easily by bus.

'So what's your news?' Mary continued.

'In here? None, but let's think . . .' Johnnie considered. 'Oh, yes, a big hoo-ha the other day. Some joker wrote "Abandon Hope All Ye Who Enter Here" over the door to the dining room. I never thought I'd miss Sister Munro, but you should have heard the roasting Matron gave us!'

'You boys!' tutted Mary. 'You're eating, though, are you? And doing your exercises?'

'What I can,' sighed Johnnie. 'My ribs still hurt, so I'm not too hot on crutches. But once they've mended properly and the plaster comes off, I can start proper exercises to build up the muscle again. Roll on the day – this is driving me crazy!'

'I know it must be, love. But you're young and fit. That'll help.'

'Yes, well, I intend to keep it that way—' He broke off. 'Hello, what are you doing here?'

'The usual rapturous welcome! Hello, Mrs Anderson.'

'Penny!' exclaimed Mary. 'Got the afternoon off?'

Penny plumped down on the other chair and fanned herself with her hand. She was wearing a halter-neck dress, emerald green with white spots, that showed off her dark hair to perfection. A white cardigan was draped modestly over her shoulders, but Mary had still noticed heads turn in her direction as she'd swished down the ward, and she'd seen Johnnie notice it too.

'It's such a lovely day! Far too nice to be slaving away on that station in a serge suit,' Penny said in answer to Mary's question. 'I felt all devilish when I woke up, so . . .' she lowered her voice '. . . I rang in sick. Wicked, I know, but worth it. But the bus was so hot and sticky! Shall we take him outside, Mrs Anderson?'

'No, not me, dear. I'll leave you to it.' Mary gathered her bag, gloves and gas mask.

'Oh, no, you don't have to go! Don't let me chase you away, please—' Penny began.

Mary smiled as she stood up.

'It's quite all right. I can come any afternoon. You've had to perjure yourself to get here!'

'Well, if you're sure . . .'

'I'm sure. I've told Johnnie all my news, such as it is.'

'Oatmeal sausages for tea at home tonight,' reported Johnnie. 'Yum-yum!'

'Cheeky.' Mary tapped him on the wrist. 'You try cooking

155

with rations!' She turned to Penny. 'To be honest, there's a nice wool shop nearby I've been dying to have a look in. And a little dress shop that doesn't look too pricey. I'll see you tomorrow, son.'

'Thanks, Mum.' Johnnie held out his cheek for a kiss. 'Be good, and don't spend all your coupons!'

With half the country's factories turning out uniforms, parachutes and bandages, everyday clothes had begun to be rationed. The government had allocated coupons for one – one! – complete set of new clothes per person, per year, right down to underpants and socks.

'I'll try not to!'

'Bye, Mrs Anderson,' Penny smiled. 'See you soon.'

Together they watched Mary go.

'Right,' said Johnnie, indicating his wheelchair. 'I wouldn't mind some fresh air. Let's go walking.'

'Pushing, you mean,' grimaced Penny. 'I'll have muscles like a stevedore soon!'

There was plenty of pushing for her to do. The RAF had commandeered a big old Arts and Crafts-style house with gardens and parkland that stretched to a good few acres. There was a rose garden, a walled garden, a knot garden and an ornamental lake. The owners, apparently, were condemned to living in the gatehouse.

'How far do you want to go?' Penny asked, putting on her sunglasses when they got outside.

'The lake, I think,' said Johnnie. 'I fancy a swim.'

'Ha ha. Still . . .' She gestured to what he was wearing. 'At least you're half dressed for it.'

Johnnie grinned. 'Yes, if I had to break a leg, best to do it over the summer when shorts are regulation issue.'

'And they look very fetching with your pyjama jacket.'

'What the best-dressed man is wearing this season, I hear.'

'Along with a plaster cast, I suppose,' Penny retorted. 'I must tip off Savile Row!'

She started pushing, Johnnie helping with the wheels. He craned round to look at her.

'You look very lovely, as always.'

'What, this old thing?' said Penny dismissively. She'd never known how to take a compliment.

'I saw all the other chaps reining in their wolf whistles. You watch that fellow Kemp in the bed opposite – what a roving eye!'

'You tell him to keep his eyes to himself. Oof! Thank goodness, nearly there – oh, and look, someone's kindly left us a couple of chairs. I'll help you hop over to one, if you like.'

'I'll be fine,' Johnnie insisted. 'I've got to learn to do things for myself.'

'Good!' smiled Penny. 'I don't really see myself as your handmaiden for life.'

There were two canvas chairs with wooden arms at the lip of the lake. Penny parked Johnnie beside one of them and put on the brake. She sat down herself, then noticed he'd lifted his good leg to unlace his shoe. She took off her sunglasses to scrutinise him.

'What are you doing?'

'I may not be able to swim, but I'm jolly well going to paddle.'

'Johnnie, don't be ridiculous!'

'Look, if you hadn't had a bath for a month, you might be more sympathetic.'

He was already struggling to stand, leaning on the arm of the chair. But the ground was unstable, the chair wobbled, and so did he, towards the water.

Penny was on her feet in a flash, throwing her arms around him, pulling him back onto the bank and holding him tight. She could feel his heart beating as fast as hers and she knew he'd scared himself too.

'You idiot!' she cried, fear making her sound angry. 'Imagine if you'd gone in, broken your other leg, bust a few more ribs and got your plaster cast soaked! You are such a fool, Johnnie!'

Johnnie looked down at her, her cardigan slipped from her shoulders, her hair disordered, her eyes fiery.

'Marry me.'

'*What?*'

'Marry me,' he said. 'And not just for saving me from drowning.'

'What?'

'You're a wonderful girl, Penny, wonderful. You've been terrific through all this, terrific through everything, putting up with me even before I crocked myself, and I know how worried you were on every mission I flew, even though you tried not to show it and tried not to hector me about it. I may be the most annoying person in the world, and an idiot, but you make me at least a bit better, and I'll try not to worry you quite so much in future. I love you. I always have, I think, ever since we first met. I love you and I admire you so much for what you've done, leaving home and coming to Brockington and finding a job and – well, everything. So will you? Please? Marry me?'

Penny looked at him, trying to take it all in.

'They haven't put you on some experimental drug, have they? To speed up your recovery?'

'What? No!'

'You're serious?'

'I'm deadly serious.'

They were still standing on the very edge of the lake, arms around each other. Penny disengaged herself, holding his hands.

'I need to sit down. And so should you.'

She sat and steadied the other chair beside her while he sat too. He looked at her quizzically.

'Well? It's a simple enough proposition, Penny. Or do you need time to think about it, like some Victorian maiden? Or—' The thought suddenly struck him. 'We've never talked about it. You're not against marriage, are you? Some girls are these days.'

Penny turned sideways towards him.

'I'm not thinking about it, I just can't believe it. It came from nowhere!'

'Not really. And it may not seem like the right time, in the middle of a war, but if we wait, when will be? And as for proposing, it seemed like the perfect moment to me, wobbling on the edge of the lake.'

'Well . . .'

'I mean, Mike set the bar so high with his blooming romantic Easter surprise . . . How could I match that in the state I'm in? Even if I could have got hold of a ring, what am I going to do, conceal it in a bedpan and propose at visiting time? And we toast our engagement with Lucozade? At least this is original.'

'Yes, I'll give you that,' Penny conceded.

'Thanks! But you still haven't given me an answer.'

Penny laughed and slid her arms around him.

'Oh, Johnnie! You really are a fool. I've loved you from the very start as well. Of course I'll marry you. There's nothing in the world I'd like more.'

'Well, thank goodness for that!' Johnnie blew out a breath. 'Talk about spinning it out. You nearly gave me a heart attack on top of my other ailments.'

'What about the heart attack you nearly gave me, almost falling in the water?'

Johnnie grinned.

'Are we having our first row as an engaged couple?'

'Yes,' said Penny, not meaning it, 'and it probably won't be the last! Come here, you.'

Their kiss was interrupted by shouts from behind them.

'Oi! Anderson! Get your filthy hands off her!'

Johnnie and Penny pulled apart. Johnnie groaned.

'Kemp and Foster. The bad boys of the ward on their daily constitutional.'

'They can be the first to congratulate us.' Penny turned and called to the two men approaching. 'I hope you've brought champagne. We've just got engaged!'

Chapter Nineteen

'Well, I didn't see that coming, but congratulations!'

Carrie leaned in and kissed her brother. Penny hadn't been slow to share the good news. Johnnie said nothing, but he smiled inwardly. So much for Carrie's famous second sight! He was more sceptical about it by the day, but he'd never say anything. He wouldn't have dreamed of bursting his sister's bubble.

'Thanks, sis.' He smiled. 'There's one good thing anyway – I'll finally get to meet her dad. We'll have to go and see him when I'm a bit more mobile. I mean, the deed's done, but even as a formality, I ought to ask his permission. Mike asked Dad before he proposed to you.'

'Hmm, yes, that's true,' said Carrie circumspectly.

She knew Penny had still said nothing to Johnnie about who she really was. It put Carrie in a very awkward position, torn between respect for Penny's right to privacy and her brother's right to know the truth about the girl he was going to marry. Whether the full story went any further than that was up to Penny and Johnnie themselves.

'Or if Penny thinks that's too old-fashioned,' Johnnie went on, 'I, or we, should at least telephone the old boy so I can introduce myself. I can't very well let the first contact Mr Edwards and I have with each other be at the wedding.'

Carrie was biting her tongue so hard her mother could have used it as a colander. This was such a mess, and it was getting more and more muddled! There was no Mr Edwards, there was only Gerald Eversleigh, a knight or baron or lord or at least a sir – Carrie had never been quite clear exactly what his title was. But whatever rank of the nobility her father had, Penny had accepted Johnnie's proposal under completely false pretences.

'Anyway, as I say,' Johnnie continued, 'I've got to get back on my feet. Two feet. And I want you to help me. I don't know what Pen's told you, but we only want a quiet do – register office – and it makes sense to do it while I'm on sick leave. Then we get a decent amount of time together before I'm back in business.'

'So where do I come in? Penny's already earmarked me to be her best woman – she won't call it a bridesmaid. Trust her!'

'You've got to help me walk again,' said Johnnie. 'I'm persevering with the crutches, but it's darned slow going. I don't intend to hobble back up the aisle, and I don't want to be propped on a stick in the photos either.'

'The Leaning Flyer of Brockington?'

'Ha, funny! Penny says she doesn't mind – we can show the kids what Daddy did in the war and all that – but I'm not having it. So once I'm properly up and about, whenever you visit, we're practising my walking. But you're not to tell Penny.'

'Fine. As long as you don't overdo things, of course I'll help you.'

It was something Carrie could agree to, at least, and she

was touched that Johnnie wanted her help, even if it involved her in keeping yet another secret. But she'd have to tackle Penny again about telling Johnnie her real name. Much as she'd tried to understand Penny's reluctance, and her desire never to have anything to do with her father again, she couldn't let her brother begin his married life on a lie.

In the event, she didn't have to.

'I've got something to tell you,' Penny said as Johnnie pored over the list of potential dates for their wedding she'd brought along. The weather had turned rainy and they were sitting in the day room at a table covered with a half-finished jigsaw of the Tower of London and an abandoned game of patience.

'Oh, yes?' Johnnie was studying the list while absent-mindedly turning over cards and adding them to the existing lines. 'What day of the week do you fancy? Dad and Carrie are going to have to shut up shop anyway, so it makes no difference to them—'

'Never mind the shops, can *you* shut up a minute? I can't marry you—'

Johnnie stopped what he was doing. 'What?'

'Let me finish!' Nerves were making Penny touchy. 'I can't marry you until I've told you something.'

'You look very serious, Pen. What is it?'

Johnnie sounded serious too. It was no time for their usual light-hearted back-and-forth.

'I'm not who you think I am.'

Johnnie gave a minute shake of his head.

'I don't understand.'

'I'm not Penny Edwards,' Penny explained. 'My real name is Penelope Margaret Geraldine Eversleigh. The Honourable Penelope Eversleigh.'

Johnnie laughed.

'You're having me on.'

'Why would I do that?' said Penny impatiently. 'And why do it now? It's taken me six months to work up to telling you, that's why!'

Johnnie burst out laughing. 'What? So this is why you've been so coy about your father. You're a lady!'

'I'm not Lady anything—'

'No, I know. I said *a* lady. And yet you're the least ladylike person I can think of! Oh, Penny. Why ever didn't you say?'

'Isn't it obvious?' Penny was laughing herself now, with relief. 'I thought it'd scare you off.'

'You don't think much of me, do you?' Johnnie took her hand. 'I love you, whoever you are, you twit! But this is incredible. Come on, let's have the full story.'

So Penny told him, all about the sad death of her mother and her ridiculously hidebound and traditional father and how he'd wanted her to marry a drippy but very wealthy neighbour in the hope of securing their family pile for the future, because of the silly business of her not being able to inherit it in her own right.

'Because I'm a girl!' she said. 'It used to make me mad, but I don't give a fig about it now. It's never made me happy, all that money and privilege. I'm the happiest I've ever been in my whole life in Brockington, meeting normal people and doing something useful instead of learning flower arranging and how to make canapés and making inane conversation at dances with boys with floppy hair and no chin!'

Johnnie felt his own chin speculatively.

'So you're marrying me for my chin.'

'That may be part of it,' said Penny gravely.

'You are a funny one.' Johnnie leaned over and kissed her. 'So that's that, is it? You don't want your father anywhere near the wedding, or anywhere near you, for the rest of your life?'

'In short, yes.'

Johnnie sighed. 'Well, it's your call. But don't you think he must be sick with worry about you? Don't you—'

'No!' Penny stopped his mouth with her fingers. 'Please, Johnnie, I've told you the truth, and you say it makes no difference. That's all I wanted to hear. I can't talk about it any more. I've told you how it is, and why it is.'

'And what about my mum and dad? How far do you want this to go?'

'That's up to you – they're your parents. I can quite see you might want them to know. I think your dad'd take it fine. I'm not so sure about your mum, though.'

Johnnie considered this.

'Hmm, she is a bit of a stickler – you know, conventional. But it's not like we're getting married in church, is it? We're not, you know, doing anything wrong in the house of God.'

'No ... we're not doing anything wrong anyway. I'm totally legal. I've changed my name by deed poll, but I've got my original birth certificate to show them at the register office if I have to.'

'Let's have it out in the open then. I mean, not *that* open – we'll keep it in the family.' Johnnie thought back to those conversations he'd had with Carrie about Penny. He'd thought at the time she'd seemed a bit constrained; now it suddenly made sense. 'But Carrie knows already, I take it.'

'Yes, but please don't blame her – I swore her to secrecy. I know she hasn't said a word.'

'No, she hasn't. Tight as the seal on a cockpit slide! But how about this, Pen? We'll tell Mum and Dad, and Uncle Charlie too, I guess. But that's it. Apart from – can Carrie tell Mike now?'

Penny smiled. 'Yes. I think that's only fair.'

Johnnie smiled and gave her a swift kiss. 'Good. You have to laugh, though. Mum thought Mike was too posh for us, all because he had an officer's pip on his shoulder and his parents' shop sounds a bit more la-di-da than ours. And now this! But just my luck, or what?'

'How do you mean?'

'I land myself a girl with a pedigree going back to William the Conqueror or whoever, and she's only gone and turned her back on the family fortune. Instead, I've got to slave away for the rest of my life to keep her in the style to which she ought to be accustomed!'

'I told you so!' Carrie couldn't help herself when Penny expressed her relief that her secret was out and Johnnie thought it was a hoot.

She dashed off a letter to Mike, telling him about the proposal – and the truth about Penny. Mary, on the other hand, was 'all of a jitter' about Penny's 'pedigree'. Carrie knew Penny was deeply fond of Mary and that she envied Carrie her mum, not having really known her own mother.

'You got to know me as Penny,' she insisted, seeing Mary's new awkwardness around her. 'I'm still the same person – just a girl like any other! I don't see having another surname at birth makes any difference.'

But Penny was about to prove just how different from other girls she was.

'Have you heard the latest?' Mary asked as she and Carrie unpegged the washing one evening. 'Says she doesn't want an engagement ring because it'd only get scratched at work. A plain gold band, that's all she wants!'

'I know, but it's up to Penny, Mum,' said Carrie mildly. 'And she's right. It would.'

'She could wear it in the evenings and for going out. I don't know, I'll never understand it.'

'You don't have to. Just be happy for them.'

'I am! She's a lovely girl, but a funny one, and no mistake.'

Carrie looked down fondly at her own ring, twinkling in the sun. Darling Mike.

In the immediate aftermath of Johnnie's accident, Mike had taken to phoning regularly once a week, but that had had to stop. Once the immediate worry about Johnnie had receded, neither of them could justify it any more. He promised he'd still try to telephone when he could, but transatlantic calls were hugely complicated to set up and terrifyingly expensive as they came out of Mike's pay.

But he was writing every week, sometimes more, and Carrie was writing back. Mike's letters described the things he was seeing and experiencing, whether it was the incredible view from the observation deck of the Empire State Building on a trip to New York or a blueberry cheesecake that was the most delicious thing he'd ever eaten. But he never made Carrie's world feel small or uninteresting, always stressing how much more these things would mean if she were there to share them with him. He always made a point of commenting on things she'd told him, like who'd bought which books, funny things she'd seen or noticed at the station or on her way to and from work and the misprint in the *Brockington Post* that meant a flat 'To Let' had come out as 'Flat Toilet'. He was following Johnnie's recovery minutely, and was thrilled about Johnnie and Penny's engagement.

Carrie sighed. She often relived the moment of Mike's proposal in the sun-washed back room, and how special it had been. How special his kisses were and how special it felt to be held by him. She longed to hold him again now, for him to hold her, to bury herself in him, to breathe him in, all of him. Only another six weeks till the beginning of August, she told herself. Not long now.

Chapter Twenty

Wiping down a table in the tearoom, Ruby was equally baffled by Penny's insistence on not having a ring. Ruby had already chosen her own engagement ring several times over, even though the day of any proposal from Eric, which she now considered a certainty, would be well into the future.

Despite her name, she had no intention of having a ruby – no chance! Blood and tears, her nan had always insisted darkly. No, at the moment the favourites were a sapphire and diamond or a simple solitaire – not a rock, but a decent size, of course. Ignorant of the terms of international conventions and the rights of prisoners, she assumed that Eric would be getting some kind of wage for the work he was doing and hoped he was saving it up. It wasn't as though there was anything to buy in the camp!

In the meantime, Ruby had bought herself a so-called 'cocktail' ring from Woolworths, a flashy thing of blue and purple stones. Hendrick had duly admired it, complimenting her on her taste. Ruby had glowed. He hadn't bought her anything more than an ice cream or a toasted teacake yet, but there was still time. Her birthday was coming up; she might drop a hint about a nice jewelled comb she'd seen in Woolies when she was choosing the ring.

Ruby looked up as the bell jangled; she was in charge out

front while Mrs Saunders laboured over the tearoom's accounts. A tall man in a dark suit with salt-and-pepper hair came in. He was followed by a shorter man, plumper and younger, in a rather crumpled suit and a bold red knitted tie. Behind them – was it rush hour or what? thought Ruby – was a uniformed constable. It wasn't George Drummond, the usual beat bobby, who popped in sometimes to rest his feet and partake of a cup of tea and a bite to eat. George must be on his holidays.

'Good afternoon,' Ruby said pleasantly, as Bette had taught her. She picked up her tray and moved towards the counter. 'What can I get you?'

'Ruby Yateman?' said the taller man.

Ruby turned, surprised.

'Yes,' she said.

He advanced towards her, as did the other man and the constable. Until then, Ruby hadn't registered that they were together.

'You are suspected of conspiring to assist the enemy in contravention of the Defence Regulations. And as such, I am placing you under arrest.'

'Eh? Me? What? No!' Ruby backed away, the tray falling from her fingers with a crash. 'It's a mistake! No, I can't be. I ain't done nothing!'

Hearing the kerfuffle, Bette appeared at the counter.

'What on earth—' she began. And then, as she saw the constable take Ruby's arm, she protested: 'What do you think you're doing? Ruby, what is all this?'

'I ain't done nothing, honest, Mrs Saunders!' squealed

170

Ruby as the constable told her to 'Come along quietly, miss, if you know what's good for you.'

'What's going on?' demanded Bette. 'What's she supposed to have done?'

'I can't discuss that with you, madam,' said the taller man politely. 'Now come along quietly, Miss Yateman.'

Her arm clamped firmly by the constable, Ruby had no option.

'I've still got me apron on!' she wailed as she was led away. 'Oh, Mrs Saunders, please, I don't understand. Please – tell Carrie. You've got to help me!'

'Well, this is a nice way to spend a sunny afternoon,' Bette said wryly as she shifted on the scuffed Rexine bench in Brockington's police station. 'Over an hour we've been here, the refreshment room closed and my accounts left at sixes and sevens, smashed crocks on the floor, and never mind being allowed to see Ruby, we haven't even been offered a cup of tea!'

Carrie lifted her shoulders helplessly. She'd stared open-mouthed as a sobbing Ruby was frogmarched away and had darted out in time to see her being bundled into the back of a police car. By the time Bette came panting up the platform, Carrie had already pulled down the roller shutter and was locking the bookshop door. They'd been lucky to jump on a bus pretty much straight away, but their haste hadn't got them anywhere except the police station foyer.

'I still can't imagine what Ruby can possibly have done to bring herself to the attention of the police,' Carrie fretted.

'Nor me. Whatever you say about her, she's as honest as the day's long,' Bette agreed. 'And she hasn't the wit to commit a crime!'

But in an airless interview room, the police didn't share that view. Gulping and clutching her grubby, balled-up handkerchief, Ruby had listened as the taller man introduced himself as Detective Inspector Dryden and the other one as Detective Sergeant Miles. Then he'd asked her to confirm her name, address and age, and Detective Sergeant Miles had written it all down. Now the inspector lit up a cigarette and the questioning proper started.

'Do you know a man called Hendrick van Roon?'

Ruby was baffled. What had he got to do with anything?

'Hendrick?' she repeated.

'Do you know him?'

Ruby nodded.

'Could you confirm that, please?'

When Ruby looked blank, the inspector said: 'You need to answer verbally, Miss Yateman, so the sergeant can take it down.' As Ruby still gaped, he elaborated: 'Say it out loud.'

'Yes,' gulped Ruby. 'I know him.' What was wrong with that?

'Where did you meet him?'

'He – he comes in the tearoom.'

'The tearoom where you work?'

'Yes.' Obviously!

'That would be the tearoom at Brockington Junction?'

'Yes.'

Honestly! Where else? She'd thought the police were a bit brighter than this.

'And when was the first time he came in?'

'What? The very first? I dunno. Oh, it was ages ago. Er . . . last year sometime. Summer?'

'Can you be more exact?'

'Not really. It were after Dunkirk. I think. Or maybe a bit before.'

The inspector sighed. It was going to be one of those interviews.

'Let's assume you've known him since May 1940. So you've known him for over a year?'

'No!' said Ruby. 'Not all that time. He was away for a while.'

'Where did he go?'

'I dunno. I never asked!'

'And he was away for how long?'

'Quite a long while. And then he came back.'

'When was that? When did he come back?'

'I dunno – wintertime.'

'Winter . . . So the end of last year or the start of this year?'

'Erm . . .' Ruby thought hard. 'It wasn't the early winter . . . so this year. It was still cold, though. Erm, March time, maybe?' She spread her hands helplessly. 'Why are you asking me all this? Have you asked him? What's it matter? Is he in trouble? And what's it got to do with me?'

'Just answer the questions as they are put to you, Miss Yateman.'

Detective Sergeant Miles yawned. The inspector sighed again. This was going to be hard going.

*

It was five o'clock when a tearful and whey-faced Ruby appeared, escorted this time by a woman police constable. Bette and Carrie jumped to their feet.

'Oh, Mrs Saunders! Carrie!' cried Ruby. 'Oh, you're here! Thank goodness. It's been 'orrible!'

'They haven't mistreated you, I hope?' Bette gave the WPC a stern glance.

'No, but they kept on and on at me! Oh, I wish you could've been in the room with me, you or Carrie. You'd have known what to say!'

'But they've released you, have they?' asked Bette. 'Without charge?'

Ruby hung her head.

'They believed me in the end, that it was all innocent. But I've had a caution.'

'Hang on, Ruby,' said Carrie. 'What was innocent? And cautioned for what, exactly?'

Head still low, Ruby mumbled something they couldn't hear. The desk sergeant was looking at them over his half-moon glasses and, with a look at Bette, Carrie shepherded Ruby towards the entrance.

'We'll go and have a nice cup of tea, Ruby, and you can tell us all about it.'

They went to Lyons; it was bigger and more anonymous than the tiny, Tudor-beamed Ginger Cat. Bette ordered tea for three and a plate of cakes, principally, Carrie suspected, so she could compare them to her own and decide they were not up to scratch. Carrie lent Ruby her handkerchief and her compact so she could repair what she could of her appearance, but all the powder in the world couldn't disguise her pink nose and puffy eyes.

'Come on, then, Ruby,' said Bette, sugaring her tea and stirring it. 'Spill the beans.'

'I'm too ashamed, Mrs Saunders,' whispered Ruby. 'I know you had your doubts about him.'

'About who?' Bette rattled her spoon into its saucer.

'About Hendrick.'

'Your Dutch friend?'

This set Ruby off. 'He's not my friend!' she wailed. 'He never was. He was just using me!'

'Using you for what?' Carrie feared the worst. 'He *was* just a friend, Ruby? You didn't ever—'

'No, no, that's not what I mean!' Ruby started to blubber again. 'Yes, I met him a few times outside of work, on a Sunday, but it was all innocent, honest it was. We just went for a walk, or had a cup of tea!' This was news to Bette, and Ruby turned beseechingly to her. 'You do believe me, don't you, Mrs Saunders? We never did nothing, just walked about and talked and that. I swear, I'd never betray Eric like that!'

Carrie broke in before Bette could open her mouth.

'So how was he using you, exactly?'

'He was using me,' sobbed Ruby, undoing all the good the use of Carrie's compact had done, 'to find out stuff about the railway! Train times, troop trains, goods trains, any kind of train.'

'Why?' asked Bette, curiosity trumping any outrage she might have felt on Eric's behalf. 'Is he some kind of crook? Planning to hold up the mail train or something?'

'A crook? I wish he was just a crook!' sobbed Ruby. 'He's a spy!'

Bit by bit, tea cooling, cakes untouched, they dragged the story out of her. Hendrick van Roon, it seemed, was not Dutch at all. He was a German called Heinrich Rosshart, who'd taken the identity of a dead Dutchman. He'd come to England with his fake passport, his cover story, his passable English and a wide brief. He was responsible, apparently, for general information gathering, and also for training other agents.

'He told me he was teaching English to refugees,' Ruby bleated. 'And I believed him and thought what a nice bloke he was. I thought he was helping people. When really he was helping them Nasties!'

Carrie had never been sure whether Ruby's rendering of 'Nazis' was intentional or a slip of the tongue, and this wasn't the time to find out.

'But how did they link him to you?' demanded Bette. 'All right, you may have met him outside work a few times, and I could say something about that, you silly girl, letting your head be turned! But they might as well have accused me of collaborating with the enemy – I've served him his tea and cakes enough times. Ooh, if I could lay my hands on the little rat! When I think of the cheek – how we'd try to make apple turnovers, special, on his regular day, 'cos he liked them . . . Well—'

'Oh, don't, Mrs Saunders, don't!' wailed Ruby. 'It was the apple turnovers that did it!'

Carrie had been lost in thought, marvelling that two people she knew – Penny and now this Heinrich fellow – had so successfully changed their identities and kept everyone fooled for so long. Yes, it was wartime, everything was fluid, and people were driven to desperate measures for personal or political reasons, but while she could understand and sympathise with Penny's situation, and there was nothing underhand about it, she was horrified to think that thanks to Heinrich Rosshart, Brockington station might have been a chink in the country's armour. What made it even worse was that it was Ruby, so naïve and so trusting, he'd so cynically targeted.

'Sorry – apple turnovers led the police to you?' she asked.

Ruby heaved a gusty sigh and, having exhausted the absorbency of Carrie's handkerchief as well as her own, scrubbed at her face with a corner of the tablecloth, removing all the powder she'd just applied. The salmon-pink streaks would add a bit extra to the J. Lyons laundry bill this week.

'It was a note,' snuffled Ruby, 'that I sneaked into his inside jacket pocket, ooh, weeks back! I'd forgotten all about it, but they showed it me. All it said was that I'd have what he wanted when he next came in.'

'And you meant a turnover?' Bette asked.

'Yes, of course I did! But the police thought . . .' She gulped. 'They thought it was secret stuff about the railway that I was going to get from Mr Bayliss's office!'

She dissolved again.

Bette looked at Carrie, her eyebrows nearly hitting her hairline.

'But how did the police link the note with the tearoom in the first place?' Bette asked. 'If it was a scribble on a scrap of paper?'

'It wasn't, it was on the back of a sheet off me order pad, Mrs Saunders,' Ruby answered, her eyes still moist. 'I'm so sorry.'

Carrie patted her hand.

'We know you are, Ruby,' she said, with a meaningful glance at Bette, who gave a little movement of her head. Agreement or disagreement? It was hard to tell.

'There's a lot I could say,' Bette began, 'but none of it'd do any good, it's too late now. I don't know what the police think they're about. Didn't they show the note to this Heinrich feller before they picked you up? What did he have to say about it?'

But Ruby's shoulders were heaving again – there'd be no getting any more sense out of her, so Carrie had to provide an answer.

'Maybe he never even found it. Or perhaps he denied all knowledge. But then, he would, wouldn't he? Still, the refreshment-room heading on the pad would have given them the link with the station, and when they quizzed him a bit more, he must have given them Ruby's name. And since they'd picked him up for being a spy, they had to investigate everyone he'd had contact with.'

'I hope they shone a light in his eyes and puffed smoke in his face, like they do in the pictures,' said Bette viciously. 'He'll hang for this, won't he? And quite right too! The slimy little rat!'

Ruby was muttering something and the other two strained to hear.

'I'm so ashamed,' she whispered. 'You're right, Mrs Saunders, I did let my head be turned. And it'd serve me right if you told Eric all about it and he breaks off with me. If you want to, you're well within your rights. I don't deserve a good man like Eric, straight I don't!'

'Oh, don't talk such codswallop,' said Bette sternly. 'I wouldn't dream of telling Eric. Why would I want to worry him with this sorry tale, stuck where he is? As long as you've learned your lesson, what the eye doesn't see, the heart doesn't grieve over, that's my motto.'

Ruby at last raised her puffy, tear-stained face.

'Do you mean it? Oh, Mrs Saunders, thank you! Thank you! That means the world to me. And I have learned a lesson, really I have!'

'It's a lesson to us all, Ruby,' said Carrie soberly. She thought back over the conversations she'd had with her customers, who, trusting her, often divulged details of their movements, their lives and sometimes their war work – conversations that could easily have been overheard. 'You see it on the posters – "Careless Talk Costs Lives" – but it's meaningless till you realise just how easy it is to do. I think we'll all be more careful in future.'

Chapter Twenty-one

Mike's last letter had said he might be able to telephone that evening, but Carrie never knew whether the call would come or not. It had happened before that she'd waited, but the telephone had remained silent and she would have to wait for another letter from Mike to learn that he'd suddenly been summoned to a meeting and another date would be fixed for them to speak. But this time, happily, the arrangement worked.

Mike was calling from the British Embassy, so it was supposedly a secure line. But, mindful of her own advice, Carrie kept to the barest details of Ruby's unfortunate adventure. She didn't mention Ruby or Hendrick van Roon, aka Heinrich Rosshart, by name. That would have to wait till Mike was home – which wouldn't be long now.

'Honestly!' Mike exclaimed. 'It's been non-stop since I left – Johnnie's accident, Penny proposed to, Ruby in trouble—'

'It just shows, you should have stayed,' Carrie teased. 'And you thought America was where all the action was.'

'Huh,' Mike replied. 'Have a meeting, write a report, send it off, read some bumf, write another report, send that off, have another meeting . . . So it goes on.'

'Oh, poor you,' mocked Carrie. 'Don't pretend you're not swanking about at embassy parties and living like a king!

Mum's latest discovery is oatmeal sausages. If it wasn't for those parcels you're sending, I don't know what we'd be reduced to.'

'There's another on the way,' said Mike. 'Tinned stuff – butter, jam, something called pressed chicken roll. They eat a lot of chicken here. I thought it was worth a punt.'

'Thank you,' said Carrie wholeheartedly. 'It's a lifeline. But I'd still rather have you than a rolled chicken.'

'And I'd rather be there, trust me.'

'I know. So . . .' Carrie began.

'What?' asked Mike.

Carrie had to ask.

'Penny and Johnnie have set a date, the twenty-sixth of July. Johnnie would love you to be best man. It's hard to pick out just one from his RAF friends.'

'Ah,' said Mike. 'That would be an honour.'

'So, what do you think?' asked Carrie. 'It's only a few days before you're due back anyway. Is there any chance they'd let you go early? They're both really hoping you'll be back. And so am I.'

'Ah, well,' said Mike awkwardly. 'That's the thing.'

'What thing?' Carrie was immediately on the alert.

'I was going to tell you. Far from coming back early, my tour of duty, as they call it . . . It's been extended.'

'What? Oh, Mike! For how long?'

'That's the other thing.' He sounded even more awkward. 'They can't say. Or they won't. Please, Carrie, don't think I haven't tried.'

Carrie bit her lip. She mustn't give in. She must be strong. Other girls had it much worse – their fiancés, boyfriends and

181

husbands could be sent away for years at a time. If Mike had been sent to North Africa or the Middle East, that would have been her lot. And at least in America he wasn't under fire.

But at the same time, never mind Penny and Johnnie – she and Mike were supposed to be getting married! Carrie and her mum had intended to start planning the wedding as soon as Mike left, but Johnnie's crash had sent everything into a spin. It would have been unthinkable to start fussing over flowers or dresses in those worrying first few weeks. And then Johnnie had gone and proposed and the wedding in the forefront of everyone's mind was his and Penny's.

As soon as she'd met Carrie, Mike's mother had sensitively written to Mary to introduce herself, and after a couple of letters had been exchanged, she had telephoned to ask what Carrie envisaged for her dress. Would it be long or short, a traditional wedding dress or something she could wear again? Then they'd had a frank conversation about Jane as bridesmaid. Jane, a convert after Carrie had sent her a copy of *National Velvet* and a couple of books about animal care, was now, apparently, happy to do it. She wanted to, in fact, Mrs Hudson said – but had vetoed anything silly, frilly or pink. Fair enough, thought Carrie.

'I'm sorry she was so difficult that day you came,' Mrs Hudson apologised. 'She adores Mike, you see, she's always worshipped the ground he walks on.'

'And I was an interloper,' said Carrie. 'Yes, I realised that.'

'But those books – she hasn't had her nose out of *Pig Keeping* since it arrived. She wants us to get a pig now!'

'Oh, I'm sorry!' laughed Carrie. 'A lot of people are keeping pigs, though.'

'Hmm. We're resisting so far,' said Mrs Hudson. 'We can't very well go to the shop stinking of manure. But I'm pleased Jane wants to be a part of the wedding.'

'So am I,' said Carrie sincerely. 'We really hoped she would – it'll make Mike's day. He's terribly fond of her too. Please thank her.'

Mrs Hudson had offered to make both dresses, but realising that it would be more sensible for Mary to make Carrie's in view of getting the fit right, she said instead that she would provide the material. With clothes rationed and everyone fighting over what they could get for home dressmaking, that was no mean offer.

'I put some fabrics by at the beginning of the war for favoured customers,' Mrs Hudson revealed conspiratorially. 'And if you're not a favoured customer, dear, I don't know who is!'

The fabric samples had duly arrived, but they were still sitting in their envelope on the sideboard.

'Carrie?' Mike's voice at the other end of the line brought Carrie back to the present. 'Have we been cut off? Are you still there?'

'I'm here.'

'I'm sorry. I'm sick of saying sorry to you for what happened last year, for going away again, for not being with you when you were so terrified for Johnnie, but most of all, for this.'

'It's not your fault,' Carrie said, heroically managing to keep the wobble out of her voice.

'I'll keep telephoning when I can,' Mike said. 'And writing. I know it's not the same, it's nowhere near good enough—'

'Of course it is,' said Carrie. 'It's all we can do.'

She thought of what her dad had said on that awful weekend of the Blitz. 'We've all just got to get on with it. And stick it, and stick it, and stick it.' She'd sworn that she would. And so she had to keep on doing it.

The tears only came when they'd finished their call.

'Oh, love, I'm so sorry,' Mary said, holding her while she cried. 'It's so hard for you.'

'No, I'm being soft,' Carrie snuffled. 'It's just disappointing, that's all.'

'Of course it is,' Norman soothed. 'Now, what can we do to cheer you up? A quarter of Brazil-nut toffee? Fruit bonbons? A Walnut Whip? I know, a Turkish Delight – you love them! Or all of them, if you like!'

'Oh, Dad!' Carrie couldn't help laughing through her tears. 'It's not like when I was a child of five and fallen out with my best friend!'

'No, true, things were simpler then. Not that it seemed that way at the time, eh, Mary?'

'I've got a better idea,' Mary replied. 'Let's *do* something. Let's have a good look at those fabric samples Mrs Hudson sent, Carrie. And when we go with Penny to sort out her wedding dress, we'll find a pattern and start making yours. Then you'll have something concrete to hang on to, so you can feel your wedding really is going to happen.'

'Concrete?' quipped Norman. 'That's a novel fabric for a wedding dress, I must say!'

'Oh, you!' tutted Mary. 'It's all right for you. I suppose you think you're wearing your siren suit and tin hat to the wedding! Go and bring us through a couple of Turkish to keep us going while we look at this material. Yes, Carrie?'

'Yes,' nodded Carrie. 'Good idea, Mum. But make mine a Walnut Whip, please, Dad!'

Mrs Hudson had sent some beautiful fabrics. Mary laid out squares of satin and organza, shot silk and lace, while Carrie sketched out her dream dress. All evening, fuelled by tea and chocolate (the chocolate kept well away from the samples), they talked bodices and necklines, ruching and contrast panels. With the fabric chosen – slipper satin – all they needed was a pattern to work out how much material they should ask Mrs Hudson to send.

Penny had already booked the following Saturday afternoon off to go shopping for her wedding outfit, and Uncle Charlie agreed to mind the stall so that they could turn it into a joint shopping expedition for Carrie's dress pattern too.

In the morning, Penny enjoyed teasing Ruby, who, recovered from her ordeal at the hands of the police, was avidly excited about the wedding.

'Where are you getting your dress?' Ruby asked as Penny collected her mid-morning tea and toast. 'Lovells? Or there's a lovely bridal shop on West Street, you know.'

Along with the town's three jewellers, the shop always featured on Ruby's window-shopping trips.

'Lovells?' said Penny in amazement. 'For something I'll only wear once? Do you think I'm made of money?'

Penny was, of course, made of money, or had been, though Ruby knew nothing about any of that. But Penny was now surviving on a porter's wage – far less than a man would have earned for doing the same work, of course, which made her fume.

'The WVS have got a perfectly good rummage sale at the Scout Hut today,' she declared, feeling in her pocket to pay for her elevenses. 'I'm sure I can find something there.'

Ruby was so scandalised she almost dropped the milk jug.

'From a rummage sale? For the best day of your life?'

'Well, that's as maybe,' concurred Penny, 'but surely what comes after is equally important, if not more so. Living with the person and liking them for the rest of your life as well as loving them, I mean.'

She handed over the money and picked up her plate and cup, leaving Ruby dumbfounded, but with much to think about. She might try that line out on Eric when she next wrote, she thought, or something like it.

'You are mean to tease Ruby,' said Carrie when Penny told her the gist of the conversation. They were on the top deck of the bus into town. They were meeting Mary there – at Lovells, of course.

'She's got such a rosy, romantic view of things,' said Penny in exasperation. 'I mean, I'm not sniping at you – of course you'll have a traditional wedding dress, and you're going to look an absolute knockout.'

'I hope so.'

'You will. But you're getting married in church, you're getting the material for free and the only expenses are the pattern and your mum's time. I want to look presentable for Johnnie, don't get me wrong, but there's other things to

186

spend our money on – we've got to find somewhere to live, and the furniture's bound to be ghastly, if there's any at all. We'll want to decorate and jazz it up a bit.'

'True. Gosh. Mike and I haven't thought that far ahead.'

'Well, it's tricky, isn't it. With Mike's American stint being open-ended now.' Penny touched her friend's hand briefly. 'I am sorry about that, you know.'

'It is what it is,' said Carrie. It was the form of words she'd come up with to close off the subject. There was really no point in dwelling on it. 'I'd rather it wasn't this way, but there's nothing he – or I – can do about it.'

'That's my girl,' said Penny, squeezing her hand briefly before letting go. 'Look sharp, this is our stop!'

They jumped off the bus before it had quite stopped, to a 'Hey!' from the conductress. Mary came forward to meet them.

'Are you trying to break *your* legs before the wedding now?' she tutted. 'We've just about got Johnnie better!'

'Sorry, Mum,' Carrie apologised. 'It's exciting, that's all!'

Gliding up on the escalator, Penny clasped her hands.

'Right,' she said. 'Here we go! I fancy an off-the-shoulder number in a bold colour, purple, maybe, or emerald.' Mary would have stumbled if Carrie hadn't steadied her, but Penny laughed. 'Your faces! Don't worry, it'll be a nice demure day dress or a suit.' They stepped off the escalator onto the velvety carpet. 'Come on, this way!'

Slanting glances at each other, Mary and Carrie followed in her wake.

'Nearly gave me a heart attack,' whispered Mary. 'But at least she seems to know what she wants.'

Penny proved to be more adept at pointing out what she didn't want.

'Nope. Nope. Nope,' she said as the saleswoman, a terrifying personage with spectacles on a chain and a viciously corseted figure, led them from one display to another.

'How about this? It's a lovely colour.' Carrie held out a bias-cut dress in a soft, buttery yellow.

'Aioww, yess, that's a mowst popular style,' said the saleswoman, who, like all the Lovells staff, had been taught to speak in a 'refined' accent.

'It'd look great on *you*.' Penny held the dress against Carrie and turned her to the mirror. It did suit Carrie, bringing out the gleaming gold of her hair. Then Penny tried it against herself. 'On me, the style's OK, but the colour! I look like a patient from the liver ward.'

'It is a bit draining on you,' Mary had to agree.

Back onto the rail the dress went, and the hunt continued. Even the saleswoman, with all her years of experience, began to look defeated and excused herself to attend to another customer who looked more promising.

'I like this, but the colour's too much like what Johnnie'll be wearing.' Penny was holding up a saxe-blue crêpe dress, simple but elegant, square-necked with a scalloped trim, and the same on the short sleeves. 'We don't want to look like a double act, even if we are about to become one.'

'But look!' Carrie darted to another rail. 'They've got it in another colour.'

She held up the same dress in a muted, dusty pink.

'Hmm.' Penny tipped her head to one side as she

considered. 'Well, it's better, I agree. And at least I can see me wearing it afterwards.'

'Try it on,' Mary urged.

A younger salesgirl sidled towards them. She was still working on her 'refined' vowels, but, Carrie thought, she'd go far – she'd spotted an opportunity. She led Penny off to the fitting room.

Carrie and Mary flopped onto a spindly-legged French Empire-style sofa and Mary eased her feet out of her shoes.

'I'm exhausted!' she said. 'Goodness, she's hard to please!'

But she sat up when Penny emerged from behind the curtain.

'Oh, Penny!' Carrie scrambled to her feet. 'It's perfect, don't you think?'

'Not bad,' agreed Penny. She turned in front of the mirror; they could tell she liked it. She stood on tiptoe. 'With heels and some decent stockings . . .'

The salesgirl stood by, wisely realising that the sale was as good as made – no need to over-egg this pudding.

'You'd be mad not to have it,' said Carrie.

Penny checked the price ticket and reeled back.

'*How* much? And that's on top of my coupons?' She tutted. 'Trust me to get proposed to after clothes rationing's come in! Why couldn't Johnnie get on with it?'

For a moment, the salesgirl looked panicked. But again Penny was only joking.

'I'll take it, thanks,' she confirmed, and the salesgirl was wreathed in smiles.

At the counter, she folded the dress into tissue paper and put it in a smart navy and white Lovells box – they were down to the last of the pre-war stock, she explained. Then she clipped out Penny's coupon and Penny handed over the money. Carrie noted a secret smile as she did so. Penny knew she looked gorgeous.

Then, with much relief, it was off to Haberdashery for Carrie's pattern. After the hoopla Penny had put them through, it was a much simpler task and they hit on one almost straight away. It was a simple style with a sweetheart neckline, a dropped waist narrowing to a V, elbow-length sleeves and a very full skirt, which Mary insisted she'd have to modify. Carrie didn't want her future mother-in-law to think she was taking advantage.

Their trip concluded with tea in Lovells' restaurant, where models paraded the latest summer fashions as the trio ate their scones.

'Nothing like getting married for giving you an appetite!' said Penny, slathering on strawberry jam.

Carrie smiled, but her stomach flipped at the thought of her own wedding, whenever it might be: of walking down the aisle towards Mike in the dress she could now envisage, turning to him, lifting her veil and taking her vows. And the day would come.

Last year, it had been ten months from the day Mike had left to the day he returned and for most of those there'd been no contact at all. Carrie hadn't known where he was or if he was even alive. At least this time she knew exactly where he was and he could keep in touch. Carrie hugged that thought to herself as her mum and Penny chattered away. He'd be back; they'd be married; that was all that mattered.

Chapter Twenty-two

With the wedding a couple of weeks away, Johnnie was making great strides – even if not quite literally. He still needed a stick for support, but was confident that on the big day he'd be able to leave that behind to walk out of the register office with his bride on his arm. Whenever she knew Penny wasn't visiting, Carrie went to see Johnnie to help him practise without the stick.

'If Sister Munro could see me now!' he said smugly as he and Carrie completed their second circuit of the lawn one evening. Carrie knew they were safe: Penny was on a first-aid refresher course.

'I bet she misses you too,' smiled Carrie.

'I was her favourite patient by the end,' Johnnie said. 'Extra helpings of custard and everything.'

'Your fatal charm, I suppose,' said Carrie wryly.

'Obviously,' said Johnnie. 'Can we sit down for a bit? It's so hot still!'

July was proving to be a scorcher.

'Sure.'

They found a strategically placed bench under a tree. Johnnie sat down gratefully and mopped his brow.

'I want to talk to you about the wedding,' he said. 'I'm

really sorry, sis, that mine is happening before yours. I know it's not what any of us expected.'

'Oh, don't be silly,' said Carrie, but she was touched. Johnnie could be very thoughtful. 'It's not your fault. It's not Mike's fault – it's nobody's fault. Except Hitler's. And he was never going to be invited!'

'Hardly,' said Johnnie. 'Anyway, he's got a prior engagement now he's gone and invaded Russia. Let's hope it's his undoing, like it was Napoleon's.'

That might be too much to hope for, but at least the fact that the Luftwaffe were tied up elsewhere meant the incessant air raids on British cities had tailed off. It had taken Carrie a while to get used to having an uninterrupted night's sleep, but she wasn't complaining.

'Look,' she said. 'Can I say this once and for all? I'm not going to be the spectre at the feast on your wedding day. I wouldn't dream of it. I couldn't be happier for you and Penny. And as far as mine goes, Mum's already started making my dress!'

She meant it as well. Mrs Hudson had promptly sent the fabric and Carrie had already tried on her dress in its tacked-together form. Even then, Norman had been speechless at the sight of his daughter transformed.

'I've spoken to the vicar at All Souls about how to book the church and the hall for the reception,' Carrie went on. 'I can't think about flowers or food or getting there because I don't know when the wedding'll be. I'm touched that you are, but, please, stop worrying about me!'

'If you say so.'

'I do. If you want to worry about anything, worry about

Penny turning up, your speech and your best man's speech. I dread to think what stories Peter's going to tell about you!'

In the absence of Mike, the pilots had put their names in a cap for best man duties and Peter had won. All Johnnie's RAF friends would be at the wedding, the ones Carrie had met and others.

'I'll get my own back when Peter and Heather name the day,' grinned Johnnie. 'Well, thanks for that, Carrie. I'm glad you won't be sobbing into your posy, thinking "It should have been me!"' He shifted slightly on the bench into a more comfortable position. 'But what I really want to know is, who's this guest Uncle Charlie's bringing to the reception?'

Uncle Charlie was going to give Penny away, as it was assumed that Norman would be supporting a tearful Mary. But Carrie hadn't heard that he was bringing anyone.

'What? He's not said anything to me!'

'He asked me the other day when he popped in. One of his many girlfriends, I assume.' Johnnie shrugged. Uncle Charlie was something of a ladies' man. 'I'm fine with it. But I wonder who the lucky lady is?'

A week before the wedding, there was a terrific thunder-storm. It looked as if the fine weather had broken. Even Penny was glum.

'I'll be getting married in gumboots at this rate,' she lamented. 'And my beautiful dress will be ruined!'

It took a few days to warm up again, but by the time the day dawned, there was enough blue in the sky to make a pair of sailor's trousers, as Mary was quick to observe.

Penny had spent the night before the wedding at the

Andersons', while Johnnie, released from his convalescent hospital two days before, had taken a room at the County Hotel in the centre of Brockington. The reception would be there, too: it was only a short walk from the register office.

As they got ready, Carrie was touched to see her friend's hand shaking as she tried to apply her lipstick.

'I'm going to look like Koko the Clown!' Penny wailed.

'Hold still.' Carrie took the lipstick – Sweet Rosebud – and defined Penny's mouth for her. 'There. Totally kissable.'

'Why didn't we just elope?' moaned Penny. 'I hear Gretna Green's very nice this time of year.' She picked up the pink rose and spray of maidenhair fern from Carrie's chest of drawers. 'You'll have to fix this for me as well. Look, I'm shaking like a leaf!'

Carrie took the corsage and pinned it to Penny's dress. She hadn't been able to justify a whole new outfit herself, but she had a corsage, too, on her best summer dress: navy with tiny white flowers and clever reverse-print collar and cuffs. Mary would be in her serviceable grey costume, but had splashed out on a new hat in a daring shade of magenta. Johnnie would be in his dress uniform and Norman had dusted off his navy chalk stripe. And everyone knew Uncle Charlie wouldn't let them down. He was always nattily turned out.

'I wonder if Peter's having to help Johnnie with his tie?' mused Carrie. 'Keep still or you'll end up stabbed – or I will!'

Amazingly, they got downstairs without injury and Norman and Mary saw an entirely new Penny – pretty, demure and clearly nervous.

'You look a million dollars!' said Norman, taking her hands. 'Doesn't she, Mary?'

'An absolute picture!' Mary agreed, choked. 'Johnnie's going to be so proud!'

Moved, Penny nodded her a thank you.

'Is that the taxi?' said Carrie brightly, though she knew it wasn't. After all her efforts, she didn't want Penny ruining her makeup.

Finally, the taxi did arrive and carried them in triumph to the register office. Peter was waiting for them.

'He's safely in there, don't worry,' he told Penny.

'He'd better be!' retorted Penny as Norman shepherded Mary inside. The journey had seemingly restored her usual verve. 'Where's Uncle Charlie?'

'Right here!'

Uncle Charlie loomed up behind them in a pristine cream linen suit, pale blue shirt and a startling pink tie. After almost two years of war, Brockington wasn't looking its best – the streets weren't swept, the Town Hall was sandbagged and the floral clock hadn't been planted up. But with his slicked-back hair and bouncy confidence, Uncle Charlie rose far above their surroundings – he looked as if he'd just stepped off a millionaire's yacht.

'Well, don't you look the bee's knees?' he said to Penny. 'Brushes up pretty well, doesn't she?'

For once, Penny accepted the compliment gracefully.

'I'll get inside,' said Peter, giving them all a mock salute. He swooped and kissed Penny. 'You look lovely,' he said. 'Johnnie's a lucky chap.'

Uncle Charlie crooked his arm and offered it to Penny.

Carrie handed over the little bouquet of roses and carnations that Mary had put together. ('Not too big. Don't forget I'll be lobbing it straight at Carrie!' Penny had pointed out.)

'Ready?' Carrie asked.

Penny nodded, pressing her lips together, nerves evidently getting the better of her again. Carrie knew the feeling. She had it when she thought about her own wedding day – as if a box of butterflies had been released in her stomach.

'Peter's right. You look wonderful,' she said, nudging her, 'sister-in-law!'

Penny cried, she actually cried, when, after the short service, Johnnie refused the stick that Peter was offering him and gave Penny his arm. To the tears and cheers of the assembled company, the newly married couple made their way slowly to the door. But once there, Johnnie restrained Penny for a moment as his fellow pilots, followed by the other guests, preceded them outside.

'What's going on?' asked Penny. 'Do you need a rest? Do you want to sit down for a moment?'

'No, I want you to myself for a moment,' answered Johnnie, dipping his head for a kiss.

'You've been practising on the quiet!' Penny smiled when she emerged. 'Walking, I mean. Keeping secrets from me already!'

'Ah, I'm full of surprises!' Johnnie smiled back. 'I need to be, to keep you on your toes!'

'Seeing you on yours is enough for me,' said Penny fondly.

Then Johnnie motioned her to carry on out into the bright

sunshine to hear Peter give the command 'Raise swords!' as the pilots duly formed a ceremonial sword arch.

'Ladies and gentlemen,' Peter intoned, 'it is my honour to present to you Pilot Officer and Mrs Johnnie Anderson!'

There were whoops and cheers as the happy couple made their way under the arch while Mary and Carrie flung their confetti – old stock from the shop – all over them. Mary had wisely put away a few boxes ('just in case') at the start of the war, realising from her experience of the Great War how such fripperies became luxuries, then scarce, then rare, then impossible to find. And she'd been right: confetti had all but disappeared.

Laughing, ducking exaggeratedly under the swords and fending off the shower of paper hearts and horseshoes, the newly married pair made it safely down the register office steps as Peter gave the command to resheathe swords. Uncle Charlie had captured the whole thing on his camera, and now he drew Penny and Johnnie to one side for a couple of photographs without the sandbags and Splinternet-taped windows in the background.

Carrie stood by, watching. It was strange, but wonderful, to see a softer side to her much-loved brother and her almost equally loved friend. Mary joined her daughter, still dabbing her eyes.

'Wasn't it lovely?' she said.

'It's not over yet, Mum.'

They still had the reception to come.

The hotel had given them a small function room upstairs, overlooking the garden. There were two circular tables, each

197

laid with gleaming glass and silverware, place cards revealing that one was for one for family, one for friends. Johnnie's pilot friends and their girlfriends headed for theirs, the women putting their bags down while the men fetched drinks. Carrie waved to Heather, Sue and Sally and indicated that she'd come over in a minute; her mum was still a bit tearful and Carrie thought she'd better stay with her parents for now.

'What must this be costing?' Norman whispered. 'RAF pay must be better than I thought!'

Carrie knew, but didn't say what Johnnie had told her: he'd been on full pay while he was in hospital and ten weeks with no bar bill represented, he admitted, a considerable saving.

'Where's your lady friend, Charlie?' Norman turned to his brother with a cheeky grin. 'Don't say she's stood you up!'

'She'll be here,' said Uncle Charlie smugly, accepting a glass from a passing waiter. Just then the door opened. A woman stood on the threshold, scanning the room. She was petite and pretty, her pale auburn hair framing a delicate face with porcelain skin, set off by an elegantly draped dress in duck-egg blue. Uncle Charlie saw her and moved across at once as Johnnie turned, saw who it was and gasped.

'Sister Munro!' he cried.

After the initial shock came the meal and the speeches, and as they mingled afterwards, the reception had an even more celebratory atmosphere.

'Talk about upstaging the bride,' Penny accused Uncle

Charlie. Sister Munro – or Jean, as they must get used to calling her – was on the other side of the room, talking to Johnnie and marvelling at his progress since leaving hospital.

'Yes, sorry, pet,' Charlie grinned. 'You don't mind, do you?'

'Mind? We just want to know how on earth you managed it, when everyone else retreated with frostbite after an encounter with her.'

'You're forgetting my irresistible appeal,' Charlie shot back. 'Melts the iciest heart!'

'Go on,' Penny teased. 'Confess! How long's this been going on?'

'I was visiting Johnnie in the hospital, too, you know,' Uncle Charlie explained. 'And, fond as I am of my nephew, it seemed a travesty to traipse all that way, petrol costing what it does, without mixing, well, pleasure with pleasure, as it were. Jean happened to be coming off duty one evening as I was leaving, I offered her a lift . . . and, well, as I'm a gentleman, I'll leave you to fill in the rest.'

'Yes, perhaps you'd better,' said Penny circumspectly. 'But "dark", "horse", "you're" and "a" are the words that spring to mind!'

Carrie's parents were also discussing Norman's brother and his new lady friend.

'Is it serious, do you think?' Mary whispered.

'He seems quite smitten,' Norman reflected. 'And she's an absolute stunner. Could be another wedding in the family as well as Carrie's, for all we know!'

Standing to one side, Carrie looked around at all the happy, smiling faces, listening to the chatter and the laughter. Johnnie and Penny were back together now and Carrie watched them, not enviously – she'd never begrudge either of them a moment's happiness – but wistfully. A look, a smile, a touch, all the little signals that made you feel like the only person that mattered, the only person in the room, the only person in the world. Everything she'd had with Mike – everything she ached for. But their time would come.

Chapter Twenty-three

Johnnie and Penny left that evening for their short honeymoon – a night in a country pub. It was strange for the family to see his room cleared of all his personal things for the last time. Penny had found them a part-furnished flatlet at the top of an old house that had been divided up. The rent was as steep as the stairs, but it was their own space and that was what they wanted. Mary had donated what she could spare in the way of crocks and cutlery, and Carrie and Penny had combed every second-hand shop and jumble sale in the area. They found all sorts of treasures – a set of dimpled water glasses, a lampshade (only slightly dented) and a colourful blanket to cover the dull moquette settee. Johnnie's RAF friends had come up with a set of bed sheets and two new pillows – the landlady's were stuffed with bricks, Penny maintained. The landlady provided a single gas ring, but Uncle Charlie had procured (no one dared to ask how) a two-ring tabletop cooker.

'So I can make a pot of tea *and* cook egg and chips at the same time,' Penny told Carrie. She freely admitted her cooking skills were minimal. 'Maybe I should have gone to finishing school and learned cordon bleu cookery after all!'

Johnnie and Penny's homemaking focused Carrie's mind, though. Where would she and Mike live when they were married? She knew it was inevitable that he'd be posted away again; he must have all his strength back by now, with all that good American food. She could carry on living at home, and her parents would love it, but what about when Mike had leave? They'd want a place of their own, wouldn't they?

But at least Carrie's wedding dress was taking shape. Mary was inserting the sleeves this week and Carrie stood patiently as her mother made sure the gathers on the shoulders were evenly matched. As she stood there, she couldn't help imagining her walk up the aisle on her father's arm, Mike at the altar in his dress uniform, with Johnnie by his side as best man, perhaps both of them turning to get a glimpse of her as she approached. Her stomach flipped at the thought. If only Mike were here and it could be soon! But every day was another day crossed off the calendar towards his return and a day closer to it actually happening. That thought, along with the continued success of the bookshop, gave Carrie hope and she counted her blessings. She'd had to become good at that since the start of the war. A chance find of a set of place mats with 'Cries of London' on them, the cork backing not peeling too badly, the station cat meticulously washing its face, a baby's sudden smile, the smell of a new book, the deliciousness of fresh green peas from the garden, the feel of her wedding dress against her skin, and the memory of Mike's touch ... Despite the war, Carrie had everything to look forward to and she counted herself lucky.

With Penny and Johnnie safely married and ensconced in married bliss in their little love nest under the eaves, August eased into September and life at the station and in the Anderson household resumed its normal rhythm. Except that in the tearoom, something was amiss.

'Over five weeks now and no letter from Eric,' Bette complained to Carrie one day. 'And Ruby the same. We can't understand it.'

'There's often delays in the post from the camps, though.' Carrie handed over the money for her cup of tea. 'And then a whole clutch arrive together.'

'That's how it was at first,' Bette agreed. 'But then we seemed to get into a sort of rhythm.' She sighed. 'Anyway, there's not a lot we can do about it.'

'I suppose not. Unless the Red Cross can help?'

'I've written to them. But they must get hundreds – thousands – of requests a day. And they're stretched as it is.'

'I know. Well, tell me if you hear anything, won't you?'

Carrie took her tea to a table. The sun of early September was peeping through the tearoom window and she basked in it like a cat. Uncle Charlie was minding the bookshop, still grinning at the trick he'd pulled by bringing Sister Munro to the wedding. Mike would be back soon, surely. All was as well as could be in Carrie's world. It wasn't to last.

Just the next day, Carrie's early-morning customers seemed particularly disgruntled, handing over the money for their books and papers with barely a thank you, let alone the usual pleasantries. She couldn't understand why.

'No tearoom today,' Professor Mason explained when he arrived. 'Missing their early-morning dose of caffeine, no doubt.' Professor Mason, who was also a vegetarian, drank only a particular brew that he got from a Chinese herbalist in Soho.

It was almost nine when Carrie found a harassed-looking Ruby turning the refreshment-room sign from 'Closed' to 'Open'.

'No Mrs Saunders,' Ruby said shortly. 'I couldn't open before, I had the bread and milk to put away and the sink was blocked again. I'll have no time to bake – I'll have to be out front all day, serving, clearing, the lot. I'll need as many arms as an octopus!'

'Has Mr Bayliss heard from her?' asked Carrie, concerned. 'She hasn't telephoned?'

'Not a peep – I asked.'

'I'm sorry, Ruby. Maybe she's been taken ill.'

'She was fine yesterday, you saw her.'

'Yes . . . though something like food poisoning can come on quickly.'

'Don't say that! What if it's something she's ate from the tearoom!'

'Let's not run ahead.' With Ruby's capacity for drama, Carrie wished she hadn't mentioned it. 'I'll pop in tonight and check on her.'

A train clanked in on the opposite platform.

'Blow it,' exclaimed Ruby, 'there's the ten-to. I'll have to get on.'

'See you.'

But Carrie was puzzled. It was very unlike Bette not to have explained her absence. At six o'clock, she locked the stall, telephoned home from the call box outside the station to explain she'd be late and set off on her mercy mission, armed with the latest *Woman's Own* and *My Weekly*.

Bette lived in a terraced cottage near the station. Carrie knocked on the door, puzzled and not a little worried by the fact that the curtains at every window were still drawn. There was no reply. She bent and peered, then called, through the letter box.

'Bette? Are you there? It's me, Carrie. Can you come to the door?'

No reply. Carrie tried again.

'Bette, please, we're worried about you. Are you all right?'

Finally, from deep inside the house, came the sound of footsteps shuffling along the hall. The bolt on the front door was drawn back and the door opened a crack. In the gloom of the hall, Carrie could hardly see Bette's face, but her hair, released from its usual tidy bun, straggled around her shoulders. She was still wearing her business dress from the day before. Had she not been to bed?

'Bette, you look dreadful – what's happened?'

Bette stood back, opening the door wide enough for Carrie to come in. She led her down the hall and into the back room. The blackout curtains were drawn, presumably from the night before, but Carrie could detect a chair pulled back from the table. There was no sign of any meal having been eaten, though. Instead, Bette's usually pin-neat room was a mess. The sideboard drawers were hanging out and the table was covered with papers and photographs.

'Can I draw the curtains?' Carrie asked. 'Or put the light on?'

Bette sank down on the chair with a brief nod. Carrie took down the blackout and the evening sun filtered into the room.

Carrie pulled out a chair and sat next to Bette. She took her hands, which were icy cold.

'Bette, talk to me. What's the matter?'

In reply, Bette took a letter that had been placed by itself on the table and handed it to her. It was on official headed paper. It must have been waiting for her when she got home the previous evening.

Without a clue to its contents but already with a chill in her heart, Carrie took it and read:

Dear Madam

We regret to inform you that we have received news of the death of your son, Private Eric Saunders, on 15th July 1941 in an accident close to Stalag XXA, Pomerania, Poland. Our information is that a transport vehicle in which he was travelling with other prisoners skidded off the road after heavy rain. We have no further information at this time. Please accept our sincere condolences.

Yours faithfully

It was signed with an indecipherable squiggle.

Tears sprang into Carrie's eyes.

'Oh, Bette, no . . . I am so sorry.'

Bette closed her eyes, then, to Carrie's horror, she laid her head on her arms on the table and howled. Carrie edged her chair nearer and put her arms around Bette's heaving shoulders. She sank her own head onto Bette's and let the older woman weep.

What a ghastly, cruel irony, Carrie thought, for Eric to die like this, not as the result of enemy action, but in a stupid, random, unlucky accident. Poor, poor Eric, poor Bette and, oh no, poor Ruby.

Carrie rang home again to explain the situation and tell them that she was going to stay with Bette overnight.

'I can't leave her,' she told her mum. 'She's completely gone to pieces.'

'I'm not surprised,' Mary sympathised. 'What a dreadful thing to happen. So . . . so blooming pointless!'

'I know.'

Carrie made tea and toast. Bette sipped the tea, but shook her head at the toast.

'I couldn't,' she whispered.

There was nothing Carrie could say, nothing else she could do. At eight o'clock, she led Bette upstairs and put her to bed. She knew that Eric's room was next door, kept exactly as he'd left it, waiting for his return. She suspected it would stay like that for ever now, a permanent shrine to him. There was no way that Carrie could sleep in there.

'I'm going to stay,' she told Bette. 'Anything you want in the night, you call me. I'll be downstairs on the settee.'

Bette nodded dully and closed her eyes. When Carrie

looked in an hour later, she'd fallen asleep – she must have been exhausted – but at two in the morning, Carrie was awoken by footsteps on the stairs. Bette appeared.

'Is it true?' she asked. 'About my Eric?'

There was no more rest for Carrie that night. She sat holding Bette's hands till the morning. The day she'd have to break it to Ruby.

Chapter Twenty-four

'Where've you been?' Penny demanded when she saw the dark circles under Carrie's eyes the next day. 'And isn't that what you were wearing yesterday?' She looked teasingly at her friend. 'Is there something Mike should know about?'

'Don't joke,' said Carrie shortly. She explained how she'd spent the night and how she'd left Bette that morning – still in the same sorry state.

Penny's manner changed at once.

'I can't believe it,' she said. 'That's terrible.'

'It's not over yet,' Carrie told her. 'I'll have to tell Ruby. She's not going to get an official letter.'

'This damn war!' Penny burst out. 'It's just so much misery, and all because one man's got some ludicrous idea that he deserves to rule the world!' She clenched her fists, as if, given the chance, she'd like to beat Adolf Hitler about the head. 'And it's the little people, the Erics and the Bettes and the Rubys – they're the ones that suffer, here and in every other country, on both sides. And there's nothing we can do about it!'

'Except defeat him,' said Carrie.

'We need America for that,' Penny replied. 'So it's all down to Mike. Let's hope he can pull it off.'

'And quickly,' said Carrie, thinking to herself: for all our sakes.

Leaving Penny keeping an eye on the bookstall, Carrie went first to Mr Bayliss.

'I can't imagine Ruby's going to take the news any better than Mrs Saunders,' she said flatly. 'So I think you can anticipate that the refreshment room will have to close for a few days. Ruby worked her socks off to keep it open yesterday, but once I've told her, I doubt she'll be in a fit state to do anything today. And quite possibly for a few days beyond. Mrs Saunders certainly won't be back for a while.'

Even Mr Bayliss looked moved, and for once he agreed without any huffing and puffing. He lent Carrie his own fountain pen and produced a sheet of paper so she could write out a notice for the tearoom door saying: CLOSED UNTIL FURTHER NOTICE — STAFF BEREAVEMENT. Then, her mouth set in a firm line, Carrie went to find Ruby.

'Did you go last night? What did Mrs Saunders have to say?' Ruby demanded as soon as Carrie reached the counter. She'd obviously had a busy start to the day. Her cheeks were flushed, her apron grubby and there were dirty crocks on several tables. The glass cases that normally held an array of cakes and sandwiches were half-empty.

'You're going to have to close up, Ruby,' said Carrie. 'I've squared it with Mr Bayliss. Mrs Saunders won't be in for a while.'

'She must be took bad!' exclaimed Ruby. 'What is it? Is she in the hospital?'

Carrie nodded in the direction of the three occupied tables.

'I'll explain everything as soon as these people have gone. In fact, I'm going to ask them to leave.'

'You what?'

Ruby's mouth opened and closed like a guppy's, but Carrie had already gone, bending low to explain the situation to the customers. Hurriedly, they collected their things, shooting concerned glances towards Ruby. They understood. By now it was a rarity for the war not to have touched anyone, whether they'd lost a member of their own family, a friend, a neighbour or even an acquaintance, and to many of the regular customers in the tearoom, Bette and Ruby were more than that.

Carrie went to the door, turned the sign from 'Open' to 'Closed' and sat at a vacant table, motioning Ruby to join her.

'What the heck is going on?' Ruby demanded, sitting down.

Carrie took a deep breath. This was going to be one of the hardest things she'd ever done.

'I'm sorry, but I've got some bad news for you, Ruby,' she began. 'The same news Mrs Saunders has had, which is why she hasn't come in. It's about Eric.'

Ruby heard the news in total silence. Having expected an immediate flood of tears, Carrie instead found herself having to repeat it.

'You do understand, don't you, Ruby? Eric's dead. I'm so sorry.'

211

'I don't understand, no,' Ruby shook her head. 'How could it happen?'

'I told you. It was an accident.'

'I don't mean that, I mean why? Eric had never done nothing to hurt no one, so why him?'

'Oh, Ruby. I don't know. I can't answer that.'

'Well, someone should,' cried Ruby, animated at last and the tears beginning. 'Why is it only good people that bad things happen to?'

'That's not quite true,' said Carrie. 'Good things happen to good people, and bad things to bad people, as well.'

'Oh yeah? I don't see much of it in this war! Do you?'

Again, Carrie had no answer. All she could do was offer a handkerchief as Ruby put her face in her hands and wept long and loud.

'It was awful,' she told Penny when she finally returned to the stall, having sent Ruby home and stuck the notice on the tearoom door. 'No wonder the telegram boys can't stand it for long, seeing people's faces when they deliver bad news.'

'I don't need to ask how she took it,' Penny replied. 'I heard the wailing from here.'

'She was inconsolable,' said Carrie sadly. 'Just like Bette. It was a funny relationship, her and Eric, all by letter, but I do believe she really did love him.'

'I'm sure she did,' said Penny.

'Poor Ruby hasn't had much luck in life, has she?' Carrie sighed. 'She's the youngest but one in that huge, chaotic family of hers. No attention, not much money, not much fun.

All she ever wanted was someone to notice her and "be nice" to her, as she put it to me once . . .' She trailed off.

'And she finally gets Eric – who from what I've heard had all the gumption of a door, to be honest – to be her boyfriend,' Penny continued, 'albeit from a thousand miles away. And then this!' She scuffed her foot along the platform. 'I feel so guilty for having so much – for being so happy and having your lovely brother. There's no justice, is there?'

Carrie shook her head.

'It doesn't seem that way at the moment,' she said.

The injustice, the waste, the stupidity of Eric's death hung over the station. Bette always wore a dark dress in her capacity as tearoom manageress, but Ruby threw off her pastel blouses and gaudily patterned headbands and appeared in a severe black serge frock. Lord knows where or how she'd acquired it, it was far too old for her, but she obviously thought it was appropriate.

On their first day back, before they opened up, Bette produced a length of black crêpe and handed it to Ruby. Ruby knew what was expected. She climbed up on a chair and draped it over the top of the framed photograph of Eric in his uniform, which hung in pride of place on the wall. Nothing was said until Ruby got down, then Bette laid a hand on her arm. She'd had a lot of time to think in her days off. In fact, she'd done nothing but.

'I know you're grieving too. I know you cared for him.'

'Oh, I did, Mrs Saunders, I loved him, I really did!' cried Ruby.

'I believe you,' said Bette. 'And I'm sorry your little . . . romance has ended how it has.'

'I don't want anyone else, ever,' Ruby asserted. 'I'll never look at another man, I swear! I know I'll never find one as good as your Eric.'

'You're far too young to be saying that,' Bette counselled. 'You're a good girl, Ruby,' she added generously. 'You will meet someone else. And you should.'

Then she took a deep breath.

'Meantime, we've got a business to run. So you get in the kitchen and start on a batch of scones. I'll get the urn on the go and when it's hotted up and we're good and ready, I'll take the notice off the door. Best foot forward, eh? It's what Eric would have wanted.'

Ruby bit her lip. If Eric's own mother could be this brave, surely she could be too.

'Yes, Mrs Saunders,' she said.

Chapter Twenty-five

'Hey, you!' Johnnie crossed the room – their one room – to where Penny was stirring a pan. 'What's cooking?'

'Secret recipe,' said Penny. 'A sort of stew. Want a taste?'

'I'd rather have a taste of you.' Before she could protest, Johnnie spun her swiftly round and kissed her. Gravy flew off the spoon onto his jacket.

'Now look what you've done!' Penny laughed. 'What's your CO going to say?'

To everyone's relief, Johnnie was still on ground-based duties. He was in the control room and, to everyone's surprise, wasn't even chafing against it. ('He can see the advantage of a safe berth now he's married,' Norman concluded.)

Johnnie sucked at his sleeve.

'Delicious,' he declared. 'But not as tasty as you.' He made to pull Penny closer, but she pulled away.

'Your dinner will burn,' she said. 'I didn't queue for half an hour for a tiny bit of shin of beef which is probably half gristle for that!'

She turned down the heat to a simmer as Johnnie drew back the cretonne curtain over the cupboard where they kept the glasses. He produced them and went to the pantry for two bottles of beer.

'Let's have an aperitif,' he said, opening the bottles and pouring. 'I've had quite an interesting day.'

'Oh yes?' Penny took off her apron and they moved to sit down, Johnnie with some relief, though he tried not to show it, as his injured leg was still stiff and sometimes painful. He put his arm round Penny's shoulders and took a sip of his beer.

'Yeah, we had a visitor. An American.'

'Really? Top brass from their air force? They're finally coming in on our side?'

Johnnie shook his head. 'If only. He's a journalist, name of Gus Grayling. He's on a local paper, *The Daily Oklahoman*, and, well, maybe it was a load of flannel, but he was also talking about syndication, submitting stuff to other papers as a freelance. A series of articles about the home front.'

Penny made a disparaging noise.

'Not the "plucky Brits" line again! Ed Murrow tried to flog that one to America all through the Blitz.'

The American war correspondent Ed Murrow's broadcasts had been a powerful propaganda tool and had gained quite a few sympathisers in the States. Sadly, they hadn't produced any commitment to action.

'There'll be a bit of that, I'm sure,' Johnnie agreed. 'He interviewed a lot of us – without us giving anything away, of course – about our war so far, our family situations, what we put on hold to fight for our country, our hopes for the future . . .'

'All good, stirring stuff.'

'Yeah. Thing is, I mentioned the family shop and then

Carrie and her bookshop. And that really grabbed his attention. You know, books as a morale booster.'

'He should come and meet her. Hear it from Carrie herself.'

'That's what he wants to do. So, do you think she'd be up for it?'

'Come on,' cried Penny. 'She eats, sleeps and breathes that bookshop! Of course she would. And . . .'

'And what?'

'I think it'd do her good. We've all been a bit down since Eric was killed, Carrie most of all – she's closer to Bette and Ruby than I am. And with Mike still away and no fixed date for him coming back, so no wedding date . . . Need I go on?'

'Great. That's all I wanted to hear.' Johnnie kissed the top of her head. 'I'll fix it up.'

They clinked glasses.

'How long's my dinner going to be?' Johnnie asked. 'Because if it's going to be a while, I've an idea how we could fill the time . . .'

The Penguin rep, Mr Parfitt, was delighted when Carrie told him about the prospective interview.

'That's excellent, my dear,' he enthused, his little silver moustache twitching with excitement. 'Marvellous publicity!'

Mr Parfitt was over retirement age, but he had come back at the start of the war when younger reps had been called up, and he admitted it had given him a new lease of life.

'Gardening and the bowls club were never going to be enough for me,' he'd confided. 'I just couldn't get excited about growing the biggest dahlia or the heaviest leek. But give me a new raft of paperbacks to sell and I'm away!'

217

Despite problems with the supply of paper and ink, the Penguins had kept coming, with four or five new titles released pretty much every month. For the interview, Mr Parfitt promised to make sure that Carrie had all the latest in stock, and she in turn promised to pick out a few bestsellers. *Pygmalion* was doing well, as was *Murder of My Patient*, less surprisingly so. Murder mysteries were unfailingly popular – Carrie enjoyed them herself. When so much that was going on was beyond comprehension, there was something reassuring about a mystery that could be solved within a couple of hundred pages.

When Johnnie first suggested the interview, Carrie had been intrigued. She couldn't help being proud of what she'd achieved at the bookshop, and her regulars had often said it deserved a wider audience. Carrie had tried to get the local paper, the *Brockington Post*, interested, but they were very lukewarm. They had plenty to fill their reduced number of pages with all the robberies in the blackout or, in better news, the sums raised from tombolas and whist drives for Warship Week or the Spitfire Fund.

'It's only for *The Daily Oklahoman*,' Carrie warned Mr Parfitt. 'That's the paper this Gus fellow's attached to. But it's a daily, and Johnnie says it covers quite a big area. And he's talking about submitting the article to other papers too, apparently.'

'Syndicated,' replied Mr Parfitt. 'I have no doubt it will be!'

'I'll make sure the stall's looking its best,' Carrie assured him. Johnnie had told her that Gus had hopes of selling the story as a photo feature.

'It always does,' Mr Parfitt beamed back. 'And your smiling presence won't do any harm either.'

Carrie had brushed off Mr Parfitt's compliment, but on the day that Gus Grayling was due, she took a bit of extra care with her appearance. It was October now, but the weather, though chilly, was bright and sunny. Carrie had taken to wearing trousers for work – so many women were wearing them, from land girls in their corduroy breeches to factory girls in their dungarees. They were practical for bending to pick up the bundles of newspapers chucked off the down train early in the morning, and warm when standing on the stone floor of the shop all day. She pulled on a pair in fawn whipcord with a fine-knit lemon sweater that she'd been amazed to find in a second-hand stall on the market – only one small hole in the side seam, soon darned. Her dark blonde hair had taken on honey-coloured highlights over the summer, and though she often tied it back or put it up for work, today she left it loose around her shoulders, held away from her face by a couple of tortoiseshell combs. She dabbed a bit of powder on her nose and gave herself a slick of coral-coloured lipstick. Finally, she clasped Mike's locket around her neck and slid her engagement ring onto her finger.

Beyond teasing that he'd have rolled-up sleeves and a green eyeshade, like a newsroom hack in *His Girl Friday*, Johnnie hadn't given her any description of Gus, but Carrie would have known Gus Grayling a mile off as he stood on the platform, looking around.

There was no green eyeshade or pencil behind his ear, but he did have a camera around his neck and a small attaché case. He wasn't as tall as Mike – not many men were – but he was well built and broad-shouldered in a smart suit and a trilby with a striped band. Everything about him was sharp and neat and – what was the phrase? – clean-cut. In contrast to the shabby air that most British men had by now, with their out-at-elbow suits and fraying collars, everything about him shouted 'American'.

He spotted the bookstall and swung down the platform. Even his walk was American – not a swagger exactly, but something loose-limbed and confident. All in all, he exuded good health and well-being – the classic product of hearty American food and good living.

'Carrie?' he asked, taking off his hat and holding out his hand. 'Gus Grayling. Thanks so much for agreeing to talk to me.'

He spoke slowly in a low drawl, and Carrie had to smile. Close to, his blond hair was brush cut and his eyes were a clear blue. He was an American from central casting.

'How do you do,' she said formally, shaking hands over the counter.

'Oh my gosh,' he smiled. 'You're so British! I feel like getting my notebook out right away!'

'Feel free,' Carrie smiled back. 'I don't know what my brother's told you, but I run this place by myself, so I have to mind the shop. But you're welcome to come this side of the counter and we can talk.'

'Really? I can play shop? Will you let me serve someone? I'd love that!'

Laughing, Carrie let him through the little side door and

indicated the stool where she took the weight off her feet between customers.

'Have a seat,' she said. 'But as I expect my brother warned you, once I get going on books and the bookshop, the only problem is shutting me up.'

'My shorthand's pretty good and my pencil's nice and sharp,' Gus grinned, getting out a notebook and a propelling pencil. 'So fire away. Tell me how you got into reading yourself, and we'll take it from there.'

'I did warn you,' Carrie said, almost an hour later, when Gus was easing his cramped fingers.

In between his jottings, she introduced him to Professor Mason and Miss Cattermole, who was thrilled when Gus served her a magazine. A posse of Boy Scouts, come to collect bottle tops and cans from the tearoom, bought copies of *The Beano*, *The Dandy Comic* and a couple of Puffin books. The Scoutmaster, a teacher, held forth about the importance of getting children, especially boys, interested in reading from an early age and Gus noted down every word. Mr Parfitt, who 'just happened to be passing', praised Carrie so lavishly for what the bookshop was doing to inform, educate and entertain, she might have been the Ministry of Information, the BBC and Cecil B. de Mille rolled into one.

Then Gus posed Carrie in front of her colourful display of Penguins – orange-banded covers for fiction, green for crime, dark blue for biography, pink for travel. It seemed a lot of work just for *The Daily Oklahoman*, and she said so.

Gus wagged his finger at her.

'Now I've met you, forget *The Oklahoman*! I'm darn well

gonna sell this story all over – newspapers *and* magazines.'
(He said it '*maga*-zines', of course.)

'In America?' Carrie exclaimed. 'My fiancé's there – he might even see it!'

'Hold still!' Gus squinted through the lens and pressed the shutter. 'Got it! Just a couple more for safety's sake . . .'

After that, they were 'done', as Gus put it. Except . . .

'I should give you sight of what I've written,' he told her. 'I'm so used to doing it with officialdom, I don't see why I shouldn't extend the same courtesy to you, as you've given me so much of your time. And so you can pick up on any inaccuracies, of course.'

'Well, I'm here every day,' said Carrie. 'When you've typed it up, just call in again.'

'Does it have to be here?' Gus winced as a train screeched to a halt at the far platform. They'd already had to interrupt their chat several times to allow for some deafening arrivals and departures. 'Couldn't we meet after work for a drink?'

'Well . . .'

Carrie hesitated. It wasn't that she thought she was irresistible, and on the face of it there was nothing wrong in meeting Gus one evening. But all the same, what if he got the wrong idea? That wouldn't just be embarrassing, it might scupper the article appearing at all. And that would be a crying shame.

'So British!' Grinning, Gus broke into her thoughts. 'Miss Prim and Proper! Look, I'm not a complete jerk. I get that you're engaged. I'm attached myself, to a girl back home in Oklahoma City. Lucille and I, we've been together since high school.'

Somehow that made it all right.

'In that case,' said Carrie, 'thank you. I accept.'

'OK. I'll write this up directly, while it's fresh in my mind and I can still read back my shorthand. Then . . .' Gus consulted a pocket diary. 'Hmm . . . rest of this week I'm with a bomber squadron over in Lincolnshire.' ('Lin-coln-*shire*.')

'Right.'

'So, shall we say Friday?'

'Friday will be fine.'

'Great. You close up at six, I think you said? I'll call for you.'

'All right,' smiled Carrie. 'See you Friday.'

'Till Friday then. So long!'

And with that, he strolled off down the platform.

Was he playing up the Americanisms? It almost seemed like it. But Carrie was still smiling as she turned her attention to the passengers who'd streamed off the down train and were now emerging from the underpass.

'Sixpence, please,' she said to a serious-looking young man in a corduroy jacket and a neckerchief who was holding out *The Case for Family Allowances*, a popular Penguin.

Mr Bayliss, nearby, was scrutinising him closely. Someone had scrawled 'FIGHT WAR NOT WARS' across the latest army recruitment poster and he clearly had the young man in his sights as a possible culprit. On the far platform, Penny was busy with her sack truck, trundling away a pile of boxes that had come off the train. A group of soldiers moved aside to make way for her, ribbing her and wolf-whistling. Penny tossed her head and ignored them.

Back to work. Back to reality.

Chapter Twenty-six

Friday was always a busy day for Carrie and the Friday of her proposed drink with Gus was no exception. As well as the regular morning commuters, and the Brockington wives travelling up to London to the hairdresser or manicurist – or, in some cases, as Carrie had initially been shocked to learn from Bette, to meet their lovers – troops were heading off on weekend leave. All in all, she barely had a moment to turn round. Uncle Charlie wasn't available, and she had to ask Penny to bring her a sandwich from the tearoom, and later to mind the stall while she nipped to the Ladies.

'Excited about your date?' Penny asked when Carrie returned.

'It's not a date!' Carrie replied. 'But I must say I deserve a drink. I've been run off my feet today.'

'That's nothing. Think how busy you'll be when this article comes out.'

'In America?' Carrie smiled. 'Nice idea, but I can't see people booking a passage on a transatlantic liner to buy a sixpenny paperback from me!'

Gus arrived promptly just as Carrie was closing up. The weather had turned chilly and he was wearing a beige trench coat and a soft hat – shades of Humphrey Bogart, thought Carrie.

'Good day?' Gus asked her.

'I've been meeting myself coming back!' Carrie parroted one of her mum's favourite phrases and Gus laughed.

'Then let me take you away from all this,' he said, hamming up the line. 'Where do you recommend?'

Carrie had expected him to ask, so had given it some thought. The obvious place was the Station Hotel nearby, but that held special memories for her – she and Mike had had their first drink together there. So she suggested her local, the Rose and Crown. She felt Gus would appreciate its elaborate Victorian tiling and its etched and frosted windowpanes advertising Stouts and Ales.

She wasn't wrong. Gus marvelled at the Saloon Bar, divided into little booths by dark wooden panelling topped with stained glass, the olde-worlde gas lamps with their fluted glass shades, and the marble-topped tables. He produced his typed-up article from an inside pocket and Carrie studied it while he fetched the drinks.

She hadn't been expecting to find fault, and she didn't. He'd conveyed exactly her enthusiasm and her expertise in choosing the books and matching them to her customers. Professor Mason got a look-in with some fulsome praise, and unbeknown to Carrie, Gus had obviously stopped other passengers on their way in and out of the station and asked if the bookstall was important to them. To a man and woman, they said it was. 'I don't know what we'd do without it' was a typical response.

'I couldn't have asked for more,' she smiled when she'd read it.

'I can't show you the photos, I'm afraid,' Gus said. 'I've

225

sent the film off to be developed and the picture desk will have first sight of them. But, you know, I'm thinking now I could sell this article on both sides of the pond.'

'What, it could appear in this country as well as in the States?'

'Why not? I'd just angle it a little differently.'

'That would be wonderful!'

'I'll see what I can do.' Gus tucked the article back in his jacket pocket. 'But that's enough business for one night. Tell me about this fiancé of yours.'

So Carrie told him all about Mike (her 'fee-on-*say*', as Gus pronounced it) and how the bookstall had brought them together ('Why didn't you say before – that's a great human angle!'). She told him how Mike had gone missing in France for such a long time, about his injury and being hidden and helped by the Resistance, how he'd finally made his way home, their reconciliation at Christmas and their engagement this year. She told him about his current posting, or at least what she could say about it. Finally, she produced the photo of Mike in his uniform that she kept in her handbag. Gus studied it closely.

'As I expected,' he said, returning it. 'He looks – and sounds – a great guy. And he's obviously crazy about you.'

'I hope so,' Carrie confirmed happily. 'I know I am about him. I can't wait for him to be home. And your Lucille? What's she like?'

In response, Gus took a photograph from his wallet – a pretty girl with dark hair that curled to her shoulders and a wide smile showing off straight American teeth.

'She's a beautician,' Gus said, tucking the photo away.

'Aims to have her own business one day. She's a smart cookie like you, Carrie.'

'I'm sure she is.'

Lucille looked like the kind of girl who knew where she was going, and Carrie warmed to them as a couple. They weren't unlike her and Mike.

She gathered up her gloves, gas mask and bag.

'And now I really should go,' she said.

'So soon?'

Carrie shrugged. 'Well, it's been very nice, but I've seen the article, and—'

Gus wasn't slow on the uptake. He stood up.

'I'll walk you home.'

'There's no need. It's not far.'

'What do you take me for? I'm not some hick from the sticks. Just shut it, and lead the way.'

Carrie gave in, and they walked the few streets to the corner of Harold Road. As they stood there, Carrie had a sense of déjà vu. This was where she'd parted from Mike after their first evening and he'd kissed her goodbye. But Gus didn't try for, or seem to expect, even a peck on the cheek. Instead, they solemnly shook hands. How very British – he was learning!

'Thanks, Carrie,' he said. 'It's been fun getting to know you a little better.' Then he looked around and lowered his voice. 'I'm off to Scotland for a couple of weeks,' he confided. 'To Scapa Flow, and the fleet. I've got clearance.'

'That's exciting.'

'I'm sure it will be. And then I'm going to tour around a little, see what stories I can turn up.'

'Maybe you'll find the Loch Ness monster,' Carrie suggested mischievously. 'That'd be a scoop!'

'Or what a Scotsman keeps under his kilt, I believe that's another mystery,' Gus grinned back.

'Well, good luck,' Carrie said. 'And do let me know when or if you place the article, especially if it's outside *The Oklahoman*, won't you?'

'You betcha!' said Gus. 'And trust me, with the photos as well, it's when, not if. Watch this space.'

And with a wave, he was gone.

Carrie made her way home, smiling. Americans!

'How did it go?' Johnnie asked.

He and Penny were entertaining Carrie in their tiny flatlet. They only had a card table to eat off, which they folded out of sight when not in use. Johnnie had to perch on the wooden arm of the settee because they only had two upright chairs, but Penny had pulled out all the stops for their first 'dinner party'. She'd covered the baize tabletop with a cloth patterned with crocuses, and served up a lentil stew livened up with the addition of powdered ginger, cinnamon, a couple of dollops of pickle and a few chunks from a tin of pineapple, one of their more unusual wedding presents.

Carrie spooned up her lentils, which were very tasty. She'd never say as much to her mother in case it hurt her feelings, but Penny's improvisations were a vast improvement on Mary's oatmeal sausages.

'This is very nice,' she said, 'and, since you ask, so is Gus. And the article was spot on. All the customers he spoke to sang the bookshop's praises. One woman even said how a book of poems I'd recommended had helped her over the loss of her friend in the Blitz.'

'There you are. Books as solace and support. You won't get a better example than that,' declared Penny.

'And escape,' added Carrie. 'Gus found a naval rating who said he couldn't have survived his last tour of duty without his copy of *Cage-Birds* to keep him calm. He bred canaries at home, apparently. His kid brother's looking after them for him now. Gus says it's stories like this that really hit home what we're going through.'

There was a moment of silence while they all imagined the small boy tending the even smaller birds as they chirped away merrily, unaware.

'Anyway,' Carrie broke the silence. 'Gus is hoping to sell the article to a magazine in America, as well as his newspaper, and maybe slant it a bit differently and sell it over here too.'

'Your fame will spread!' smiled Penny. 'You'll have as many branches as W.H. Smith soon.'

Carrie thought back to the chain of bookshops she and Mike had planned on their night away, and smiled a secret smile.

'I'm quite happy where I am, thank you,' she said. 'One shop is quite enough for now.'

Chapter Twenty-seven

Uncle Charlie was the brightest and breeziest soul, and he had even more to be cheerful about now he had the lovely Jean Munro on his arm. He'd brought her to tea at the Andersons' a couple of times since the wedding, and Jean had them in stitches with the things that some of her patients got up to.

'Not to mention certain determined visitors sneaking in through the side door!' she teased. She gave Carrie the same icy stare that had chilled her the first time they'd met, except this time she meant it in jest.

For two women whose lives had been very different, Mary and Jean got on very well. Mary's brother had been gassed in the Great War and she'd nursed him at home for two years until he died, so she had some idea of what Jean's work entailed. Off duty and out of uniform, Jean was nothing like the gorgon she was in the hospital. Uncle Charlie, meanwhile, was basking in the glow of the family's approval.

So it was a surprise to Carrie when he arrived one day looking both gaunt and grave.

'Is something wrong?' Carrie asked as he brushed the rain off his hat before coming round behind the counter.

Uncle Charlie put his hat down with more than usual care on a stack of yesterday's papers.

'I need to talk to you, love,' he said slowly. 'I've got some bad news, I'm afraid.'

'What is it?' Carrie asked anxiously. 'You're not . . . you're not ill? Or . . . you haven't broken things off with Jean?'

Uncle Charlie made a dismissive gesture.

'No, no, nothing's wrong with me and Jean. She's been marvellous. She understands.'

'Marvellous . . . ? Understands what?' Carrie was getting more and more alarmed.

Uncle Charlie took out his cigarette case and lighter and lit up. His hand was shaking.

'You are ill!'

'No, I'm not. I just don't want to say it.' There was an agonising pause while he drew deeply on his cigarette and blew the smoke towards the ceiling. 'I'm in trouble, Carrie. Deep trouble.'

'Not with the law?'

Carrie knew her uncle could sometimes sail close to the wind. He was the one who'd given Johnnie and Penny the precious tin of pineapple as a wedding present – and that hadn't been all. He'd come up with all the sugar and dried fruit for the cake, cigarettes for the tables and, for a corkage charge by the hotel, all the champagne.

'No,' Uncle Charlie said now. 'With the bank.'

Carrie went cold. Uncle Charlie had put up the money to start the bookshop – the deposit on the rent, the insurance, buying the stock. Norman and Mary, much as they might have wanted to, hadn't the wherewithal to help; the family shop just about kept its nose clean as it was. The rest of Carrie's start-up funds had come from the bank, a loan taken out by Uncle Charlie in his name but on her behalf. Carrie had been punctilious about paying him back, but she still owed him a substantial sum.

'You need your money out.'

'I'm so sorry, love. The bank's called in the loan. Typical of a bank – lend you an umbrella when the sun shines, take it away when it rains.'

'And it's been raining at the garage?'

Charlie nodded. 'It's been pouring. A monsoon. Me and Des have raised all we can against the place – it's mortgaged to the hilt and we can't pay that off either. And we're not green enough to go to loan sharks.'

'But you were doing so well!'

Considering the restrictions on private motoring – at least Uncle Charlie didn't seem to have become involved in forging petrol coupons, thank goodness – the business had seemed very resilient. Car sales had virtually ceased – no one was buying cars any more. But there'd been a private-hire business on the side, and on the repairs front, the garage had a contract for maintaining certain official vehicles, which meant regular money coming in.

'"Were" being the operative word,' said Uncle Charlie regretfully. 'It's a miracle we've survived as long as we have, to be frank. But everything's conspired against us these last few months. No one's buying cars, of course, haven't been for ages. And then there's petrol. It's been scarce since Dunkirk, when the government got so scared of invasion they cut the supply in the south by almost half. And it's got worse. We've had more days without than with. We had to let the forecourt attendant go in the summer—'

'You never said!'

'I didn't want to worry you, did I, till I had to. You know me, cheerful Charlie, I thought there might still be a way out. But things are only going to get worse. Soon there'll be no fuel at all for private motoring. We might have weathered that, just about, but our young mechanic's been called up and the older bloke can't do it all on his own – he should have retired two years ago. And you know that maintenance contract we had? That's stopping at the end of the year.'

Carrie knew what this meant for her. Only a few days ago, on that jolly evening with Penny and Johnnie, she'd been revisiting her dream of a chain of bookshops. Now even hanging on to the one she'd got looked hard enough, and the dream of expansion was a complete fantasy.

But Carrie wasn't one to give up that easily; she'd put two years of hard graft into the bookshop. And Gus Grayling's article, while yet to appear, had reinforced just how vital it had become to her customers – a lifeline, in fact – never mind what it meant to her.

'I'll go to the bank myself,' she declared wildly. 'I've got two years of solid trading, doesn't that count for anything?'

'I'd like to think so, love, I really would,' Uncle Charlie said sadly. 'But unfair as it is, you know that's not how it works. You're a single woman, and a young one, not twenty-one yet, and even if you were a man ... Banks don't like taking risks in good times, and these are hardly good. The war's in a desperate state – look at Greece and Malta. The campaign in North Africa's bogged down in sand, there's U-boat attacks left, right and centre, and look how thinly the RAF is spread – we're bombing Berlin, Boulogne,

Ostend . . . yet it doesn't seem to be making much difference.' He hung his head. 'I'm just so sorry I've made such a mess of things for you.'

Carrie had never seen him look so crushed, and her heart went out to him.

'Don't keep saying sorry! I wouldn't be here if it wasn't for you. You must never think that!' She put a hand on her uncle's arm. 'You must do whatever you have to do to salvage your business—'

'Carrie, have you been listening? Love, there's nothing to salvage. We're going to liquidate the garage – that's better than being declared bankrupt. We'll pay off what creditors we can, the ones with the loudest voices, the ones who've been sending the hard boys in—'

He stopped: he'd said too much.

'What?'

Uncle Charlie made a face.

'I wasn't there, but Des got beaten up last week, and the office trashed.'

'You're not serious?'

'Why do you think I'm going out with a nursing sister – I might need treatment!' Uncle Charlie took refuge in a dash of black humour, then added, in case Carrie misread it, 'Only joking. That's not the reason. Like I said, Jean's been a brick.'

'I'm glad you've had her to talk to about it.'

'Me too. We, er, she's going to transfer her post to a London hospital and we'll find a small place together. I can't afford the flat any more. But I'm not going to be a kept man. I'll find something!' he added fiercely. 'I've got my pride.'

'Of course you have, and of course you will.'

The rain had turned to drizzle and Uncle Charlie glanced out at the station clock. 'Time for the ten-twenty-three,' he said. He knew the train times almost as well as Carrie.

Carrie nodded. Her head was fizzing with all she'd been told, and what on earth she could do about it. Not for the first time in the six months he'd been gone, she wished desperately that Mike was there, to listen to her, to comfort her, to advise her, but most of all to hold her close and tell her everything would be all right, that they'd get through this together. As she truly believed they would.

'I'll find a way to get you your money,' she said.

'What about your mum and dad?' asked Charlie. 'I'm on my way to talk to your dad now, to explain. Not that I expect or want him to help me, but for you ... might there be a way?'

Carrie shook her head.

'I don't think so,' she said. 'Everyone round our way is cutting back. And you talk about things getting worse ... newspapers are already only a couple of sheets and the Cadbury's rep says sweets are bound to be on ration by next year.'

Uncle Charlie picked up his hat.

'I'm so sorry, love,' he said again. 'You've got a brilliant little business here. You've worked your socks off to make it what it is, and you don't deserve to suffer because of me.'

'It's not you, though, is it?' said Carrie vehemently. 'It's not your fault! It's the war! The war that's killed people, innocent people, here and all over the world, injured Johnnie

235

and Mike, sent Mike to America, got us all penny-pinching and living on lentils and saving scraps!'

She hadn't known how tired she was of the war until she said it. She'd worked so hard at keeping up a front, putting on a brave face, one foot in front of the other, all through Mike being sent away last year and this, all through the Blitz, all through the dreariness of the food and her gas mask bumping against her hip and stumbling around in the blackout and scrimping and saving and reusing everything.

'Ever thought of writing a book instead of reading them?' said Uncle Charlie. 'I couldn't have put it better myself.'

'Not very patriotic, though, is it?' said Carrie wryly. 'It may be what everyone's thinking, but it's not what you can say. I'd be arrested for sedition. And that's no way to keep the bookshop going.'

'Do you really think you can?'

Carrie looked around her little shop, the carefully arranged newspapers, the monthly and weekly magazines, the lovingly displayed paperbacks. Her Title of the Month (*Kipps* by H.G. Wells this time, something nice and light) and the latest Puffins, *Flowers of the Field and Hedgerow* and *A Book of Trains* – she had to stock that one! Her eyes travelled over the small basket of reductions, the slightly battered books and last week's or month's magazines, the assortment of stationery she kept for those urgent letters or postcards that people might have to write before a sudden departure or recall to base, the string for a bulging parcel. Let it all go? See the bookstall shuttered again, as it had been on the day war broke out, which had inspired her to revitalise it? Not on your life. Not on her life!

'Watch me,' she said.

Carrie wasn't sure how she got through the rest of the morning. She was desperate to speak to Mike, whatever it cost to telephone, even though she should be saving, not spending. Surely this counted as an emergency? But she couldn't telephone till she got home tonight. By then, it would be early afternoon in Washington. If he were in a meeting, he might not be able to call her back until late evening in England, if at all, and if she was waiting at home by the phone, she couldn't go and unburden herself to Penny and Johnnie. Meanwhile, her parents would be fretting, knowing how devastated she was, but unable to do anything practical to help. So who could? Hang on – there was one person . . . Gus!

Carrie had heard nothing from him since he'd disappeared up to Scotland over two weeks ago, apart from a postcard of Loch Ness with a serpentine-looking monster scratched on it in pen and a scrawled *'Scoop of the Year!'* on the back. There was no indication of when he'd return.

Carrie had been hoping his article would appear as soon as possible, on either side of the Atlantic. Now she hoped it wouldn't. If he hadn't placed it yet, he could include the threat to the bookshop and – why not? – an appeal to save it. There was surely some book-loving philanthropist out there with money to spare! When it came to her bookshop, Carrie wasn't proud. She'd accept money from anyone and anywhere – as long as it was legal, of course.

She pinned on a smile and did her best for her customers, but by the time the lunchtime rush had subsided, she had a blinding headache. She needed a glass of water and an aspirin and she had neither. Bette would have some in the tearoom, but Penny had taken a day off that she was owed, so there was no one to mind the stall. Carrie sank onto her stool and put her burning forehead in her hands.

'Carrie, dear? Are you all right?'

'Oh! Miss Cattermole!' Carrie looked up. 'Yes. I've got a bit of a headache, that's all.'

'Oh, you poor dear! Let me see . . .' Miss Cattermole delved in the knitting bag that she was never without. 'Yes, here we are, my aspirins, and shall I fetch you a glass of water from the refreshment room?'

'That would be so kind.'

Miss Cattermole pattered off and returned with the water. Carrie downed two aspirin and emptied the glass.

'You do look pale, dear,' worried Miss Cattermole. 'Is something the matter? You don't seem yourself.'

'Oh, I'm sorry.'

Miss Cattermole's kindness and concern seemed to embody everything that the bookshop stood for. All Carrie needed now was for Professor Mason to turn up with one of his quotations – 'the slings and arrows of outrageous fortune', perhaps – and she'd be totally undone. She tried to blink back the tears, but they fell anyway. With surprising speed and hitherto unsuspected decisiveness, Miss Cattermole hurried round behind the counter and took Carrie in her arms. And Carrie blurted everything out.

'Oh my dear, if only I could help!' Miss Cattermole looked distraught. 'I only have my pension . . . I have a small sum in War Savings, if I could access that . . .'

'Oh, please, I wouldn't dream of it . . . I didn't tell you for that!' Carrie exclaimed. 'You're so kind, but I'm not giving up. I'll find a way.'

'Of course you will!' Miss Cattermole assured her. 'We need you here, Carrie. Myself and all your other customers. We won't let you close!'

Chapter Twenty-eight

'Oh, Carrie, darling! That's dreadful.'

Carrie was at home. She'd requested her call the moment she got in, but inevitably Mike was in a meeting. Finally, at almost eleven o'clock at night, he phoned back and she told him everything.

'If only I were there!' Mike went on, frustrated. 'What can I do to help?'

Carrie was exhausted. Her head still ached and some of her earlier fighting spirit had evaporated.

'I don't know. What can you do, from over there?'

'Lots, I'm sure.' Mike was thinking aloud. 'I've got a regular income. I can contact my bank, try to arrange a loan and then hand it to you. Oh, no, they'd want to see me . . . Perhaps I could wire you some money in the meantime, and then, in the longer term, divert some of my pay . . . I'd have to refer upwards for that—'

'It'll all take ages!' Carrie burst out. 'Uncle Charlie's on the brink. He was trying to cover it up, but he's been hiding it for months!'

'Oh, Lord.' Mike sounded distraught. 'I don't want to be here, Carrie. I want to be with you. You shouldn't be going through this on your own.'

'When *are* you coming back, Mike?'

She'd tried to stop asking him. Mike was doing important work there, however modestly he played it down, and she had a pathological fear of seeming needy, but she couldn't help herself.

'Oh, darling. Believe me, I keep asking. But the answer's always a flat no – well, that's not true. Oh damn it, I can't say what I'm told, but . . . they're not going to let me go just yet.'

'You've gone and made yourself indispensable, I suppose.' Carrie managed to say it lightly, without a hint of bitterness. 'You shouldn't be so flipping good at everything!'

'I'm not being a very good fiancé, am I?' Mike said regretfully.

Carrie smiled. She'd told him about Gus, of course, and how he pronounced things. She loved to hear Mike say 'fiancé' the English way.

'Don't talk rubbish,' she said. 'I've got no complaints.'

'Well, you're an angel. You should have.'

'When you've just sent me that lovely perfume?'

The bottle of Worth's Je Reviens had arrived just last week. It was light and springlike, smelling deliciously of jasmine. And on the note with it, Mike had written: *'Je Reviens means "I'm coming back". And I will.'*

'I want to smell it on you,' said Mike. 'I want to kiss wherever you put it, the hollow at the base of your throat, and the place behind your ears . . .'

'Oh, Mike.' Carrie felt her bones turn to water at the thought of him kissing her again.

She turned as the chenille curtain that separated the little hall from the back room was pushed aside and her dad's head poked through. He tapped his watch and gestured

241

upstairs to show that her mum and he were going up. Carrie nodded and mouthed that she wouldn't be long.

'I have to go,' Carrie said. 'I just – I wanted you to know.'

'I'll think about what I can do,' Mike said urgently. 'I'll get on to it right now. I'll do what I can.'

'I hate asking.'

'You didn't ask, I offered,' Mike said. 'And I mean it. Think of it as a down payment on our future, OK?'

'I love you.'

'I love you too. Now you get some sleep. That's what you need.'

'I will.'

'Promise? No lying awake, worrying?'

'I'll try.'

'I love you, Carrie.'

'I love you too. Night-night.'

'Night, darling.'

There was the usual pause. The undersea cable was the thread that connected them; neither wanted to be the first to sever it.

'You go first,' Mike said gently. 'Go on.'

'OK. Night.'

'Night.'

Carrie replaced the receiver carefully, not wanting to hear the click as the line was cut. Then she obediently went upstairs to bed.

In her room, Carrie undressed slowly. As she did, she scanned the small wooden bookcase that held her most treasured books: Rosamond Lehmann, Winifred Holtby . . . She knew she'd have to read herself to sleep. On the bamboo table beside her bed she had *The Rich House* by Stella Gibbons, which promised 'the love affairs of six young people on the eve of the war', but tonight didn't feel like the time to start a new novel. Instead, she took from the shelf an old favourite.

She got into bed, opened her book and read:

It is a truth universally acknowledged, that a single man in possession of a good fortune, must be in want of a wife.

Despite everything, it brought a smile to her face, as it always did. Clever Jane Austen! Carrie sighed and settled down to immerse herself in the faraway but enticing world of the Bennet sisters.

Mike was right – what Carrie needed most was sleep. He really was as good at everything as she'd joked. When she woke the next morning, amazed at having slept through, she couldn't have felt more different. All her resolve and determination were back. She was going to save what she'd worked for and she arrived at the station feeling almost light-hearted.

'I'm calling a meeting,' she told Penny. 'In the tearoom tonight, after hours. Bette and Ruby too. I've already asked them to stay on.'

'Why? What is it?' Penny demanded.

'You'll see,' said Carrie.

That evening, when the sign on the refreshment-room door had finally been turned from 'Open' to 'Closed' and Ruby had swept up, the four friends gathered round.

Bette brought a fat brown teapot to the table and was followed by Ruby with a tray of cups and a plate of jam tarts. Penny, who was always hungry – well, she did a hard physical job – fell on them straight away.

'Right,' said Carrie when the tea was poured, 'I declare this meeting open!'

'What's it all about?' said Ruby. 'I hope I can still catch the early show. It's *Dangerous Lady*.'

'This won't take long,' Carrie reassured her. 'But it is important. It's an SOS, well, SOSB – Save Our Station Bookshop!'

Penny stopped brushing crumbs off her uniform jacket and sat forward.

'How come?'

'You what?' said Bette as Ruby looked nonplussed.

Without going into detail, Carrie explained that Uncle Charlie needed to withdraw his capital.

'I've got to find another source of funding – and quickly – if the bookshop's going to survive,' she explained. 'So if anyone's got a brainwave going spare – or a few pounds, for that matter . . .'

'A collection tin on the counter!' suggested Penny at once.

'And on the counter in here!' Bette chimed in.

'Not a tin, a bucket!' said Ruby, not to be outdone now she'd grasped what was going on. 'I don't know what any of the passengers'd do without you, Carrie! I don't know what any of us'd do!'

Carrie had already thought of a collection tin. She had baulked at the idea of asking for money from her customers, some of them already hard-pressed, but she couldn't afford

244

to be proud. And – as the posters constantly hectored about saving string, paper or scraps of food – every little helped.

Bette frowned.

'That won't raise enough, though, will it?' she said. 'I had a bit put by, Carrie, you could have had it and welcome, but the Red Cross do so much for prisoners . . . My Eric couldn't praise them enough. So after he died, I went and gave it all to them.'

'I never knew that, Mrs Saunders,' said Ruby in awe.

Carrie was touched. 'Bette, that's so kind, but the Red Cross deserve it – even more than the bookshop.'

Penny looked at Carrie regretfully.

'I wish I had more to offer,' she said. 'If things were different – if I hadn't gone and . . .'

Carrie knew what she meant. If Penny hadn't turned her back on her wealthy family and come to Brockington with a new identity, she would have been wealthy in her own right. But then they'd never have met, and she'd never have met Johnnie – the whole notion was ridiculous.

'If you and Johnnie hadn't overstretched yourselves with the rent on your little flat and decorating it and everything, you mean,' Carrie said pointedly, to spare Penny her remorse. 'Don't be silly – you had to make a home.'

'We might be able to stump up something,' Penny offered, grateful for Carrie's understanding. 'But it won't be a lot, I'm afraid.'

'I've got nothing to give,' said Ruby disconsolately. 'I had about three bob in my Post Office book, last time I looked. You can have it, though, Carrie, sure as I'm sat here!'

'Oh, Ruby, you are sweet, but I can't take your money,'

said Carrie. 'I honestly didn't mean any of you to start subsidising me. Mike's seeing if he can get some kind of loan or advance from the army. But there is something we can do together. Who's got an old sheet they can spare? We've got a bit of paint at home – we'll do a Save the Bookshop banner!'

Bette was sure she could find something, and the meeting broke up with everyone promising to keep their thinking caps handy.

'If all else fails, you can always sell that perfume Mike sent you on the black market,' suggested Penny as they stood on the platform while Bette locked up. 'And the three pairs of stockings he sent for your birthday.' Then, with a grin, she added, 'What, jealous, me? Not a bit of it!'

That same night, Bette cut and hemmed half a sheet ('It had gone in the middle anyway, only good for rags!'). She brought it straight round to the Andersons', and by the light of a storm lantern, in the little shed where Johnnie used to do his woodworking, Carrie daubed the SOSB message with some leftover paint that matched the shopfront. The next day, Penny helped her hang it, to the perturbation of Mr Bayliss, who told her it made the station look untidy and then castigated the collection tin, already rattling with coppers and the occasional threepence or sixpence from concerned customers, as a 'begging bowl'.

'Have you contributed yet, Mr Bayliss?' asked Carrie archly. As if!

He was the only person not to be upset by the news. He knew perfectly well that the crisis was nothing to do with her ability as a businesswoman, but that didn't stop him sounding smug when he asked one day how long Carrie thought she could keep going. Professor Mason happened to be at the bookshop at the time. He turned on the five-foot-four-inch stationmaster with all the superiority of his age, education and height.

'Carrie's bookshop is going nowhere, if we customers have anything to do with it,' he pronounced. 'And I should have thought you'd be rather sorrier to lose a facility that enhances the experience of travel from this station, which, with its delays and cancellations, is challenging enough! When the railway offers its paying customers a better, faster and more reliable service, there might be less need for books and periodicals to distract the travelling public from the privations of war. But as that day is some way off, if indeed it ever returns, Carrie's bookshop is a vital asset. And I promise you, we, her loyal customers, will be lying down across the tracks if it closes.'

'It's nothing to do with me! I don't have any say in it,' Mr Bayliss spluttered.

'If that is the case, kindly refrain from making either comment or enquiry.' Professor Mason turned back to Carrie. 'Now, where were we? Ah, yes, *The Second Penguin Crossword Puzzle Book*. I'm not surprised you need to reorder.'

More than slightly pink, Mr Bayliss waddled off.

'Thank you.' Carrie turned to the professor.

'Silly little man, small in stature, a clear case of Napoleon syndrome,' declared Professor Mason crisply. 'Take no notice. By the way . . .' He fished in the well-worn briefcase that he always carried. 'We held a little discussion in the refreshment room, myself and some of the regulars, and we want you to have this.' He placed a small cloth bag on the counter. 'We know it's not enough, not nearly enough, but if it helps to cover one or two weeks' overheads it will buy you a little time.' As Carrie stood stock still, he added, 'It won't bite! Take a look!'

Stunned, Carrie pulled open the bag's drawstring and peeped inside – more coins. A lot of coins.

'I can't accept this!'

'Well, I can't give it back,' said Professor Mason. 'It started out amongst us regulars, but it transpired that Hermione Cattermole has been approaching passengers on the trains.' Carrie gaped and he went on, smiling broadly: 'Yes I know, with her little lace jabots and her knitting, who'd have thought it! But she went up and down, first class to third, and told anyone who'd listen, even people who never disembark here, let alone buy a book, about your plight. And this is the result.'

'But that's illegal!' squeaked Carrie. 'Wouldn't it count as begging?'

'If anyone had caught her, yes. But who's going to suspect little Miss Cattermole of being an insurrectionist, hmm? But there was no harassment, the donations were all quite freely given. So I'm afraid you have no choice but to accept.'

'I don't know what to say.' Carrie's throat was tight.

'Then say nothing, simply lock it in your cash drawer,' smiled the professor. 'Well, my work here is done. Goodbye.'

And with a flourish of his briefcase, he disappeared towards the station exit.

That night, with her parents' help, Carrie counted out the contents of the bag, silver and coppers. There was even, at the bottom, a half-crown coin. Carrie suspected Professor Mason of that.

'Well!' Norman exclaimed. 'Look at that little lot! Hey, Mary, perhaps I should have a whip-round for our shop!'

'Dad, don't! I'm so embarrassed.'

'You didn't ask for it, love,' Mary reasoned. 'The best thing you can do is accept it graciously.'

'I'll have to, but it's still nowhere near enough to pay off Uncle Charlie, the same with the tin on the counter. My best hope is this money of Mike's.'

Mike had managed to telephone again. He'd wired what money he could, and had spoken to his superiors about leveraging a decent loan from the army, or an advance against his expected pay. But that would take time. The wheels of army bureaucracy ground even more slowly than those of a delayed train.

Meanwhile, there'd still been no word from Gus, and Carrie couldn't understand it. Nor could Johnnie.

'I thought better of him than this,' he puzzled when he called by the bookstall on one of his rest days. 'Maybe it's true what they say about journalists – you can't believe a word they say. Or promise.'

'He's probably found far more exciting things to write about than my little bookshop,' Carrie said bravely, but she was disappointed. She, too, had thought better of Gus. He could have let her know either way.

'But if it was a little feature story before, it's hot news now!' said Penny, clutching an umbrella and a bedraggled teddy bear. She was on her way to the Lost Property store. 'Have the *Brockington Post* got back to you yet?'

'No,' said Carrie disconsolately. She was badgering them every other day, but they kept claiming they had no space. 'Professor Mason's going to have a word when he drops in his next crossword. It's galling having to write out a headline about an escaped budgie when what I really want to put is "Boneheaded *Brockington Post* Refuses to Save Bookshop".'

'Huh! I'd write it anyway,' said Penny.

'Yes, you would,' grinned Johnnie. 'Carrie's a bit less devil take the hindmost than you!'

'Thanks, hubby!' Penny swatted him on the arm.

Carrie left them to their good-natured bickering: it was the hallmark of their relationship.

She had other things to think about. One thing was puzzling her above all else. Mr Parfitt was her staunchest champion. He'd been shocked and sorry to hear about Uncle Charlie's difficulties and the inevitable outcome for the bookshop. Deep down, Carrie had nurtured a vague hope that as she'd done such sterling work for Penguin, he'd appeal to them for support.

Publishers, like everyone else, were struggling, but Allen Lane, Penguin's founder, was a canny businessman. As he provided special editions for the forces, the government allocated Penguin extra supplies of paper, which was how they could release five or six new titles every few months. But if news of the bookshop's possible demise had reached Allen Lane's ears, he'd done nothing about it.

On the other hand, Carrie had always known it was a long shot. Mr Parfitt was one of many reps, and no doubt his colleagues had tales of other struggling bookshops. But if the silence from Allen Lane was understandable, Mr Parfitt's was less so. In fact, he'd disappeared, just like Gus. A brisk, younger rep had replaced him and when Carrie asked after Mr Parfitt, she was told brusquely that he'd been 'called away'.

'And I've had to take on half his round, along with another poor sucker, who's got the other half. Don't talk to me about wartime economies!' said the new bloke, stuffing Carrie's (much-reduced) order in his briefcase and speeding off.

Mike, Gus, Mr Parfitt . . . So much for Je Reviens. Carrie's perfume, which she'd taken to wearing every day as a sort of talisman – it made her feel closer to Mike – was acting more like fly repellent. She was sure that wasn't at all what the makers had intended.

Chapter Twenty-nine

November was almost over. The Town Hall put a Christmas tree on the cantilevered canopy at its entrance and the WI announced a tea party for old-age pensioners. The Salvation Army arrived on the station, unpacking their instruments, playing carols and rattling their tins. As a catering outlet, the tearoom still got more or less regular supplies of flour, fats and sugar, and Bette and Ruby added mince pies and spice biscuits to their menu. After checking with Bette (she was definitely learning), Ruby finally cast off her black dress for a red and green tartan number, albeit with a black velvet bow at the neck.

'It's a relief actually,' she told Carrie. 'I'm not any less sad about Eric, but he doesn't know what I'm wearing, does he, bless him. And black's a really draining colour on me.'

On the wireless, *The Kitchen Front* offered tips for creating a 'delicious' Christmas dinner with the little that was available.

'Who are they trying to fool?' said Mary, who'd made her Christmas pudding with grated parsnip and carrot in place of sugar.

Yes, Christmas was coming, and though she tried her best, Carrie had never felt less festive. Last year had been difficult enough: she'd finally been close to accepting that, after all, Mike must have been killed at Dunkirk. Then, in a

Christmas miracle, he'd turned up on the doorstep on the day itself. And this year he was away again.

'I sometimes wonder if Mike and I will ever spend Christmas together,' she mused to Penny. 'We've never had a summer together either. We've only ever had autumn, winter and the start of spring.'

'Well, you've got all that to look forward to, haven't you?' declared Penny in her usual matter-of-fact way. 'Think of all the clothes he's never seen. I'm sure Johnnie's sick of mine!'

You could rely on Penny for a sideways look at things.

Meanwhile, Carrie scraped together what she could to pay back Uncle Charlie and to keep the bookshop going. She was sustained by the money Mike had wired, her own Post Office savings, a small contribution from Johnnie and her mum and dad, the collection tins, Miss Cattermole's cloth bag, and strict economies. No more cups of tea or treats from the tearoom: Carrie brought in a flask and sandwiches. She'd never taken much of a wage; her payment was the pleasure the bookshop gave her. Now she cut even that to the bone. As with the books, she reduced her papers and periodicals order, though that could prove a false economy: what she didn't have, she couldn't sell, so her turnover and profits would be less.

'And a Very Merry Christmas to All Our Readers,' she muttered when the December magazines came in, all with the same jolly greeting.

One morning, she was on the customer side of the counter, writing the daily poster for the *Brockington Post*. It had finally squeezed in a tiny snippet about the bookshop's possible closure, but, unsurprisingly, Carrie had not been killed in the rush of local millionaires appearing with fistfuls of notes.

The *Post*'s headline of the day was RED TAPE HOLDS UP HOSPITAL and Carrie couldn't help but smile. The subeditor had obviously missed the double meaning – or perhaps he was as frustrated as Carrie with the so-called newspaper he worked for and was having a subtle dig.

'Surprise!'

Carrie was so startled that the 'H' of 'HOSPITAL' zigzagged across the sheet.

'Gus! You made me jump!'

'I like to make an entrance,' Gus winked. He was wearing a shiny grey suit, a narrow tie and a soft-collared shirt. Carrie had ink on her fingers and was dressed for winter on the stall: furry boots, whipcord trousers and two sweaters, the top one an old one of Johnnie's, belted at the waist. But she didn't care what she looked like – it was simply good to see him after all this time.

'I know it's been a while,' he said, putting her thoughts into words. 'But boy, have I got news for you!'

Carrie pushed the poster aside.

'Where have you been? Is everything all right?'

'It's a long story. But don't you want to hear about the article?'

'Of course I do. The thing is, Gus, I've got news too – something's happened—'

But Gus wasn't about to be interrupted.

'To answer your questions in order,' he lowered his voice, 'I've had a thrilling time. I got myself embedded on one of

254

your ships, an escort vessel. I've been to the Baltic, Carrie, with a convoy – the Baltic and back!'

'No!'

'Oh, yeah. But before I went, I sent off the article to various newspapers and magazines, here and in the States, just like I promised. I didn't expect to hear straight away, but when I got back and checked my mail – we've done it! *The Oklahoman*, of course, they love it. In fact, it may have been in already. And – wait for it – the *New York Sun* is going to run it! How about that?'

'That's amazing, Gus, but the thing is—'

'I know, I know, you want to know about UK coverage. Here goes. I think we've got a good chance with the *Daily Mail*. I'm talking to a guy there – they still do the odd human interest feature and—'

'Gus, listen! Things have changed. The bookshop might not be here much longer.'

'Whaaattt?'

'If you'd let me get a word in . . . Uncle Charlie, who helped me set it up – he needs his money out. He's had to liquidate his own business and he's got creditors on his back. The loan he fixed on my behalf isn't paid off either, and . . . well, I've got to find a way of staying open or my little Penguin bookshop won't be here at all!'

'Oh, jeez.'

'I know! Can you amend your article? You never know, perhaps someone who loves books and believes in them as much as I do might be so taken with the story they offer to chip in! As long as it's legal, I'd take it, I really would. I've just – I've got to keep it open, Gus.'

Gus rubbed his forehead.

'I never saw this coming.'

'Neither did I. I found out while you were away, but I had no way of contacting you . . .'

'No, of course not. And there was I having a rare old time on the high seas. And I mean high. The waves out there! And the cold! Tell your mom to keep knitting those scarves for sailors – and your Miss Cattermole.'

'Miss Cattermole . . . I must tell you. She organised a whip-round – a collection – on the trains. If I don't pay myself anything and hardly order any stock, I can keep going till Christmas. But then that's it!'

Desperation and distress sent Carrie's voice up an octave.

'OK, look,' said Gus. 'This is what we do. I'll cable the *New York Sun* and ask if I can add a rider about the bookshop being in difficulty. There's a lot of wealthy people in New York – bankers and stockbrokers, attorneys, businessmen – someone might just reach for their wallet.'

'And the *Mail*?'

'I'll call them too, straight away! See if the same applies.'

'Thank you. It's a slim chance, wafer-thin, but it's a chance.'

'You're right. OK, well, I have work to do. I'll let you know how I get on, and we'll have another drink sometime, huh? I'm getting quite a taste for your weirdly warm English beer. And Carrie . . .' He stepped towards her, arms out wide. 'Come here. You'll get through this, I know you will.'

He wrapped her in a huge hug. Carrie closed her eyes. It was so long since she'd been held by a man who wasn't her dad or her brother. The temptation to give in to it, to lean in and sag against him, was almost irresistible, but Carrie fought it. Gus wasn't Mike. Gus wasn't as tall, and he was bulkier. The cloth of his suit was slippery, not the rough khaki of Mike's uniform jacket, and he smelled different, some kind of spicy aftershave, whereas Mike always smelled cleanly of shaving soap. She stepped away.

'Better?'

Carrie smiled.

'Yes. Thank you.'

He wasn't to know.

'OK,' Gus went on. 'I'll go and make that call, send that cable.'

He turned to go, almost colliding with a man who was approaching.

'Hello, there, sir!' he said.

'Mr Parfitt!' cried Carrie, startled for the second time that morning.

Mr Parfitt raised his hat and smiled.

'Carrie. Mr Grayling,' he said.

And for the second time that day, Carrie asked:

'Where have you been? Is everything all right?'

'I certainly hope so,' smiled Mr Parfitt. 'Have you got a moment, Carrie? And you may like to hear this as well, Mr Grayling.'

Gus demurred. 'I've got a couple of things to do. Carrie's told me about her predicament. I need to see if I can get my article amended to include an appeal for funds.'

'Ah. No, hold your horses there, young man. The situation has changed.'

'Really? Don't tell me Penguin are going to put in some money to keep the bookshop going?' Carrie gasped.

'No, no, my dear. That would be setting a very dangerous precedent. No, I'm happy to say I can offer you a new partner in the bookshop.'

'Wow, that's great!' said Gus. 'But how? Where? Who?'

'You're looking at him,' said Mr Parfitt simply.

'You, sir?'

It was a good job Gus was there, Carrie reflected afterwards, because she'd been entirely robbed of the power of speech. Mr Parfitt explained.

'The reason I've been away is that my sister – you remember, Carrie, I have mentioned her? She unfortunately passed away.'

'I'm so sorry,' Carrie managed.

'Sorry to hear that, sir,' echoed Gus.

'That's kind, but it was what they term a merciful release. Inoperable cancer, you know. Anyway,' Mr Parfitt continued, 'she was housekeeper for a wealthy family who provided for her very generously. As such she had few expenses and, well, how can I put it? Every penny she had – a not inconsiderable sum – has come to me.'

Still silent, Carrie was absorbing every word.

'Well, as I've indicated before, Carrie, retirement holds no appeal whatsoever.' Carrie nodded and Mr Parfitt permitted himself a brief smile. 'As a world cruise is out of the question at the moment – and frankly, would not be on my agenda even if it were possible – I can't think of any better use for the money than to invest it in a tidy little business in which I already have an abiding interest.' Still

Carrie said nothing, and Mr Parfitt said anxiously, 'Oh dear. I hope I'm not being presumptuous. I hadn't really thought . . . I may not be your ideal partner. You may have been hoping for someone younger. Or perhaps you've already found a backer?'

He glanced at Gus, who gave a grin and a shake of his head.

'No, she hasn't. But I think, sir, that for once Carrie is lost for words.'

Finally, Carrie found her voice.

'Oh, Mr Parfitt! I can't believe it! I – I don't know what to say! You'd really do that?'

'Nothing would give me greater pleasure,' said Mr Parfitt. 'Or – because I've seen your accounts – a better return on my money. Shall we shake hands on it?'

Relief, joy and disbelief flooded through Carrie. She would have flung herself at Mr Parfitt for her second hug of the day, but she knew it would embarrass him. Instead, she took his outstretched hand in both of hers.

'Thank you! Thank you, thank you, thank you!' she said and couldn't help adding, 'I could kiss you!'

'Oh, I don't think that'll be necessary,' said Mr Parfitt, blushing.

'If only I had my camera. So British!' smiled Gus.

It didn't take long for word to spread around the station. Penny had been watching the arrivals at the bookshop as she went about her work and as soon as she had a moment between trains, she nipped into the tearoom to pass it on to Bette and Ruby.

'Gus, the American, turned up first, and then Mr Parfitt! And now they've all got their heads together.'

Ruby rushed to the door and craned out.

'Gus is slapping Mr Parfitt on the back ... blimey, he nearly sent him off the platform! Oh, and Carrie – she's heading this way!'

Leaving the tearoom customers staring, the three of them congregated in the doorway as Carrie approached.

'I had to tell you,' she cried. 'Miracles do happen! Mr Parfitt is going to put money into the bookshop. It's saved!'

The friends fell on each other with tears and laughter. No words were needed – at least, not until Mr Bayliss came out of his office to supervise the arrival of the next train.

'Mothers' meeting?' he enquired sarcastically.

'Businesswomen's meeting,' said Bette, adding, 'Carrie's found a new backer for the bookshop. We always knew she could do it!' And knowing his views about Carrie, she added pertly, 'I'm sure you'll want to congratulate her.'

Mr Bayliss twitched his nose like someone detecting the smell of drains. He managed a curt nod in Carrie's direction.

'You'd better get back to it, then,' he snapped sourly, and strutted off.

'I swear to God,' pronounced Bette, 'the only thing that'd make him crack his face, Carrie, was if your toes were made of cheese and the rats were eating them! What a misery!'

The four women looked at each other and laughed. Nothing – especially not Lucius Bayliss – was going to bring them down today.

*

Mary and Norman were almost as bowled over by the news as Carrie – so much so that Norman sent Carrie down to the off-licence for a few bottles of beer to celebrate. The three of them toasted the bookshop's future with a pale ale for Norman and shandies for Carrie and her mum.

'I'm over the moon and back!' cried Mary tearfully. 'The hours you've put in there, and the pleasure you've brought people, Carrie ... No one deserves this more than you!'

'Hear! Hear!' echoed Norman. 'Look at the way the customers rallied round, and your pals on the station. Shows what an asset you are.'

'Oh, shut up, the pair of you,' Carrie said affectionately. 'You're making me blush!'

The little celebration, and the unaccustomed alcohol, meant that tea was delayed as Mary had forgotten to put the potatoes on. It was Mike's night for phoning – it had become a regular thing again since the crisis at the bookshop – and the family were still eating when the phone shrilled.

Carrie jumped up.

'Keep mine hot!' she cried, flying to the telephone and snatching up the receiver.

'A transatlantic call, will you receive it?' said the operator dispassionately.

'Of course, put it through, please!'

'Hold the line, please.'

There was the usual agonising pause of clicks, whistles and hums and the fear that the line would drop before Carrie heard Mike saying, 'Carrie? Are you there?'

'Yes, I'm here, I'm here!'

'How are you, darling? I've been thinking about you so much.'

'And me you. Mike, the thing is—'

'I know, I know, the shop. Before you go any further, in case we get cut off, I'm working really hard on that loan. Over here on this semi-diplomatic thing, I'm not strictly speaking with my regiment, so the problem is finding the right person to speak to—'

'Well, don't! Forget it! Don't bother! Mike, wonderful news. You don't have to ask the army or anyone for a loan, or advance, or sub or whatever! I've got a new partner!'

'You have? Who?'

Her words somersaulting out, Carrie told him everything that had happened, starting with Mr Parfitt and his astonishing and generous offer and ending with the other good news about Gus's articles appearing, hopefully, in titles on both sides of the Atlantic.

'Hang on, I'm trying to take all this in. You're sure about this? Mr Parfitt? And Gus has come good as well?'

'Yes, and yes! Isn't it amazing? I feel like the White Queen in *Through the Looking-Glass* – you know, believing six impossible things before breakfast. Or in my case, two before lunch!'

'It's incredible. Oh, that's fantastic, Carrie – when you've been through so much. I so wish I'd been there when things looked bleak – and now to share your moment of triumph. Oh, I'm giving you a huge hug and the longest, longest kiss. Can you feel it?'

'I can feel it. I'm hugging and kissing you back, Mike.'

'I know you are. And one day you will be for real. Soon, I hope.'

'Oh, me too.'

Mike smiled down the line.

'If you knew how different you sound! All the energy and spark and loveliness is back in your voice. I can just picture you, eyes shining, that huge smile of yours, that glow you have about you . . .'

Carrie both loved and hated it when he got wistful like this. He'd rallied her as best he could all these weeks. It was her turn now, even though she wanted him back by her side more than ever. She desperately wanted to ask if the British mission to get America into the war was actually making progress, what he was actually doing day by day, but she knew she couldn't. Hadn't she sworn to be even more careful in what she said after Ruby's experience? Didn't every other government poster caution: 'YOU NEVER KNOW WHO MIGHT BE LISTENING'? So instead, she said:

'We're not the only couple who're apart. And you're doing valuable work there, Mike. I know you can't talk about it, but you know you are, and I know you are. And you're making a difference, I'm sure.'

'Yes, yes, I know.'

'It can't be much longer now till you're home.'

'I really hope not. As soon as I possibly can.'

Chapter Thirty

All the Christmas decorations that had looked tawdry to Carrie's jaundiced eyes during the weeks of worry now took on a magical air. The strips of lametta and paper lanterns in the refreshment room made it look like the transformation scene from a pantomime. The crêpe paper chains and sprigs of holly that her dad had placed in his shop window around the faded dummy boxes of Black Magic and Milk Tray looked like something from a Victorian Christmas card, and the effort he'd made even though the outside of the window was trellised with anti-blast tape made her heart swell for him. The smile that Mike had referred to was never off her face.

As the news spread among her regulars, they shook her joyfully by the hand and congratulated her. Only one small boy asked for his contribution (tuppence) back as 'you don't need it no more'. He did, he said – he wanted to put it towards a Christmas present for his little sister. Carrie handed it over gladly.

'You are a mug,' said Penny. 'A present for his sister, I don't think! He promptly spent it in the chocolate machine, I saw him. And how do you know he gave you a contribution in the first place?'

'Penny, I'm surprised at you!' Carrie scolded. 'I don't

care if he did or not. Haven't you heard of the season of goodwill?'

Nothing, but nothing was going to dent her spirits. Then it happened.

It was the first Sunday in December, and Carrie was at a loose end. She wrote to Mike, then she darned a hole in the elbow of a sweater and poked through a couple of pulled threads in another. She polished her shoes; she experimented with a new hairstyle that she'd seen in *Woman* magazine. Her mum was at church, her dad in the shop. It wasn't time yet to peel the potatoes or scrape the carrots. What could she do? Suddenly she remembered.

On the day of his surprise return, that astonishing day when his reappearance had been trumped by Mr Parfitt's arrival, Gus had left her some magazines.

'My mom sends them to keep me in touch with the States,' he explained. 'They're right across the board – from her *Ladies' Home Journal* to *Life* magazine. I'll never have the time to read these back numbers – there's more arriving by the hour. I thought you might like them.'

'Thank you. I'll be fascinated!' said Carrie.

But since then, so much had been going on – discussing how their new partnership was going to work and drawing up a contract with Mr Parfitt, spreading the good news among her customers and generally wafting about on cloud nine – that Carrie hadn't opened a single one. They were still rolled and wrapped in their paper sleeves.

Energised, she got out her bike and pedalled to the station. It was always quiet on a Sunday, with the refreshment room and the bookshop closed. Carrie opened the side door of her little shop. She lifted all the magazines onto the counter and ripped off the paper wrappers.

She'd take them all home, she decided, and read them in comfort. Her mum would love the *Ladies' Home Journal* – a nice change from *Woman and Home* – and her dad would be interested to see them too. But first she couldn't resist a quick flick through.

She started with *Life* magazine. Gus had told her a bit about it. It had carved out a niche in what it called 'photojournalism' – not much text, just photographs with captions. It had followed the war closely since its outbreak, which could only be helpful to British efforts to get America to join the fight. Elbows on the counter, oblivious to the cold draught from the half-open door, Carrie was captivated by the immediate difference from British magazines, even the outstanding *Picture Post*. The typefaces were quite different and the layout was bold.

She turned the pages in something like a trance. The photographs were striking – bomb damage in London, a tattered curtain, a stray cat; tanks on manoeuvres, a shell-shocked soldier staring blankly, a queue of men at the field canteen.

Moving on, Carrie peered at a photograph of the Woolworth heiress Barbara Hutton in a stunning satin evening dress and white fur stole. *'Miss Barbara Hutton is noted for her philanthropy,'* said the caption, *'having donated generously to the Free French Forces.'*

Good for her, thought Carrie. It made a change from the speculation about her supposed romance with Cary Grant that filled the pages of Ruby's *Picturegoer*.

Idly, Carrie turned the page.

Carrie read the headline and glanced at the photographs, then looked again, more closely. It couldn't be. It couldn't be! But there he was. Mike, her Mike, dancing with a slim, dark-haired young woman in a backless evening dress, his hand partly resting on her naked flesh. Mike in profile with a faraway look on his face; the woman with her head close to his and a look of triumph.

'*Anglo-American relations are aided by Lieutenant Michael Hudson, attached to the British delegation,*' said the caption.

Carrie felt sick. And as if that wasn't enough, there they were again, at the same event, in the background of a photograph of Howard Hughes and the Vice-President. There was Mike with the same girl, seated at a table, heads together in animated conversation.

Feeling as though she might fall down, Carrie gripped the edge of the counter. The fundraising dinner had been in October. So all these past weeks when Mike had been so sweet, so supportive, he'd actually been seeing someone else? It hardly looked as though the woman he was with – and not just with, but dancing with, dancing closely with and, well, almost canoodling with at the table – was a casual acquaintance.

A day ago she'd have sworn it was impossible that Mike would or could ever betray her with someone else. But he'd been gone over six months – did she really know him any more? So much could happen, so much could change a person in that time. By his own admission, he'd found it hard to deny his natural male instincts with her. Maybe in America, where everything was different and nothing was off limits and his fiancée was thousands of miles away, he hadn't had to try too hard. She'd heard myriad tales of the strongest relationships ruptured by separations caused by the war. Why should she and Mike be any different?

Carrie jumped as someone spoke.

'Who's there?' said a voice. 'Is that you, Carrie?'

It was PC Drummond, the beat bobby, doing his rounds.

Still shaking from what she'd read, Carrie pulled the door wide.

'It's only me,' she managed.

'Oh, Carrie, love, that's all right then,' beamed PC Drummond. 'I saw the door ajar, thought it was odd.'

'I was just leaving,' Carrie mumbled. 'But thank you for checking.'

He touched the brim of his helmet and went on his way.

Carrie picked up the magazine and stumbled out behind him, shaking so much she was hardly able to get the key in the lock. She wasn't sure she could control her bike, so pushed it all the way home.

Her dad was still in the shop; at church, her mum would be singing the final hymn. If it had been a weekday, the Post Office would have been open and Carrie could have sent a telegram. Today, there was no other option but the fantastically lengthy and even more fantastically expensive process of placing a telephone call to America. Swallowing the sick feeling she'd had since seeing the photograph, she went to the telephone in the tiny hallway and lifted the receiver. She asked the operator to place an international call to Mike's office in Washington. Though it was Sunday, and early in the morning in America, someone would be there, even if not Mike: war was no respecter of hours of the day, or days of the week. She could leave a message, and she didn't care who saw it. Mike had publicly humiliated her – if he faced a few shocked looks from colleagues who might see the message on his desk, too bad.

It took an age – even longer than usual – for the connection to come through, but finally she was connected to Mike's office. A man's voice – young, polite, English, but not Mike's – answered. Carrie asked for Mike, but sure enough, he wasn't there: he was off duty that day, she was told. Pushing down sickness and panic at the thought of what he might be doing, where he might be doing it – some hotel room? – and with whom, Carrie asked to leave a message.

'Of course, miss,' said the voice. 'Who shall I say is calling?'

'Carrie,' she said. 'He'll know who I am.'

'Carrie,' repeated the voice. 'Very well. And the message is . . . ?'

'Just tell him . . . Just tell him this: "I've seen *Life*. We're finished."'

'"I've seen life. We're finished,"' repeated the voice, sounding puzzled, not to mention awkward. 'I'm sorry, I'm a little confused. By "life", you mean . . . ?'

'The magazine.'

'I see! *Life* magazine. So to clarify . . . may I add that word to the message?'

'Yes, perhaps you'd better,' said Carrie. She was grateful. It was hard to think straight. 'Thank you. That's all.'

*

Mary bustled in twenty minutes later, full of church news.

'It was Bob Mansfield's birthday, bless him, nearly ninety and still playing the organ every Sunday— Carrie? What's the matter?' Her mother stopped halfway through taking off her coat. 'You're as white as a sheet. You're not well.'

Carrie was sitting in her dad's chair by the fireplace, the magazine on her lap, staring at the empty grate. Coal was soon to be rationed and the fire was only lit in the evenings, but that wasn't why she was shivering uncontrollably.

'I've had a bit of a shock,' she said dully.

'Carrie, for goodness' sake, tell me what's gone on!' said her mother, pulling up a chair beside her. 'You're worrying me.'

In reply, Carrie held out the magazine. 'At the back,' she said. 'Some charity ball.'

'What? Oh – this is American, isn't it?'

Mary took *Life* and riffled through.

'Next page,' said Carrie, and when Mary had turned over, 'There! Under the bit about Barbara Hutton. The photographs. Look who it is.'

Mary's mouth fell open.

'Mike . . .' she said in amazement. 'Who's that he's with?'

'If I knew that!' exclaimed Carrie. 'All I know is it's not me. I've finished with him, Mum.'

'You've what?'

'I've left a message at his office. He's not in today. I've told him it's over.'

'Oh, Carrie, no!' said Mary helplessly. 'I don't know what to say . . . Let me get your dad.'

She scurried through to the shop and was back moments later.

'What's all this?' said Norman, crouching down beside Carrie's chair and chafing her cold hands. 'Make a pot of tea, Mary, for pity's sake, there's no blood in her!'

Tea made, Mary stirred a full teaspoon of sugar into Carrie's cup while Norman poured a capful of brandy and added that as well. Then they stood over her as she took a cautious sip, and then another.

'Drink up,' chided Norman, squatting down again. 'And then we'll talk about this sensibly.'

'There's nothing to talk about,' said Carrie flatly. 'Mike's not the man I thought he was. He's been carrying on with someone else, lots of women, for all I know, possibly for the whole time he's been away. Maybe I can't blame him, maybe it's only natural for a man—'

'Don't give me that!' cried Norman. 'Mike's not any man! He's not like that!'

'How do you know?' flared Carrie. 'I know him better than you, or thought I did, and I had no idea!'

'There'll be an explanation,' said Norman. 'I know there will.'

'Well, I don't want to hear it!' said Carrie. 'I can't understand why you're taking his side!'

'I'm not! But all you've seen is a photograph—'

Carrie snatched up the magazine and waved it in his face. 'Two!'

'All right, two photographs—'

'Yes, and the camera never lies!'

'That's nonsense and you know it,' said Norman. 'Look

at that snap of me caught off guard at Johnnie's wedding – I look like Crippen!'

'Dad! This is serious! Don't you see what he's done to me?'

Carrie's voice broke and finally the tears came. She put her face in her hands and wept.

'Norman!' chided Mary. She fumbled in her sleeve for a hankie and offered it to Carrie, putting her other arm around her daughter's heaving shoulders. 'Leave her alone, can't you? Don't bully the girl!'

'I was only trying to help!'

'She doesn't want to hear it,' hissed his wife. Then mouthed, 'Not yet anyway.'

Shrugging, Norman pointed in the direction of the shop.

'Well, if I can't add anything useful, I'm sorry but I'll have to get back.' He took Carrie's hands. 'I didn't mean to bully you, Carrie, sweetheart. I'm sorry. I don't want you to do anything rash, that's all.'

'It's done, Dad!' Carrie raised her reddened eyes to his. 'It's done. I don't want any more to do with him. I don't want to see Lieutenant Mike Hudson – or this – ever again!'

And she tugged off her engagement ring and threw it in the hearth.

Chapter Thirty-one

'I don't know what to do with her,' Mary said despairingly that evening as Penny studied the two offending photographs. 'She's been up in her room all day, door locked, and won't answer us.'

Johnnie was on duty, so Penny had been invited for tea. She pushed *Life* magazine aside.

'It's potty,' she said. 'Mike would never deceive her like this! He's dancing with someone – so what?'

'I don't want to believe it either. But they do look quite . . . intimate,' Mary said awkwardly.

'Shall I go up? See if I can get through to her?' offered Penny.

'Good luck! She's beyond reason.' Norman, doing his accounts at the table, looked over.

'It's a pity Johnnie's not here, she might open up to him,' reflected Penny. 'With them being so close. But we can't leave her festering up there for ever. I'll have a go.'

Mary nodded gratefully. 'See if you can get her to eat something. She's had nothing all day. I can do her a sandwich or toast, we've got cheese, well, a bit . . . or she could have a nice boiled egg – she can have mine.'

'I'll tell her,' said Penny kindly. She knew food would be

the last thing on Carrie's mind, but it was so often the first on Mary's, along with the inevitable pot of tea.

Upstairs, Penny tapped on Carrie's door and called her name. There was a long silence. Penny tried again.

'Carrie, you can't stay in there for ever. Come on, unlock the door. Talk to me.'

Another pause, then Penny heard the creak of bedsprings, stockinged feet crossing the floor and the key turning in the lock. The door opened a crack. Penny resisted the temptation to slide her foot into the gap – too like something from a gangster film – but hooked her fingers around the edge of the door so Carrie couldn't close it again.

'I know we've all lost weight since the start of the war, but I can't get through that,' she said. 'You'll have to open it a bit wider.'

With a sigh, Carrie stood back and Penny stepped into the room. Carrie hadn't put up the blackout, but a thin sliver of moonlight was silvering the crumpled bed and dented pillow. Penny could sense, rather than see, her friend's dejection. Carrie trailed back to the bed and slumped down heavily. Penny followed and sat down, putting an arm around her.

'All cried out?' she asked. 'If not, my shoulder's available.'

'Oh, Penny,' whispered Carrie. 'I don't know what to do with myself. I can't believe it. I don't want to believe it. But I have to. He's cheated on me.'

Penny pulled her friend against her.

'I know your mum and dad have said this, and it may not look good for Mike on the surface, but . . . breaking off with him, Carrie? Doesn't he get a chance to explain?'

'What is there to explain?' All the vehemence with which Carrie had laid out her case to her parents had evaporated – she sounded utterly beaten. 'I take it you've seen the pictures. He's betrayed me in the cruellest possible way. Even if he never imagined I'd see the evidence – to be so blatant, in public . . .'

'I know what it looks like—'

'It looks like he's a complete swine. How would you feel, what would you do, if it were Johnnie? I trusted him, Penny, I trusted him implicitly. All these months. And he's been carrying on like this.'

Penny sighed. 'If he has – and that's a huge "if", because I can't say I believe it – I don't understand. Only a couple of weeks ago he was offering to bankroll you to carry on with the bookshop.'

'Yes, well, I suppose he thought when he got back he could take up with me again as if nothing had happened. And but for Gus giving me those magazines, I'd have let him! I'd have been completely ignorant.'

'Hmm.' Penny thought for a moment. 'Look, I'm going to say this, and you can shout me down . . . You're sure Gus had no idea the photographs were in the magazine?'

For a moment, Carrie became more animated.

'What, you think Gus was trying to split me and Mike up? No! He's got a girlfriend back home, for one thing, and the magazine was still in its wrapper, exactly as his mother sent it.'

'OK. Good.'

'Yes, it is good! It's good to know there's one decent man in the world.'

'Oh, Carrie, there are loads. Your dad, your brother, your uncle Charlie . . . and Mike too!'

'How can you say that?'

'I say it because I still think, until he's explained himself, as he surely will, you have to give Mike the benefit of the doubt. Innocent until proven guilty and all that.'

'And the photographs?'

'Circumstantial evidence,' said Penny stoutly.

Carrie gave a huge sigh.

'I'm so tired. I've been going over and over it, every letter, every telephone call these few past months, looking for clues, looking for some hint he was . . . going off me. The last time we spoke he . . . he said such lovely things. Now I don't know if I can believe any of them. What if it was all put on, an act?'

'It's a hiding to nothing,' said Penny. 'You'll just end up twisting things.'

'What do you suggest I do?'

'I suggest you do what your mum wants you to do. Have something to eat. I'll bring it up if you don't want to come down. And I'll bring you a cold flannel for your face.' Penny reached out and gently touched the skin around Carrie's eyes. 'As I thought, all puffed up.'

Carrie didn't answer, but she didn't refuse. Instead, she said:

'Will you do something else for me? Will you put a notice on the bookshop tomorrow, saying I'll be in late? There's something I need to do.'

'OK . . . but you are coming in?'

Carrie turned to her. She said fiercely: 'Of course I am.

After it's just been saved? The bookshop's all I've got now. I'm not letting that go.'

'Attagirl,' said Penny. She paused for a moment. She didn't want to start the whole cycle over again, but this was Penny, so she said it anyway. 'And I don't think Mike'll be letting you go either. There'll be an explanation. I bet he's cabling back right this minute.'

But there was no knock on the door with a telegram, either that night or by early next morning, when Carrie got up, dressed and crept downstairs. She'd heard her dad get up at five, as usual, but waited till she knew he'd be safely in the shop, marking up the papers for delivery. She didn't want another conversation with him or her mum, however well intentioned. The morning papers would be arriving at the station for her too, but they'd have to wait. By eight, she was at the County Hotel, where Gus was staying while he pursued a few more stories in the south-east. He'd told her he'd got leave from his paper to stay till Christmas.

The lobby was buzzing with people coming and going, chatting in groups or poring over newspapers. The receptionist was busy with guests checking out. Carrie passed unnoticed towards the dining room. Gus, she assumed, would be at breakfast. She peeped through the glass-panelled doors, but couldn't see him. The head waiter approached and pulled open the door.

'Are you looking for someone, miss? Or breakfasting yourself, perhaps?'

'Oh, no – no breakfast, thank you. I was looking for Mr Grayling. Mr Gus Grayling – he's staying here?'

'I haven't seen Mr Grayling this morning, I'm afraid, miss. You could telephone his room from the desk, perhaps?'

'Thank you, I'll do that.'

Carrie hurried back to reception, which was quieter now: there was just one man standing at the desk, his back to her. Carrie looked again. Surely she recognised that suit and the trench coat with its checked lining flung over the suitcase?

She hurried forward just as the receptionist pushed a sheet of paper over the desk.

'Your bill, sir.'

'Gus?'

He whirled around.

'Carrie!'

'You're leaving?'

Not another one! Another decent man, or so she'd thought, abandoning her – and without a word? His face was drawn; he didn't look like himself at all. But then a glimpse in the huge mirror that hung in the lobby had told Carrie that she didn't look like herself either.

'Has something happened?' she asked.

'You're asking me that? You?' Gus clicked his tongue. 'Let me settle up. I assumed I'd see you at the station. I have a train to catch.'

That was something; he was leaving, but at least he wasn't leaving without a word. But what could have happened? Had he got another assignment somewhere else in Britain? Or suddenly been recalled to the United States by his paper? Gus glanced at his bill and laid some notes and coins on the counter.

'I'll need a receipt, please,' he said to the receptionist.

'Of course, sir.'

He shrugged on his coat and crammed his hat on his head as the receptionist checked the amount and stamped the bill 'PAID WITH THANKS'. He picked it up along with his case.

'I take it you're on your way to work?' he asked. 'You're late, aren't you? Walk along with me anyhow.'

They went out into the cold, damp morning, Carrie trotting alongside as Gus took huge strides. Full of nervous energy, it seemed he couldn't get away from Brockington quickly enough.

'Gus? Tell me. What's happened?'

'You haven't heard on the wireless? Or seen a newspaper?'

'No. I—'

Carrie had been in her room since yesterday morning; today she'd crept out of the house and moved blindly through the streets. Gus stopped walking.

'The Japanese have bombed our base at Pearl Harbor.'

'Oh, Gus!'

For the last few months, the papers had reported 'tension' between America and Japan over various issues in the Pacific. Pearl Harbor was a huge American naval base in Hawaii.

Gus gave her a brief account of the facts – a newsman's account.

'It was a massive attack – they think over three hundred planes. Eight battleships, three cruisers, three destroyers and more, sunk or damaged. Thousands of Americans dead or wounded – thousands! No formal warning given, so it was against the Hague Convention, but there you go. Oh, and as a side order, by the way, the Japanese also attacked some of your territories – Singapore, Hong Kong, Malaya . . .'

'Oh no.'

'Oh yeah. So America is now at war with Japan, and Britain is too.' He paused. 'You really didn't know? And you a newsagent? How come?'

Suddenly Carrie's problems, which had loomed so large, seemed . . . not trivial, but somehow small. This was a huge development: on the one hand, having America as an ally was what Britain had been desperate for; on the other, the war had become even more serious.

'It's a long story,' she said. 'I haven't seen or heard any news.'

'That's not like you. But I have to catch a train up to London, and get on an airplane as soon as I can.'

'You're going home? You've been recalled by your paper?'

'By my paper? Who knows? I'm going home to join up, Carrie! I'd be kidding myself if I thought what I've been doing till now was still of any importance. I'm joining the fight!'

Chapter Thirty-two

Carrie and Gus were facing each other. The morning was damp and drizzly. Carrie had come out hatless and gloveless and she was shivering from the cold, from lack of food, from the shocks that just kept coming.

'You're cold,' he said. 'We've been talking all about me. You should have opened up the bookshop a good while ago. What's going on with you?'

Carrie shook her head.

'Not here.'

'OK, let's get to the station and get a hot drink inside you.'

'But you need to go, you just said.'

'I'm not leaving you like this. I know something's wrong.'

He put his arm around her shoulders and steered her along. Carrie could have wept for relief, for the feel of a strong arm supporting her, for the warmth of his body and his kindness. At the station, he swept her through to the tearoom, installed her at a corner table and, as far as Carrie could tell from the gestures and lowered voices, gently parried Bette and Ruby's concerns. Carrie had told Penny not to say anything, but naturally they'd noticed her absence and must have worried. She'd tell them in due course. First she had to tell Gus.

He came back with two cups of tea and sat down.

Carrie warmed her frozen hands around her cup and took a sip. It was hot and almost oversweet: Bette had gone mad with the sugar. Gus was looking at her, a question in his eyes. Carrie replaced her cup carefully on the saucer. She mustn't keep him long; she owed it to him to tell the story concisely. So she did – the magazine, the photographs, the inevitable conclusion, the message she'd left.

'Gee, Carrie.' Shock and concern were in his voice. 'That's awful. I'm so sorry that by giving you the magazine I was the cause of it.'

'Are you? I'm not. I'd rather know what he's been up to.'

'What *has* he been up to?' queried Gus. 'OK, apart from the pictures. What does Mike say?'

'I don't know. He hasn't replied.'

'I'm sure he will. But now you know what's happened overnight, you must see that things must be pretty busy in Washington right now.' Carrie acknowledged this with a dip of her head, but then Gus went on: 'I'm sure he can explain everything.'

Carrie's head came up.

'Not you as well. You're taking his side? All boys together?'

'No, I'm not doing that! I'm saying you should wait for his explanation. Surely that's only fair. There's got to be one.'

Carrie sighed and shook her head.

'That's what everyone says, Mum, Dad, Penny. Whatever his explanation is, I'm not sure I want it. I trusted him, Gus! I thought we trusted each other.'

'I'm just not sure you're even giving the guy a chance.'

'You *are* taking his side!' Carrie tried to keep her voice

low, but indignation got the better of her and she saw Bette look across. She lowered her voice again. 'I know what I saw. It was there, in the photographs, this woman draping herself all over him, and Mike not minding one little bit.'

Gus shrugged.

'OK. It's your call.' He rubbed his chin. 'But this is a nice irony.'

'What? Is it?'

'Yup.' He reached into the inside pocket of his suit and pulled out a letter. 'Read it.'

Carrie did. It was short and to the point.

Dear Gus

I'm sorry to tell you this, but I need to break off our under-standing. I've met someone else since you've been away. He's proposed and we want to get married. I really am sorry – I didn't mean for this to happen, but it has. Thank you for all the good times we shared which I'll always value. I wish you all the very best in life.

Lucille

Wordlessly, Carrie handed the letter back. Gus folded it and put it away.

'The original Dear John letter,' he said wryly. 'And what great timing.'

'I'm so sorry, Gus,' Carrie said quietly.

He shrugged.

'Well, at least I shan't have to worry about her pining away if I get killed.'

'Don't say that! That's no consolation!'

'No, OK. I mean, I'll still do my utmost not to be. Killed, that is.'

'Good.'

He gave a half-laugh.

'What a turn-up, though, huh? For both of us. And again, what an irony.'

His eyes met hers and held them. Carrie had always sensed that he rather liked her. Now she knew for certain.

'I'll never forget you, Carrie.'

'Nor me you,' she said lightly.

'I suppose I shouldn't ask you to keep in touch. But maybe, whatever happens with you and Mike, because I'm not writing him off yet, even if you are – no, don't say anything – well, if I let you know my address, wherever I end up, maybe you might write back? It'd be good to hear from you either way.'

Carrie gave a sad smile. This war! The situations you found yourself in . . . situations that a couple of years ago she could never have imagined.

'Maybe.'

Gus returned her smile.

'OK. Let's leave it there.' The bell clanged and over the Tannoy Mr Bayliss announced the departure of the delayed eight-forty-three. Gus picked up his hat. 'I guess I should go.'

'Yes, you must. Thank you, Gus, for everything.'

'Thank *you*, Carrie. You've sure brightened my stay in England. Even this morning, when you're upset. I'm glad I've seen you. I'm glad we had a chance to –' his eyes held hers again '– to talk.'

'So am I,' said Carrie quietly. She knew what he meant. Then she said firmly, to draw the conversation to a close, 'I'll come out with you.'

'Are you going to open up the shop?' he asked.

'What? Of course.'

'I just wondered – after all you've been through in the last twenty-four hours—'

'After what I've been through? I'm not the only person in the world, Gus! Don't you think, after all the death and destruction, all the injustice and senseless violence, people need the printed word more than ever? I mean, sometimes I think books are the last thing left that show we can still call ourselves civilised.'

Gus looked impressed.

'Well said,' he replied quietly. 'In that case, let me walk you to work.'

They went out and walked up towards the bookstall, where Penny was fending off a throng of bemused customers who were wondering where Carrie was and were ably proving her point.

'It's all right! I'm here now!' she called.

'Thank goodness!' cried Penny. 'Mr Bayliss has been going on and on, and – oh, hello, Gus.'

Gus raised his hat and addressed the crowd.

'I'm sorry, ladies and gents, blame me, I've been keeping her from her work.'

Knowing this was far from the truth, Carrie fumbled in her bag for her keys.

'Apologies,' she said. 'I'll open up now.'

But before she could, the train clanked in and the crowd,

along with Penny, dispersed. Carrie and Gus were left facing each other as the disembarking passengers eddied around them and others pressed forward to claim their seats. No one was watching as Gus took her hands in his.

'We both know things could have been different between us,' he said. 'And I mean it. If Mike doesn't come good, I'll always be here for you.'

Carrie smiled. 'Hardly. You'll be, well, you could be anywhere.'

'Literal to the last,' smiled Gus. 'Take care, Carrie.'

'You too. Take great care, won't you?'

He touched his hand to his forehead in a little salute of acknowledgement. Mr Bayliss was checking his watch and the guard was going down the train, closing the doors. Gus picked up his case and jumped on. He beckoned to Carrie through the lowered window.

'I'll chase up those articles, the *New York Sun* and your *Daily Mail*. I won't forget. My mom snipped out the one from *The Oklahoman* – she keeps all my stuff. I'll get her to send it to you.'

'Thank you. I'd love to see it.'

'Window up, please, sir.' Mr Bayliss marched up. 'This train is late enough already. As are you, Miss Anderson.'

Gus pulled a face at Carrie, who pulled a face at Mr Bayliss's back. Gus raised the window; the guard blew his whistle and hopped into his van. The train, with a fearful effort, as if the weight of Brockington's additional passengers was straining every nut and bolt, began to move off.

Still at the window, Gus waved a final time as the train pulled away. Carrie waved back, then turned to her little

Penguin bookshop and braced herself to face the day – and the future, whatever it might hold.

Work actually helped and, to her amazement, Carrie found she could function normally. She cut the strings on the early editions, whose headlines told bleakly of the latest unwelcome development in the war.

JAPAN DECLARES WAR ON BRITAIN AND
UNITED STATES, ATTACKS U.S. BASES

the *News Chronicle* stated bluntly in two huge lines of type.

Under various subheadings, the story took up most of the front page. The advertisers who'd booked space that day had wasted their money, Carrie reflected. Who on that tragic day would bother to read pleas from the manufacturers to 'Use Less Brylcreem' or buy the 'wonder tablet' Elasto –'Take It! – and Stop Limping'.

'And stop moping,' Carrie told herself sternly once the early rush had finally died down. 'Pull yourself together, Carrie Anderson!'

Her eyes still stung from crying and her naked ring finger was a stark reminder of Mike's betrayal. Her heart didn't hurt any the less and she knew she would never give it so willingly to another man, but the events overnight had jolted her from shock and devastated disbelief to dull awareness and, almost, acceptance. Shocking things happened, and were happening, all over the world. Finding that your fiancé was romancing another woman was only one of those things.

'Carrie?'

'Mum!'

'Honestly, love, what time did you go out this morning? You didn't even leave a note! And where were you in all that time before you came here?'

'Hang on . . . how . . . ?'

'I telephoned Mr Bayliss, of course, and asked him to ring back when or if you arrived! I was on the point of going to the police, Carrie. The state you were in yesterday and last night, well, you might have gone and done something stupid!'

'Oh, Mum – I'm so sorry, I never thought—'

'I know. Not like you at all! Anyway, never mind that. This has come for you.' Mary produced a telegram. 'Well, go on, take it. It won't bite!'

All Carrie's resolve evaporated. She was back where she'd been twenty-four hours ago. What would it say? That she was right, he'd fallen for someone else, her own cable version of Gus's Dear John letter?

Sensing that Carrie almost didn't dare, Mary asked: 'Do you want me to open it?'

Carrie shook her head and held out her hand. Heart lodged sickeningly in her throat, she ripped open the envelope, read, and handed the telegram to her mum.

COMING HOME ASAP I LOVE YOU
ALWAYS MIKE

Mary had the good sense to say nothing – certainly not 'I told you so'. But she gave Carrie a look that eloquently expressed it, softening as she saw Carrie trying to keep control of her bottom lip.

'Oh, love. You do realise . . . if he's managed to send a telegram, let alone try to come home, with everything that's happened in America in the last twenty-four hours, when he's perhaps needed there more than ever . . . that means something, doesn't it? He knows he's needed here.'

Carrie felt as if she was in a firefight of her own, trying to deal with so many warring feelings.

'Do you think I should tell him not to come? If he is needed there . . . ?'

'I think,' said Mary wisely, 'Mike's old enough to make his own decisions. And if the whole point of him being over there was to encourage America to join the war – well, the Japanese have done that for us, haven't they? So he might have been coming home soon anyway.'

'Maybe. Oh, I don't know what to think!'

'Well, I do.' Mary fished in her shopping bag and brought out a crumpled greaseproof packet. 'I think you need to keep your strength up. I made you some sandwiches, and there's a bit of plain cake in there as well.'

'Oh, Mum!'

Carrie almost dissolved at her mum's simple kindness.

'Save the paper, won't you, there's a good girl,' Mary went on. 'Oh, and there's this as well.' She produced Carrie's engagement ring from her pocket. 'You are a silly girl, chucking it down like that, it got all covered in coal dust. I've given it a good scrub. Look how it's sparkling!'

Carrie closed her hand over her ring and held it, the stones digging into her palm.

'Not going to put it back on?'

She shook her head. She had too much to take in, too many swings of the pendulum in the last twenty-four hours.

'Not right now.'

'Oh. All right, then.' Mary frowned, but Carrie said nothing more, so she said, 'Well, I'd better get off to the grocer. And the Post Office, if you want me to send Mike a reply?'

'I don't know what it should say.'

'What, you, who's always got a head full of words?'

'Not for this. Just leave it for now, Mum.'

'All right, love. If you're sure.' Her mother sounded less sure, but she pulled on her gloves and said goodbye.

Carrie genuinely didn't know what she would have said. She'd been through such turbulence in the past twenty-four hours, she still felt buffeted. She opened her hand and looked at her engagement ring. The three stones represented their past, present and future, Mike had said when he'd given it to her. They had a past, for sure, but whether they had a present, let alone a future, would depend on how she felt when she saw him. Whenever that might be.

Chapter Thirty-three

Carrie didn't reply to Mike's telegram, and though for the next couple of nights she expected – hoped for – a telephone call from him, there was none. But she understood why. She was following the news slavishly, and events were moving fast.

Germany and Italy had a pact with Japan, so they promptly declared war on America and America declared war on them too. As if they were drunk on the success of Pearl Harbor, there was another devastating Japanese air attack, this time on two British ships in the South China Sea. Eight hundred and forty men and officers were lost; a thousand more were rescued from the water or became prisoners of the Japanese.

On Brockington station, and in the whole country, the mood was grim. Carrie could only imagine how things were in the corridors of power in Washington and, by extension, in the British Embassy and Mike's office. The timing could not have been worse. No wonder he hadn't got a moment to telephone – or, equally, to fix a passage home.

'What's going on with Carrie? Can you really not tell us? It's Mike, isn't it? What's he done? It's only that we're worried!' Bette asked Penny, and Ruby added:

'She looked so awful the other morning when she was in here with the American feller. As if she'd heard Mike had been killed or summat. But we know he hasn't been.'

All Carrie had told them was that Mike was coming home – and they had 'things to sort out'.

'I don't like the sound of it,' Ruby went on doomily. 'Something bad's happened. They're such a lovely couple, if they split up, what hope is there for any of us?'

'They are not going to split up!' said Penny forcefully. 'Not if Johnnie and I have anything to do with it!'

'Even so. She's not wearing her ring,' Ruby said.

'She's got it on a chain round her neck, though,' added Bette. 'I saw it through her blouse.'

'There you are, then. And she's still wearing the watch he gave her.' Penny closed off the speculation firmly. 'Are you watching my toast, Ruby? I can smell burning.'

'Drat!' Ruby fled into the kitchen.

Bette wiped a smear off the urn.

'The road to true love never did run smooth,' she declared, with a glance at Eric's photograph, still draped in its black crêpe shroud. 'Especially not in wartime. There's that nice young American chappie gone off to fight and all. Where will it end, that's what I want to know?'

'None of us knows,' said Penny reasonably. 'But I overheard one of the passengers, who knows someone who knows someone who works in the government.'

'Oh yes?'

'It's what Mr Churchill said the day our ships were sunk.'

Bette was a huge admirer of the Prime Minister. She hung on every word of his broadcasts.

'And?'

'KBO.'

'KBO?' repeated Bette. 'Is it a code?'

'Sort of,' said Penny.

Ruby came back with two pieces of sorry-looking toast with the burnt bits scraped off.

'Sorry,' she said, passing the plate. 'But, you know . . .'

'Save the wheat and help the fleet,' chanted Penny resignedly.

'Well, tell us,' Bette urged. 'What you were saying. KBO. What does it stand for?'

'Oh, that,' said Penny, peering at her toast. 'It stands for "keep buggering on". Like I've got to do with this burnt offering. I hope I at least got a bit of extra marge.'

'Come on, Carrie, just half an hour – we'll go to the Rose and Crown. Or anywhere you fancy.'

'No, Johnnie, honestly, please. I don't want a drink. I don't want to go out.'

'OK, whatever you say.'

Johnnie understood: Carrie didn't want to leave the house in case Mike rang.

Penny and Mary had told him everything and as soon as he got an evening off, he came round to see his sister. Both women seemed convinced he could make Carrie see sense; Johnnie wasn't so sure. He knew his twin better than either of them did, and he knew that once Carrie got an idea in her head, she was impossible to deflect – look at how determined she'd been to set up the bookshop and, lately, to keep it going. If she was convinced Mike had betrayed her, despite the telegram he'd sent, which Johnnie had also heard about, she wouldn't be easily shifted.

All the same, Johnnie couldn't believe that every single one of them had been so wrong about Mike. Surely he wasn't the philandering kind? He and Carrie had seemed so besotted with each other. In the early days of their more casual relationship (or when they were both gamely trying to keep it casual), he and Penny had laughed about it.

On the other hand . . . what if Carrie was right? What if, against all the odds, Mike had been dallying with someone else while he was away? It seemed impossible, but Johnnie knew that a sort of madness could descend on men when they were away from home. He'd seen plenty of it in the RAF – supposedly happily married men chasing after WAAFs, chatting up barmaids and waitresses and usually making utter fools of themselves. This sort of behaviour was no respecter of rank: he'd seen it in pilots and riggers, medics, drivers and even his superior officers. But saying Mike might have been possessed by a sort of temporary insanity was hardly going to be a comfort to Carrie – if Johnnie could even bring himself to believe it.

'Look,' he began, 'I don't want to repeat what I know you've heard from Mum and Dad, and from Penny.'

'No, please don't,' said Carrie. 'I know they think I'm jumping to conclusions. But as I've said to them all, what else am I supposed to do?'

'But you've had Mike's telegram.'

'Yes, and? He's coming home, fine. He says he loves me, fine. Anyone can say things. They don't have to mean them.'

Johnnie sighed and took her hands. They were seated at

the table in the back room; their parents had tactfully removed themselves.

'Do you want to talk about it?'

'I'm not sure I do,' Carrie replied wearily. 'Even to you. I've said it all. I've been over and over it, I've read and reread his letters, I've replayed every telephone call in my head . . .' Her voice rose as she went on: 'One minute I love him, then I hate him, then I wonder if I even know him. Did I ever? I don't know what I think or believe. I'm sick of thinking about it! Sometimes, you know, my head feels as though it's going to burst. But I can't . . . I just . . . I can't talk about it any more! I don't want to think about it, but I can't stop thinking about it . . . Oh, Johnnie—'

'Shh, shh, it's OK.' Across the table, Johnnie took her hands, her ringless hands. 'I get the picture. I just wanted to help if I could. I mean, I haven't got any great insights, but I could just listen if you wanted to talk it over. But if you really don't . . .'

Carrie squeezed his fingers back.

'Thank you. Thanks for coming, and thanks for trying. I'm sorry I'm not better company. I'm just hurting too much.'

Johnnie could see that for himself. Carrie's eyes were dull and it seemed an effort for her to hold her head up. He ached for her.

'No, I'm sorry, sis,' he said. 'You did such a good job of keeping me going after my accident. I wouldn't be doing anything like this well if it hadn't been for all those hours you put in walking round and round with me. But I do know' – he'd seen this in the RAF as well, too much of it – 'that emotional damage can be far harder to get back

295

from than anything physical. Though I really do hope that what you and Mike had isn't damaged for good. Because despite what you say, I think you do still love him. You wouldn't be feeling this way otherwise.'

Carrie shrugged. 'Maybe.'

'But I'll tell you one thing,' Johnnie said firmly. 'If, when he shows his face, we do find out it's all a front and he has cheated on you, well, I'll knock his block off!'

Norman tore a sheet off the little calendar that reposed in its wooden stand on the mantelpiece. 'Friday the twelfth of December,' he announced, then squinted at the small print beneath the large red numerals. 'Day of the Virgin of Guadalupe.'

'You what?'

Mary was clearing the table. After opening up the shop, Norman always left Terry in charge and came through mid-morning for a second breakfast. Unusually, Carrie was at the table too, sewing on a button. Knowing the turmoil she'd been through, Uncle Charlie had offered to do a whole day at the bookshop.

Now divested of the garage business, he had more time on his hands, for a while at least. After Christmas, he was to start work as a departmental under-manager in Men's Outfitting at Selfridges. ('Fall in a cesspit and he'd come up smelling of roses!' his brother had marvelled. 'Always did! How does he manage it?') To be fair, Uncle Charlie was determined to pay off as many of his creditors as he could, and as such he'd already taken on two bar jobs on evenings when he wasn't with the Home Guard. Sister Munro was working at King's College Hospital in Camberwell, and they'd found a basement flat in Peckham where they lived quite openly as a couple. No Woolworth's wedding ring needed when you had Uncle Charlie's 'what the hell' attitude and Jean Munro's icy stares to face down any prying busybodies.

'I can't believe it, you've never heard of the Virgin of Guadalupe?' grinned Norman. 'Loves melon, so I hear.'

'That's cantaloupe, you clown,' tutted Mary. 'And you know it! Mike sent Carrie that menu from some embassy dinner, didn't he? It was the starter, we had to look up what it was.'

She glanced at Carrie to see if the mention of 'Mike' and 'dinner' had registered with her and revived bad memories, but Carrie seemed oblivious. Mary was worried about her daughter. She'd expected Mike's telegram to buck her up, to change her mood entirely, but it hadn't happened. Carrie had gone about the entire week like a sleepwalker, and wouldn't be drawn on Mike, his return, or her feelings about him.

Mary stacked her husband's cup and saucer on his plate and sighed. She prayed silently once more for guidance in this particular difficulty and that Carrie and Mike would see a way through, but she did wish God would give Mike a nudge and put them all out of their misery.

She often reflected afterwards that God really did move in mysterious ways, and in terms of answered prayers, it was pretty instantaneous. For at that moment, the chenille curtain was pushed aside and there he was – Mike, that is, not God. In his uniform, and as tall and devastatingly handsome as ever, despite looking exhausted – it was Mike.

Norman froze, Mary froze. Carrie's head was still lowered over her sewing.

Mike put his finger to his lips and moved quietly across the room towards her. Suddenly aware, Carrie looked up. In her surprise, her hand flailed out and the button box flew off the table, scattering its contents everywhere.

'Now look what you've made me do!' she cried, jumping to her feet. 'As if you haven't done enough already! And now you just turn up here – how dare you!'

Her hands were raised and she began pummelling him in the chest.

'Hey, hey, hey,' Mike protested, trying to grab her wrists. 'Carrie! What a welcome!'

'Don't you make light of it, don't you dare!' Carrie was like a thing possessed.

'Carrie. Calm down. Darling, stop it! Stop. Stop!'

With a defeated sigh, Carrie dropped her hands and looked up at him. Mike took her firmly in his arms and kissed her. And Carrie didn't resist.

Chapter Thirty-four

'I did say I was coming,' Mike said reasonably, when he finally let Carrie go. 'But I couldn't say when. I got the first transport I could, but I didn't know I was coming myself till Wednesday afternoon. I've been travelling for . . .' He looked at his watch. 'Do I count the time difference or not? Anyway, it feels like weeks.'

'I'll make a pot of tea,' said Mary automatically, disappearing to the kitchen with her loaded tray.

'And I'll get back to the shop.' Norman sidled away. 'You two need your privacy.'

Carrie hadn't said another word. Mike sat her down again at the table, pulling out a chair to sit beside her. They looked at each other, face to face, eye to eye.

He looks tired, Carrie thought – well, that was understandable after the week he must have had, and the travelling. He'd managed to shave, so the strong jawline that she loved to run her fingers along was as smooth as ever, but he was pale. His blue-grey eyes were shadowed purplish underneath, but, as they held hers, they still had the same loving sincerity, or they seemed to – surely that couldn't be faked?

She wanted – needed – so much to believe that what she'd seen in the photographs was something that could be explained. Not explained away, but explained, and she knew now, her frustration expended in those first few seconds after his arrival, that she'd listen to his explanation, whatever it was, good or bad. Simply seeing him, sitting so close to him, his real, vital presence, sent her heart, still helter-skeltering from their kiss, on another dizzying zigzag. She loved him so much.

She looks tired, Mike thought, and it's all my fault. She's pale, she's lost weight – she's not been eating. And I've done this to her. Never meaning to, never imagining she'd see those damn photographs . . . On top of all the anguish of being apart, on top of the worry about the future of the bookshop, I've done this to her. Her eyes were locked on to his, at the same time defiant and pleading. He loved her so much and he'd hurt her so much. Unwittingly, but he'd still hurt her. Though she'd let him kiss her . . .

Mary edged in and placed a tray of tea on the table, gave them both a brief smile and disappeared through to the shop. Carrie looked at the tray as if she'd never seen a teapot and cups before, then roused herself.

'You do still drink tea?' she said. 'It's not just coffee with you now? You haven't gone all American?'

Ouch, thought Mike, a bit of a dig. Still cross with me, then.

'I still drink tea.'

Carrie poured, adding not too much milk, the way Mike liked it. She passed his cup.

'Thank you.'

Carrie poured herself a cup and took her time stirring it. She was composing herself to hear what he had to say. She knew she loved him still, she wanted to believe him, and if

300

there was something to forgive, to forgive him, but . . . had the camera been lying? Or had he? Did that woman mean anything to him? Had he had another girlfriend, or several, while he'd been away?

'Well?' She laid down her spoon, trying to stop her hand and her voice from shaking. Everything, their entire future, hinged on the next few minutes. 'You're the one who's got the explaining to do.'

Mike leaned forward. For the first time, he noticed she wasn't wearing her engagement ring.

'I know. Please, just hear me out.'

'I'm listening.'

'OK. I couldn't say much about what I was doing over there operationally, and I know you understand that. But I can tell you now. A lot of it was just meetings, endless meetings, like I said, with the military, with politicians. But there was also a lot of soft-touch diplomacy.'

'Meaning?'

'Meaning meeting and socialising with influential people in all walks of life. What the Americans call schmoozing. What we'd call buttering people up.'

'I see,' said Carrie tightly. 'And dancing with girls comes into that category, does it? Because they're bound to be really "influential people".'

Ouch again, thought Mike, but from Carrie's perspective, perhaps fair enough. He realised, beneath her sarcasm, how deeply and profoundly she'd been hurt. He sat back, took a breath, then leaned forward again.

'She's the daughter of a senator, Carrie. He's a really important voice in the President's ear. He's a widower and she always attends functions with him. I was at that do for one reason and one reason only, to keep her occupied while my boss and my boss's boss talked to him. I was there to distract her and be charming to her.'

'Well, mission accomplished. She certainly looked charmed.'

Those wretched photographs!

'Well, I wasn't,' said Mike. 'It was a job, my duty for the evening. And I'm sorry. I'm sorry I couldn't tell you any of this. And I'm so sorry you had to find out like you did.'

'I don't suppose you'd ever have told me otherwise.'

Mike spread his hands helplessly.

'No, probably not, because there's nothing to tell. We chatted, we had dinner, she obviously wanted to dance, what could I do? She's not the only woman I've had to converse with or even dance with in the past seven months. I've made polite conversation and had my toes trodden on by half the wealthy wives and daughters of Washington while their husbands or fathers smoked cigars and drank brandy with my superiors.' He seized her hands. 'That doesn't mean I enjoyed it! And that night, when I was dancing with her, I was thinking of you. And wishing I was with you!'

Carrie looked down at their joined hands in her lap. It was true, in the photograph of them on the dance floor, Mike had had a faraway look in his eyes. Had she been really stupid in being so impulsive? Had everyone else been right all along? Was the most obvious explanation the one she hadn't seen, or wanted to see? Was she the one at fault for not trusting him?

Mike took his hands away and lifted her chin.

'I'm so sorry about it all. I can only imagine how upsetting – shattering – it must have been for you to see those photographs. But I've meant everything I've said over the past seven months. I've missed you every single day. I've thought about nothing else but getting back to England as soon as I could and being with you again, and about us getting married.'

Carrie's lip trembled.

'Where's your ring?' Mike asked softly. 'Put it back on, Carrie. Please.'

Carrie took a long time before she answered, but it wasn't because she was in any doubt about what she was going to do. She was thinking, in fact, of Gus, how she'd acted with him. Oh, she'd told Mike all about him, so her conscience was clear on that score, but if some photographer had snapped them together in the pub or laughing together at the bookstall and Mike had seen it, she could see how it might have been misconstrued when, like him and the senator's daughter, it had, from her point of view anyhow, been purely a working relationship. She knew now that even if Gus did send her his address, she wouldn't be writing back.

She undid the top two buttons of her blouse and pulled out the ring on its chain. Mike stood up and Carrie bowed her head. He gently moved her hair out of the way so he could undo the clasp. He came back to sit in front of her.

'Give me your hand.'

Carrie held out her hand as Mike slid the ring onto her finger.

'For the third time of asking, will you marry me?' he asked.

'Oh, Mike, of course I will!' she said shakily. 'I'm surprised you still want me to!'

'Don't be daft. Of course I do.'

'But I'm the one who should say sorry. Sorry I didn't listen to everyone who was telling me there'd be an explanation, sorry I jumped to the wrong conclusion and left you that silly message. Sorry for not trusting you. Sorry for all of it. I was an idiot. But I was just – I was just – in shock.'

'Forget it,' said Mike with that sudden, illuminating grin of his. 'Forget it. Maybe it's even done us a favour.'

'What? How do you work that out?'

'At a time when everything's really kicked off over there and I might have got sucked in and had to stay on for months, I could plead a family crisis and come home.'

Carrie gave a joyous, dazzling smile of her own.

'I suppose it did.'

'Good. We agree.'

He took her face in his hands and kissed her. This time, she kissed him back. Finally pulling apart, he said:

'Better?'

'Better,' Carrie confirmed. 'Much better.' She sighed happily. 'Can I ask you one thing, though?'

'Go on.'

Carrie took a deep breath.

'Will you have to go back to Washington?'

Mike grinned. 'Fair point. But no. They've already sent someone to replace me.'

'Really?'

'Really.' He looked her in the eyes and Carrie wondered

how she could ever have doubted him. 'So let's put all this behind us and look to our future, shall we?'

'Oh, yes, please. Let's.'

Mike kissed her again.

'Good. So how do you feel about a winter wedding?'

Before Carrie could reply, the chenille curtain from the hallway was thrust aside and Penny burst in, followed by Johnnie.

'Oh, for goodness' sake, say yes. Just get on with it, as soon as possible!'

'Penny!' Startled, Mike rose to his feet.

'Quite right, the way you two have dragged it out—'

'And Johnnie!' Carrie was on her feet too, equally surprised. 'What are you two doing here? How did you know . . . ?'

'I telephoned them, of course. From the box on the corner, so you wouldn't hear!'

Mary came in behind them, beaming at the success of her subterfuge. 'Your dad's gone to the off-licence for something to celebrate with.'

Johnnie was slapping Mike on the back and Penny gave Carrie a hug.

'Luckily, I'd nipped home for lunch because Johnnie was on a rest day,' she explained. 'Your mum said Mike was back and things were looking hopeful, so we shot straight round. Didn't want to miss out on the big reunion!'

'So much for privacy,' smiled Carrie. 'I hope you haven't been eavesdropping!'

'Certainly not. We just caught the end,' Johnnie assured her. 'The important bit.'

A clanking of bottles announced Norman's return.

'Here we go,' he said, unloading his booty on the sideboard. 'Glasses, son!'

Johnnie obliged and Norman poured beers and shandies for everyone.

'What's the toast?' asked Penny.

'To Carrie and Mike, of course,' said Johnnie. 'Love, luck and a long life together!'

'Carrie and Mike!' everyone chorused, clinking their glasses and drinking.

'You did drag it out, though – admit it,' said Johnnie accusingly.

'Not entirely my fault – and certainly not Carrie's.' Mike took Carrie's hand – her left hand, with its ring back where it belonged.

'And it did mean I got three proposals.' Carrie smiled up at him.

'Three?' Penny poked Johnnie in the chest. 'I feel quite cheated now!'

'Well, let's just say it's third time lucky,' Norman concluded firmly.

'And so say all of us!' the others chimed in, as Mike pulled Carrie to him for another kiss to prove it.

Johnnie put his arm round Penny. Norman squeezed his wife's hand as Mary smiled fondly.

'Oh, I do love a happy ending!' she said.

Chapter Thirty-five

'I really think it might snow!' Carrie, her eyes bright, whirled round from the window.

'Oh, surely not!' Mary, the inveterate worrier, scurried over to stand behind her. The heaped white clouds pressing heavily down on the rooftops certainly indicated a strong possibility. 'What about your dress?'

'Oh, Mum, for our wedding? It'd be perfect!'

At the mirror, Penny was setting her neat, feathered hat on her head.

'Spot the romantic!' she grinned. 'A proper fairy-tale finish. No confetti any more, so snowflakes could do the job.'

There was a tap on the door, and Norman's voice.

'What are you lot doing in there? Your car'll be here in a minute, Mary!'

'Nearly ready!' Mary called back.

They heard Norman's indulgent tut and could imagine the amused little shake of his head as his feet moved away.

'Come on, then,' said Mary. 'One last look at you, and down we go.'

Carrie stood obediently while her mother adjusted the way her dress sat on her shoulders and arranged her short veil, anchored to the crown of her head by a jewelled comb. Her long, caramel-blonde hair was loose, at Mike's request, and she was lightly made up: a tiny bit of powder and a touch of pink lipstick. She transferred her engagement ring to her right hand and felt for the locket Mike had given her on their first Christmas. Suddenly—

'Ooh! I've got a butterfly!' she exclaimed.

'Only one?' smiled Penny.

'Yes,' Carrie replied. 'But its wings are the size of elephant's ears, and it's in some kind of trampolining competition.'

It had been a month like no other, and there'd been some pretty extraordinary months – of ups *and* downs – for the Anderson family since the start of the war. This one, though, had held only one note: pure excitement.

First, for Carrie, there'd been Mike's return and their reconciliation, then Christmas and New Year. And their wedding plans, idling all this time, were suddenly at full throttle, chocks away and ready for take-off, as Johnnie put it.

Noting Penny's admonition to 'Just get on with it!' Carrie and Mike went to see the vicar the very first weekend Mike was back. He asked them if they had a date in mind.

Silly question.

'A.S.A.P!' they chanted together. Consulting the calendar and allowing time for the banns took them to Saturday, the tenth of January. Carrie looked at Mike; Mike looked at Carrie.

'I think we can wait that long,' he said.

'Just about,' Carrie added under her breath – because, after all this time, all she wanted was to be with Mike and never let him go.

So the vicar of All Saints, at his busiest time of year, added, 'I publish the banns of marriage between Caroline Mary

Anderson of this parish and Michael James Hudson of the parish of St Mary, Leamington Spa,' to his announcements at the Advent service and on the two Sundays afterwards.

Carrie was there for every one of them with her mum and dad, and Mike too. On the third reading, Penny and Johnnie came as well, and Bette and Ruby, and even Uncle Charlie and Jean. After the pin-drop moment when the vicar called on anyone who knew of any cause or just impediment, etcetera, etcetera, to declare it, and no one uttered, Uncle Charlie stood up and applauded and the whole congregation smiled and joined in. Could you kiss in church without a lightning bolt striking the steeple? Carrie and Mike did anyway.

Carrie had had long enough to plan, but while she'd been planning, the seasons had changed not once but twice. At one time she'd fantasised about a simple posy of meadow flowers, which she'd gather herself – poppies, cornflowers and moon daisies. No chance of that now, and no bronze chrysanths either, or coppery leaves underfoot. Early on, they'd settled on having the reception at the familiar and friendly Rose and Crown, a bouquet's throw from the church. The landlord's promised cold table ('Proper ham,' he'd said with a wink. 'And sausage rolls. Just don't ask me how!') had hastily been supplemented with hot soup to start, and the ham had become roast pork. While there'd be no spilling out into the beer garden at the end of proceedings, the pub's panelled function room with its figured carpet was welcoming with the red-shaded lights on, a fire in the grate and the maroon velvet curtains drawn tight.

There'd be proper wedding cake too, for Carrie and Mike to cut. To Johnnie's disgust, Mary's Christmas cake, made with the dried fruit he'd managed to get hold of from the NAAFI, had been snatched from his grasp and the cake tin hidden away for the wedding; he'd had to make do with mince pies padded out with grated parsnip.

'It's for the greater good, son,' Norman consoled him, as he sprayed dry crumbs of pastry down his shirt front. Even Mary could only do so much with all cooking fat on ration.

Tomboy Jane, initially the reluctant bridesmaid, had written to Carrie apologising for being 'such a twit' at their first meeting, and saying she loved the dress her mum had made.

'Mint green organdie, in January?' Mary had fretted. 'She'll be frozen, poor lamb!'

'She'll just have to wear a vest!' replied Carrie briskly. 'We're not waiting till the summer, not after all this time!'

Now the day was here, and Carrie couldn't help but feel a pang for poor Jane's frozen arms. Her dress of heavy white satin would keep her cosy: in any case she and Mike had their love to keep them warm.

Norman had seen Carrie's dress take shape over many months, but he'd blinked back what was surely a tear when Carrie finally made her entrance, her dress lisping softly behind her.

'Oh, love! I— love! I— I— I'm lost for words!'

If Johnnie had been there, he'd have quipped 'first time ever' but Johnnie was Mike's best man. Having had the obligatory 'stiffener', they'd be at the church by now, with Mike's parents, Jane and the other guests.

Mary and Penny departed in their taxi; now it was almost time for Carrie and her dad to leave. Carrie's butterfly had quietly folded its wings – all she wanted was for the whole thing to begin. But Norman, alternately fiddling with his cuffs and adjusting his collar, still seemed tongue-tied.

'Come on, Dad,' Carrie smiled. 'You're supposed to be reassuring me. Not that I need it.'

'I know you don't.' Norman came close and took her hands. 'You – and Johnnie – you've both of you made your mum and me so proud. We've given you the best start we could, but all along you've grabbed every opportunity, even in this blooming war – especially in this blooming war – to make something of yourselves. That you've both found someone to love and settle down with, and we can see how happy you are – well, that's just the icing on the cake.'

'Oh, Dad, don't, I'll be ruining my makeup!' Carrie's eyes were full; she leaned forwards and kissed his cheek. 'Neither of us would amount to anything without all the love and care you and Mum have given us and the way you've indulged our passions – Johnnie for flying, and me for books. I love you both to bits, and I know Mike's very fond of you too.'

'Well, that's very nice to—' But there was a rat-a-tat on the shop door – the shop closed, of course, for the occasion, as was Carrie's bookshop. 'That'll be the car. Looks like we're off!'

Carrie would never forget the moment when the first notes of the wedding march sounded and she saw Mike turn to look at her. The expression on his face could only be described as awe, and Carrie thrilled again to see him standing tall and straight in his dress uniform, her brother by his side.

Norman was grinning widely now as he saw so many friends and neighbours packing the church. Carrie, turning

311

from one side to the other, saw Alf Warburton, the chief warden and his wife, and others from the ARP, with whom her dad had spent so many long and difficult nights. She recognised her mum's friends from the Knitting Circle, the Red Cross and the WI, and her own schoolfriends, Evie and Sylvia. Both their husbands were away fighting. Johnnie's friends were there too, the group that Carrie had met and who'd been so kind after his crash.

From behind her veil, Carrie's eyes slid back to Mike – his eyes hadn't moved from her. He shook his head slightly, as if he couldn't believe this apparition was her, or that this was happening. But it was.

Closer now to the altar steps and the benevolently beaming vicar, Carrie saw Mr Parfitt, seated with Bette and Ruby, and on Mike's side of the aisle, in a mass of khaki, Stan Thompson, Mike's sergeant, who'd kept in touch during that awful time when Mike had been missing after Dunkirk. Finally, in the second pew from the front, Mike's mum and dad, both smiling encouragingly. In the front pew on Carrie's side, Mary sat with Jean and Uncle Charlie, who gave her the inevitable wink and a thumbs up.

The organ crashed to its triumphant final chord and Carrie was at Mike's side in a cloud of net and a whisper of satin. She turned to look at him.

'Just beautiful,' he said softly.

'You're not so bad yourself,' she smiled.

Carrie turned to hand her bouquet of Christmas roses, holly, ivy and winter berries to Jane, whose dress was not of mint green organdie but forest green velvet – and set off 'granny's pearls' far better than the pale fabric would have done. Jane had grinned at Carrie's surprise when she'd explained the speedy rethink – at any rate, she looked lovely and Mary would be relieved.

Carrie turned back to Mike. With hands that she couldn't help but notice were shaking slightly, he lifted her veil.

The wait was over. They were here.

'Ladies and Gentlemen, your attention please!' Everyone looked up from their coffee and cube of cake as Johnnie tapped on the rim of his glass. 'The town crier's masquerading as a sergeant major on some parade ground, so you've got me as master of ceremonies instead.'

(Shouts of 'Typical, trying to hog the limelight even today!' from his RAF friends.)

Johnnie held up his hand.

'I know, I know, the fan club's in, but you'll have to wait for my speech. First, pray silence for Mr Norman Anderson, the father of the bride!' Amid the applause, he added, 'Come on, Dad, put in a new needle and start the record!'

Norman got to his feet and produced no less than four sheets of paper from his pocket.

Carrie shot a look at her brother. Their dad was often moved to make little speeches on family occasions – he'd done so the first Christmas that Mike had spent with them – but this looked like anything but a 'little' speech.

Clearing his throat, Norman made a great play of shuffling the pages.

'I'm only going to give a short address. It was longer, but then I showed it to Mary . . . no, seriously folks, it's not that bad.'

Laughter as he put three of the pages down.

He began, inevitably, with stories from Carrie's child-hood. Some were flattering, like her soft-heartedness in popping an extra couple of mint imperials on the scale for a favoured pensioner or letting a child with only a sticky halfpenny have their full quota of sweets and making up the difference herself. Some were less so, like the time she'd nearly set the house on fire letting the potatoes boil dry while she had her nose in a book.

Still listening, holding Mike's hand under the table, glancing at him as the revelations came out, and laughing with everyone else, Carrie let her gaze slide around the room.

There were Johnnie's RAF friends and their girlfriends, the men with ties loosened and the women with their hats off. Evie and Sylvia had neatly filled a table with Mike's friends from the regiment, two couples and two single men – one of them Stan. But his chair was empty – where was he now? After the meal, everyone had got up and milled around. Oh, there he was! Sitting at what had been Ruby's seat on one side of Bette, who was flanked on the other by Mr Parfitt. Talk about a rose between two thorns . . .

Norman was up to the moment of Carrie meeting Mike. Mr Parfitt was looking highly disgruntled as Bette, smiling and rather pink, leaned towards Stan, who was whispering something in her ear. Carrie's mind took its inevitable imaginative leap in what Mike had once claimed would win her a medal in conclusion-jumping. Bette and Stan? And Mr Parfitt jealous? That'd be interesting!

But if Stan was in Ruby's seat, where was Ruby? Surprisingly, not with the younger single soldier . . . no, over by the bar, deep in conversation with the barman-cum-waiter. From Ruby's attentive expression, it looked like something more than a flirtation. Could she be picking up some tips of the trade? Or even considering a job move?

'So, despite everything the war's thrown at them in the way of separations and anxiety and injury and heartache, Carrie and Mike have a love for each other that nothing and no one can destroy . . . '

Carrie looked at Mike, and then beyond him to her mum, who was dabbing away a tear. Beyond her were Mike's dad, nodding in agreement, and Penny who, in her 'best woman' role, had taken it upon herself to charm the somewhat reserved Geoffrey Hudson throughout the meal.

Then she turned her head the other way, looking past her dad to Mike's mother, and to Jane, her boyish frame softening now she was sixteen. Beyond her sat Johnnie, scribbling notes on his speech, which Carrie knew would teasingly debunk most of her father's lavish praise. From the way Jane was watching him, it was clear that Johnnie had also been exercising his charm, and a serious crush could be developing.

Norman came to what Carrie knew was his final paragraph – bless him, she'd heard him rehearsing in Johnnie's woodworking shed often enough.

'Sometimes it takes another person to fully bring out all your best qualities.'

Carrie looked over to where Uncle Charlie and Jean were standing close together by the fireplace, his arm around her slender shoulders. She'd certainly brought out a different and tender side to him, one that the family had never seen.

'I've been lucky enough to have that with Mary,' Norman

315

continued,' and I know that Carrie and Mike complement each other in the same way. All that remains for me – for all of us – is to wish them a long, and I hardly need to say, happy, life together.'

'Hear, hear!' called Uncle Charlie.

'And so,' Norman declaimed, 'a toast—'

('Someone put the grill on!' That from one of Mike's friends, this time).

'Ladies and gentlemen, I give you the bride and groom: Carrie and Mike!'

As everyone stood and raised their glasses, Mike leaned over and kissed her, and not for the first or the last time that day.

Carrie closed her eyes and gave a happy sigh. In her mind she pictured dear old Brockington station with its soot-stained platform and distinctive canopy, and the scene of so many dramas. She spared a brief – very brief – thought for Mr Bayliss, having to manage alone today with only the morose ticket collector, Jack, for company. She thought how different her life would have been if she'd never opened her little Penguin bookshop, all the friends she'd never have met and, above all, the way it had miraculously brought her this wonderful man she loved, who was now her husband.

As Mike got up to begin his speech, Carrie looked up at him lovingly. She'd read enough books, but even more importantly, lived enough of life by now to know that in every end there is a beginning, and her new life with Mike would be just that.

THE END

Acknowledgements
and a Message from Jo

If it takes a village to raise a child, it takes a small city to produce a book, populated by a great number of talented people. This starts with my agent, Broo Doherty – endlessly kind, patient and wise. At Penguin, huge thanks to my editors Katie Loughnane and Jess Muscio, and latterly Susannah Hamilton, and the fantastic production team behind them. Lucy Thorne designed another standout cover, copy-editor Caroline Johnson and proofreader Gabby Nemeth checked the text, Faye Collins and Rose Waddilove saw the book through production and printing, while Mhari Nimmo and Georgie Townley oversaw marketing and publicity. See what I mean?

Thanks to the pandemic and an unusual route into saga, it took me a while to find my feet in the writing community, but I'd like to thank Annie Murray, Lesley Eames and the much-missed Elaine Everest for welcoming me, for reading the book in advance and for giving it such generous praise. Tracy Baines and Helen Yendall did the same – Tracy is a constant source of inspiration and encouragement on social media, and Helen is a past competition winner on my Facebook page, and an author herself. Mick Arnold kindly helped with my questions about Second World War RAF hospitals. Writers Rachel Brimble, Alison Knight, Angie Morgan and Rachel Ward have become friends since my move to the South West.

Thank you to all the new friends I've made in Somerset, who've been enthusiastic champions of my books. In tribute, I've borrowed some of their names to double as Johnnie's friends and girlfriends. I hope they like their portrayals – I know I'll hear about it if they don't!

A big hug for my husband John, daughter Livi and son-in-law Ashley for supplying tea, wine and pep talks when things aren't going so well, and tea, wine and praise when they are. And of course, my two scrumptious granddaughters, Clara (CC) and Cressie, simply for being themselves and making me smile so much.

I've loved writing all my books, and above all I love meeting you, the readers, in person at library talks and festivals, and online too, through my Facebook page @joannatoyewriter, or on Instagram and X. Thank you to all who've loved the books, told me they have, and left reviews/recommendations on Amazon, NetGalley, Goodreads or Fantastic Fiction – please keep doing so. They mean the world to me and really do help other readers to find and enjoy the books too.

With love,

Jo x

Turn the page to read the first chapter of the previous book in the series

'It's beautiful, Uncle Charlie – but you shouldn't have!'

'Ha! But I did!'

Carrie Anderson lifted the silver bangle from the velvet bed in its leather box. She'd been named for her uncle – Caroline to his Charles – and he'd always had a soft spot for her, and for her twin, Johnnie.

Johnnie was watching now, along with her parents, as her uncle clasped the bangle around her wrist and fastened the safety chain. Thrilled, Carrie turned her hand this way and that so the ivy leaves engraved on it caught the light.

'You spoil 'em, Charlie, you really do.' Carrie's father, Norman, shook his head at his brother.

'Ah, well, it's not like I've got kids of my own, is it?' Charlie grinned, leaning back in the best armchair and pulling out his cigarettes.

Carrie's mother, Mary, immediately edged the Bakelite ashtray closer to him on the little oak side table. Last time Charlie had called, he'd dropped some glowing ash on the rug. He'd been in the middle of one of his stories, as usual, waving his arms about and keeping everyone in stitches. No one else had noticed and Mary hadn't liked to interrupt and make a fuss, but she could still see the tiny scorch mark.

'Yes, very nice, Carrie, but if you've quite finished showing off, is it my turn now?' Johnnie raised an ironic eyebrow.

'Oh, go on, then, you martyr!' Carrie teased, giving her

1

brother an affectionate swipe. 'I'm five minutes older than you, though, don't forget, so it's only right I go first!'

'Hmm, so you are, and you'll be sorry about that when we're eighty!'

Carrie pulled a face at him. Privately, though, she admitted it was good of Johnnie to have waited. Uncle Charlie's gifts were always something special.

Johnnie unwrapped his own birthday present – another leather box, which he opened, gasped at, then turned around so that everyone could see the contents: a tiepin and cufflinks.

'Oh, wow! Thanks, Uncle Charlie!'

They weren't just any old cufflinks and tiepin. The links were in the shape of a plane, and there was another perched on the bar of the pin.

'Well, planes are your pigeon, so to speak, aren't they?' grinned Charlie. Having lit up, he snapped his lighter shut. 'I dare say you can tell me exactly what model they are, and what's wrong with the design!'

'I wouldn't dream of it,' Johnnie shot back. 'They're great, honestly.'

'It's really very generous of you, Charlie,' said Mary as Charlie waved her comment away – this time, fortunately, with no ash hanging from the tip of his Craven 'A'.

Trust Charlie, with his big ideas, she thought, to smoke a brand named after Lord Craven and his special tobacco mixture.

Mary had meant what she said, but Charlie's generosity only pointed up that she and Norman could never have afforded such lavish gifts. Their presents to Carrie had been a pair of stockings, some scent (only Yardley's Lily of the Valley, but it was her favourite) and a handkerchief sachet Mary had embroidered from a pattern in *Woman's Weekly*. Johnnie had had some new collars, a pot of shaving soap and a hand-knitted sleeveless jersey. Mind you, that was more than some in their street would have got for their eighteenth birthday.

The Andersons' newsagent and stationery shop provided a fair income, but there wasn't much left over for luxuries. And goodness knew, they worked for what they had, what with Norman up at five to do the papers with Carrie's help and someone having to be behind the counter till the sign was finally turned from 'Open' to 'Closed' at six o'clock. They worked hard six days a week and half a day on Sundays – especially on Sundays, so that other folk could enjoy their day of rest with the help of the *News of the World*, the *Express*, the *Mail* or the *Sunday Pictorial*. Then there was the ordering, the stocktaking and the books to balance. Almost every evening, once tea had been cleared away, Norman sat at the table in his shirtsleeves, braces hanging down, toiling away till ten o'clock or later, with Carrie helping him.

But if Mary ever tried to remonstrate, she knew what answer she'd get, and it would be a dusty one. Anderson's Newsagent & Stationer had been established in 1877 by Norman's grandfather, and passed down to Norman and Charlie by their own dad. By then, the railway had come to Brockington, turning it from a large village into a small town. But a corner shop in a not especially prosperous area hadn't been exciting enough for Charlie, of course. He'd gone off to do his own thing, which had only increased Norman's determination to keep the business going.

Mary gave an inward sigh – inaudible to anyone but her – and got up.

'So, who's for tea and cake?' she said brightly.

'Uncle Charlie's a card, isn't he?'

Family celebrations over, brother and sister were walking to their local pub, the Rose and Crown. Johnnie was counting on at least a couple of birthday drinks from the friends he'd promised to meet.

Having crossed the road, he swapped sides with Carrie to make sure he was still walking on the outside of the pavement – he was always a gentleman with things like that. Whoever finally bagged him as a husband would be a lucky girl, Carrie thought loyally, though there was no one special in Johnnie's life at the moment, nor in hers for that matter.

Six feet tall, with dark brown hair and grey eyes like their father's, Johnnie wasn't short of admirers – all the girls in the typing pool at the engineering factory where he was training as a draughtsman, for a start. Carrie had noticed the giggles and the saucy looks they gave him, and the rather less friendly looks they gave her when she linked arms with him as they walked away from the factory gates on the days she came to meet him, jealous even after they'd realised she was his sister.

With their mother's blue-eyed colouring, lighter hair and peachy complexion, Carrie had her own admirers – the dapper reps who called at the shop with their cases of samples, cheeky van drivers trying it on, and some of the customers too. But she'd given Cyril, who worked at the barber's on Harold Road, the gentle heave-ho at Easter and she wasn't in any hurry to replace him.

She replied to Johnnie's question with a shrug.

'I never know whether to believe his stories. That one about the motorist, the monkey and the bunch of grapes!'

Uncle Charlie had left the business five years ago to go into partnership with 'a pal'. He had lots of pals, did Uncle Charlie. This one ran a garage in Catford – used car sales and repairs, as well as petrol. They'd had a boom time. Everyone seemed to want a motor, or, if they couldn't afford one, there was what Charlie called a 'private hire business' on the side. People could hire a car for the day and take a run out to the countryside, stopping for lunch or a drink at one of the new mock-Tudor pub-restaurants – they called themselves 'roadhouses' – that had sprung up along the ribbon routes out of the capital.

'Quids in!' Uncle Charlie had crowed.

No wonder he could afford such expensive presents.

But Johnnie wasn't listening. His eye had been caught by a poster showing a skein of planes, one after the other, coming in to land like swans on the flight deck of an aircraft carrier.

'WHY NOT JOIN THE NEW FLEET AIR ARM?' shouted the poster. 'GOOD PROSPECTS OF EARLY ADVANCEMENT.'

Carrie stopped so Johnnie could read the small print. The advertisement was calling for people with all sorts of skills, from jig and tool fitters to blacksmiths. At eighteen – just – Johnnie was the right age, but Carrie realised with relief that he didn't fit the bill. He wasn't that interested in building or maintaining planes – he wanted to be a pilot. Desperately.

Carrie had lost count of the Sunday afternoons she'd spent cycling over to Croydon Aerodrome to hang about while her brother drooled over an Armstrong Whitworth Atalanta or logged the arrival of a huge Handley Page biplane. On one occasion, he'd ambushed a pilot who'd just flown in from Africa as he strolled through the terminal. Johnnie had quizzed him relentlessly about wind speeds and turbulence until Carrie had felt quite sorry for the chap. He must have been dying simply for a wash, a shave and a drink! But the pilot hadn't seemed to mind – two enthusiasts together – and his autograph was Johnnie's most treasured possession. Well, until today's tiepin and cufflinks, perhaps.

But learning to fly was only for the very wealthy – public schoolboys in the OTC, or people whose fathers had their own private planes. So when he'd finished school, Johnnie had done the next best thing: he'd started as an office boy at a nearby aircraft factory and by hard work and aptitude, and a bit of night school, had managed to get himself taken on as a trainee draughtsman. And as soon as he could, he'd joined the new Air Defence Cadet Corps, which had given him the chance to actually go up in a plane.

Carrie knew that if the war that had been narrowly averted last year came to anything, and things were not looking that hopeful, Johnnie would be among the first to sign up to fly. With horrible irony, war would give him the chance that life so far had denied him.

She didn't even want to think about it. She tugged on his arm.

6

'Come on, there's a pint on the bar with your name on it, remember?'

Back at home, Charlie was getting ready to leave, shrugging on his jacket with its, to Mary's eyes, rather loud check – but that was Charlie all over. She pressed a large piece of cake on him. As a bachelor, doing for himself in digs, he missed out on home cooking.

'You're a good 'un, Mary,' he said, kissing her as he placed the cake in its greaseproof paper on the passenger seat of the Rover. 'Our Norm's a lucky man.'

'Don't I know it!' Norman beamed and slapped his brother on the back. 'Drive safely,' he warned. 'No more than thirty miles an hour now, remember.'

'Tch! It's a sin with this little beauty, but there you are. That won't be the only restriction we're under soon.'

Norman frowned and gave a warning tip of his head towards Mary, but it was too late.

'I think I'll go in,' she said abruptly, crossing her cardigan over her chest. 'It's getting chilly.'

'Sorry, sorry.' Charlie looked contritely after her. 'I know she doesn't like to think of another war, but it's coming. So much for poor old Chamberlain's "peace for our time" and "peace with honour", eh?'

Norman nodded as Charlie went on.

'Hitler's already broken the agreement, marching into Czechoslovakia – he's never going to let things rest till all of Europe's under the jackboot.'

Norman knew his brother was right. While the others

were clearing up tea, they'd gone out the back for a look at the Anderson shelter that Norman and Johnnie had built the year before. They'd lifted the yard bricks to half submerge it, Carrie helping them to pile the earth they'd dug out back over the roof. With her mum, she'd sown carrots, cabbages and beetroot, which her dad tended to in his limited free time. The shelters in backyards and gardens weren't the only things that were different. All over London, workmen had dug trenches in any bit of open ground. They'd carted off the sandy soil up Hampstead way for sandbags, and the parks were decorated – if you could call it that – with barrage balloons like tethered silver whales. However much the government might still be hoping for peace, all the preparations were for war.

The Rose and Crown was the usual fug of beer, smoke and bodies, despite the doors and windows being open to the summer evening.

'Hiding in the garden,' Johnnie concluded, having scanned the bar for his friends. 'Trying to duck their responsibilities! I'll get us a drink anyway and we'll go and dig them out. Shandy?'

Carrie nodded a thank you. She wasn't really a pub person: when she met her friends, it was usually at The Ginger Cat café or the cinema, or to go to a dance at the Mecca Ballroom. Her work at the family shop didn't pay a vast amount, though she didn't mind that. What she minded more was having to give up her hopes of a more exciting career.

All her life, she'd been a reader, haunting the local library and picking up tattered copies of anything and everything at jumble sales. While Johnnie's bicycle basket on planespotting trips contained a notebook and binoculars, hers always carried a novel. She'd wanted to be a librarian herself, but there wasn't the money to stay on at school to take her School Certificate. Not to be deterred, in what she hoped would be a cunning move, Carrie had taken a job at Boots' the Chemists, hoping to progress from selling shampoo and suppositories to a position in their own lending library.

But before that could happen, her mother had fallen badly on an icy pavement and broken her hip. Carrie had had to leave her job, and with it her ambitions. Mary couldn't stand for long now, and Norman couldn't run the shop on his own. So for the last two years Carrie had been working alongside him.

' "Many a flower is born to blush unseen and waste its sweetness on the desert air," ' one of the more persistent reps had flannelled, trying to wheedle her into a night at the flicks. Carrie had refused – he looked the 'handsy' type – but a bit of her couldn't help agreeing, much as she loved her mum and dad and knew they couldn't really afford to employ anyone else.

Her dad knew how she felt. He'd cleared a space for her in the shop to start selling a few books alongside the Basildon Bond and bottles of ink.

'There you go, love,' he'd said. 'You choose a few books, I'll get 'em on sale or return, and you can have a little book corner here. We'll see how we fare.'

Carrie had been thrilled. She'd chosen a range of titles, including a lot of the classics she loved, but there weren't many takers. Everyone in their neighbourhood, men and women, worked hard. They hadn't the time or the energy – or, often, the money – for indulging in books. Those who did buy preferred Ethel M. Dell to Dickens. Not that there was anything wrong with that – Dickens did go on, and Carrie loved a nice romance as much as anyone. But she was disappointed she hadn't been able to persuade local readers to stretch themselves a bit. Books had meant so much to her. Through them she'd travelled back and forth in time, visited places she knew she'd never see for herself and experienced things she hadn't yet experienced. Love, for one . . .

Johnnie was paying for their drinks, and Carrie dragged her thoughts back to the bar. The radio that always burbled in the background blurted out the pips for the news and she sensed Johnnie straining to listen.

'Turn it up, Fred, will you?' he asked.

The barman obliged and Carrie wished he hadn't. Hitler, the BBC reported, had ordered mobilisation against Poland. The bar fell silent.

'That's it, then,' someone said. 'We've guaranteed Poland's independence, haven't we? This means war.'

Carrie looked at her glass. Condensation was running down the side, like tears.

She turned to Johnnie, her twin, her blood brother, the person she felt closest to in the world.

'You're going to volunteer, aren't you?' she asked. 'Before they even call you up. For the RAF.'

Johnnie opened his mouth, but before he could reply, Carrie went on.

'Well, you're not going on your own! I'll volunteer too. For the WAAF!'